FESTIVAL
of FEAR

ISBN: 978-1-68313-004-8

First Edition
Printed and bound in the USA

Cover photo credits:
Mac Armstrong: www.flickr.com/photos/reiver/10524212314/
Stephane: www.flickr.com/photos/stf-o/12109611434/
Cover and interior design by Kelsey Rice

FESTIVAL of FEAR

THE PAXTON BROTHERS SAGA – BOOK 1

RON PARHAM

𝓟
Pen-L Publishing
Fayetteville, Arkansas
Pen-L.com

BOOKS BY RON PARHAM:

-THE PAXTON BROTHERS SAGA-

Festival of Fear

Molly's Moon

Copperhead Cove

DEDICATION AND ACKNOWLEDGEMENTS

This novel is dedicated to the Oakland, Iowa, class of 1965, which I was a part of until moving away in my sophomore year. I hope that my portrayal of our little town stirred some nice memories in your heart.

I wish to acknowledge Russ Lamer, Bob Joseph, and Jerry Hogan as beta readers on this novel. They provided sound feedback, advice, and suggestions during the course of writing *Festival of Fear*. And Duke Pennell for his outstanding editing and countless publishing efforts that made this novel a reality.

When at some future date the high court of history
sits in judgment of each of us, it will ask:
"Were we truly men of courage—with the courage to stand up
to one's enemies—and the courage to stand up,
when necessary, to one's associates?"

JOHN F. KENNEDY, JANUARY 1961

PROLOGUE

Jimmy pulled out of the trailer park in the darkness, his old beat up Chevy Impala spitting gravel and fishtailing onto the Montana country road. Shaking uncontrollably, he was barely able to steer the car in a straight line. He reached the blacktop and careened onto the highway without looking, almost slamming into a passing big rig, horns blaring. He sped down the highway away from Helena and everything he had ever known in his life, towards the unknown. All he had with him was an old weathered scrapbook and an address.

Sirens wailed behind him, the sound growing dimmer and dimmer as he raced through the dark night towards his destiny. He had just slammed the door on one life and now was headed towards a new one, one that would be all his, not his mother's. His dark inset eyes belied his excitement, his anticipation, his need. He glanced down at the address on the piece of paper and finally smiled. His new life would begin in Iowa.

The brown Chevy crossed over the Missouri River from Nebraska into Sioux City, Iowa, the blood on Jimmy's backseat still fresh, his left eye still twitching. His pulse raced, as it always did after one of his treasure hunts. It had been a month since he left his home in Montana, driving through Wyoming and Nebraska on his way to the address in Iowa he had taped to his dashboard.

He opened his car window and tossed out the rag, as he did after every treasure hunt. The smell intoxicated him, made his left eye twitch uncontrollably, but it was dangerous to keep it in the car. He rubbed his bloodshot eyes as he drove down the dark highway that paralleled the Missouri. He looked at his face in the rear view mirror, at the dark circles under his deep-set eyes. The circles had become a permanent feature on his dark face due to the lack of sleep—and the drug.

Since leaving Montana, Jimmy's treasure hunts had become more and more frequent. He needed it like most people need food, like a drug addict needs a fix. It nourished him, energized him, and empowered him. But his latest treasure had been another disappointment, taken from the streets like all the others. The street urchins were easy to abduct, but were much too compliant, too dirty, and weak, with little or no fight in them. He needed something different, something fresh, young, and unspoiled. Iowa would be the place where he could find it, his ultimate treasure.

He stared at the white line of the highway as cars flashed by, guiding the car effortlessly, almost on autopilot, only occasionally glancing at the road ahead. It was three o'clock in the morning and he hadn't slept in two days. The smell of his last treasure wafted up from the backseat, the scent a mixture of sweat, excrement and cheap perfume. And chloroform—always the scent of chloroform. He had tossed the girl out as he crossed over the bridge that took him into Iowa, never to be found in the churning, muddy waters of the Missouri.

Jimmy flashed back to Montana, rubbing his eyes harder as he thought about the way his mother used to massage his shoulders, brush his hair, kiss his eyes before bedtime, calling him her treasure. How she would sneak into his bed at night and lie next to him, caressing him up and down, up and down. The first time, when he was a teenager, was quick and messy, but she eventually helped him delay his gratification as she taught him self-control. Towards the end he could outlast her, have her lying in bed spent, exhausted. That's when he knew he needed someone new, someone that would provide a challenge, fight back. His mother had grown old and fat, the folds of her skin becoming a growing irritant, and that infuriated him. He saw the young girls on the streets of Helena, so full of life, with young, supple bodies. He had to have one, to know what it was like to fight for his treasure. When his mother found out about it she went crazy and ranted until he couldn't take it anymore. He dealt with her the same way he did all of them, except he left her lying in her bed—the same bed where she had robbed him of his innocence so many years before. The fire was an afterthought, but a satisfying final touch, one that he could remember for the rest of his life. His mother would never touch him again.

He saw the sign ahead. "Council Bluffs—200 miles." The address on his dashboard was a small town just east of Council Bluffs, where he had been born a million years ago. His mother had taken him in the middle of the night when he was a child—just barely ten years old—never to return, until now. Jimmy remembered his father and older brother vaguely, like people from a history book, with no emotion or memories. He looked at the scrapbook that his mother had kept on his 'other' family through the years. She always bragged about Johnny, his estranged older brother, and his medals—the Purple Hearts, the Bronze Star. And she railed incessantly about his father, the small town teacher who had a thing for young boys.

Jimmy rubbed his bloodshot eyes and smiled. He wanted to meet them, to reconnect, but first he needed a new treasure. Something fresh, unspoiled, pretty and clean—she had to be clean. His left eye began twitching as he envisioned her in his mind. He had a whole new hunting ground, virgin territory so to speak. He laughed out loud as he rubbed his eyes one more time, the brown Chevy careening down the river highway towards a new life in the cornfields of Iowa.

CHAPTER 1

The black and yellow flower-covered float turned the corner, pulled by a giant green John Deere tractor, passed by the Deep Rock gas station and entered Main Street, where hundreds of people lined the street for the Fall Festival parade, smiling and waving American flags. Nick Paxton was sitting on the float with most of his high school football teammates, feeling the glow of being a small-town hero. They hadn't played a game yet, but already they were being touted as the best team in Acorn, Iowa history—a perfect blend of seniors and underclassmen, led by the senior All-Conference quarterback Allen Neal and the sophomore sensation halfback, Nick Paxton, and a shut-down defense led by All-Conference middle linebacker Steve Conner and sophomore cornerback, Tim Preston, Nick's best friend.

The float carrying the football team, all wearing their black game jerseys, came to a gradual stop, waiting for the Acorn High marching band to form in front of them. Nick, with his little brother Bo sitting at his feet, kept looking behind him.

"Who you lookin' for, Nick?" Bo asked, unable to get the grin off his face. Bo was only seven years old but insisted on riding on the float with his big brother. "Oh, I know, the cheerleader!" He shook his head as he began to sing. "Nicky's in love, Nicky's in—"

"Shut up, you little turd," Nick said, "or I'll kick your scrawny butt off this float."

1

Bo stood up and began moving his hips back and forth. "Nicky's in love, Nicky's in love."

Nick planted a fist into his little brother's arm that sent him sprawling to the deck of the float.

"Oww!" Bo rubbed his arm. "I'm telling Mom."

"I told you to shut up. One more peep and you're off this float." Nick looked around at his teammates, all of them grinning and chuckling. "What the hell you guys looking at?"

"Nicky's in love," Tim Preston said from the back of the float, smiling broadly. "Your brother's a tough little dude, Nicky."

This brought a broad smile to little Bo's face.

Nick stared at Bo, warning him with his eyes to keep quiet.

Nick saw five cheerleaders running down the street, their black-and-gold pompoms flailing in the air above their heads. His heart raced as he looked for the long blonde hair of Sarah Rogers, but as the cheerleaders ran by the float, she wasn't with them.

"Where's Sarah?" he yelled at one of the cheerleaders, Susie Daniels.

Susie stopped in front of the float and shrugged her shoulders. "I thought she was with you."

Nick shook his head. "No, Tim and I went to pick her up but she wasn't ready so she told us to go ahead."

Nick's voice was drowned out by the band, which began blowing horns and banging drums, getting ready for the start of the parade. He stood up and peered behind him, but didn't see her.

"She'll be here, Nicky," Tim said, smiling. "I think Bo's right, Nicky's in love."

Tim Preston was the only person, other than his mother and Sarah, who Nick allowed to call him Nicky. Anyone else who tried it would get a knuckle sandwich or a smack on the arm.

Nick almost fell backwards as the tractor pulling the float lurched forward. The parade was starting, the band was playing "America the Beautiful," and everyone lining the streets began clapping and cheering. Nick looked backwards one more time, then turned and put on a fake smile and began waving along with the other players. *Where the hell is Sarah?*

Jimmy sat in his father's dirty black Ford pickup under the shade of a large oak tree at the end of the street, watching for any activity. He figured everyone in town would be going to the festival, but there were always one or two stragglers. He drummed his fingers on the steering wheel, patiently scanning the hillside street on the outskirts of Acorn. He had picked the area specifically because it was on the outskirts of the small town, so there wouldn't be too many prying eyes to worry about, especially on Fall Festival day. The street was lined with two-story houses with large porches and lawns on one side and a wooded area on the other. He knew the area well and had been scouting it for a week. He had seen several young teenage girls walking to school. It was a prime hunting ground.

Suddenly a girl rushed out her front door a few houses down from him, dressed in a black-and-gold cheerleader's outfit, her pompoms and long blonde hair flailing in the air as she ran down the sidewalk. Jimmy smiled, started his truck, looked around, and slowly pulled out into the deserted street. *A cheerleader, that's something different.* He reached over to the passenger seat for the bottle and rag, getting ready. As he pulled up about ten yards behind the young girl she darted into the street right in front of him. He slammed on his brakes as she stopped and stared at him, her hands on the hood of his truck. He stared back for what seemed like an eternity, and then she ran across the street and disappeared into the woods. He peered into the woods, his hand on the bottle, and thought about running after her but changed his mind when he saw a car coming up the street. He took his hand off the chloroform bottle, grabbed his red baseball cap and put it on low over his face. The car passed without the driver looking at him.

He smiled again as he thought about the cheerleader. Her eyes were mesmerizing, haunting, and she was so fresh, clean and pretty. She had seen his face, so now it was inevitable. He had plenty of time, and he knew where she lived, the cheerleader with the long blonde hair. His left eye began to twitch as he rolled the bottle between his fingers.

CHAPTER 2

The band and the football team float slowly made their way down Main Street. Another seven floats followed behind, all decked out with artificial flowers, streamers and banners, the typical small-town parade. Many of the people lining the street were in overalls—farmers and their families in town for the annual fall festivities, the beginning of the harvest in rural Iowa. The corn and oats and other crops were ready for harvest, and the leaves on the big oak trees so prominent in the area were beginning to change color, from green to yellow, orange, and red.

Nick looked out at the crowd of people on the sidewalks as they passed Luther's Grocery Store and the Lincoln Nickel and Dime, where he grew up buying penny candy and reading Superman comic books. He spotted his little brother Ethan, waving a small American flag, being held by their dad, with his mom standing beside them. Nick waved at them and got a scream from Ethan back. He loved his little brother, who was only three years old, and wished Bo could be more like him. He glanced down at Bo, who was standing up, doing his swivel-hip dance for the adoring crowd. Nick grabbed him and pulled him down.

"What're you doing?" Nick said.

"Givin' 'em a show," he said. "Better than just smiling and waving, like you."

"Well, cut it out. It's embarrassing me," Nick glanced at his teammates, who were all cracking up at the sight of little Bo doing his thing. "They think you're a clown, Bo. Is that what you want?"

"Yeah, just call me Clara Belle the clown, like on Howdy Doody," Bo said, laughing as he danced on the float.

Nick gave up and looked again at the cheerleaders in front of the float. Still only five. No Sarah. He felt a hand on his shoulder and turned to see Tim.

"Not like Sarah to be late for anything," Tim said. "Was she okay when you went to her house?"

"Yeah, I guess. I didn't actually see her, just heard her from the bathroom. She said to go ahead and she'd be along in a few minutes."

"You probably should have waited for her," Tim said.

Nick dropped his gaze and stared off into the crowd. "She told me to go ahead . . ."

"Well, don't worry about it, Nicky. She's fine and she'll probably join the parade up ahead somewhere."

Nick looked up and down the crowded street, hoping to see Sarah running, with her long, blonde hair flowing behind her. That made him smile, thinking about how she brushed her hair back, laughing that cute little laugh. *Nick's in love is right.*

The parade turned right, past the Acorn State Bank and Big Oak lumber yard, the crowd beginning to thin out. They passed the food booths set up on either side of the street and he smelled the Maid-Rites and hot dogs cooking. His mom made the best Maid-Rites around. Some people called them Sloppy Joes, and she would be manning one of the booths, making her special recipe. Nick's mouth began to water at the thought.

Finally, the band stopped playing and began to disperse. The tractor pulled the football float off to the side of the road near Chautauqua River Park. Bo jumped off before it had come to a stop.

"Bo, where you going?" Nick yelled.

"To get one of mom's Maid-Rites," he yelled back over his shoulder.

Nick jumped off the float and stretched his back. Tim came up beside him, slapping his back.

"Well, you ready for our first game Friday night?" Tim said.

Nick finally smiled at the thought of their first game. "Oh yeah, wish we could play tonight."

"Naw, tonight we gorge ourselves on hot dogs, and—"

"And my mom's Maid-Rites," Nick said, grinning broadly.

Tim laughed. "Let's go."

Nick saw the cheerleaders standing close by and walked up to Susie Daniels. "Any word from Sarah?" he said.

Susie shook her head. "No, nothing. Hope she's okay."

Nick's smile faded as he looked back up the street towards the crowd of people mingling around the food booths. "Me too."

"Nick, look who's here," Tim shouted as he pointed back at the park.

Nick stared into the park and saw the long, blonde hair and black-and-gold pompoms. He took off like a shot and stopped next to the jungle gym.

"Sarah, where the heck have you been?" Nick said.

Her face was covered in sweat, her breath coming in big gulps. She put her arms on his shoulders and looked up at him with her big, blue eyes.

"I wish we had a girl's track team. I think I'd be pretty good," she said, still breathing hard. "I just ran a five-minute mile, and through the Palmer woods."

"Through the woods? Are you crazy?"

She took a deep breath. "Do it all the time, great shortcut to downtown. Cuts off about half a mile."

Nick relaxed and smiled at her, brushing sweat from her brow. "Nice job, but you missed the parade."

Sarah laughed as only she could, her head thrown back, her blonde hair flowing, her white teeth flashing. "Who cares, I'm here now. Let's go eat!"

"Okay, but why wouldn't you let me wait for you at your house?"

"'Cause you're the big football star and I didn't want you to be late," she said, tilting her head and smiling. "I'm a big girl. I can take care of myself."

Nick wanted to kiss her, to hold her, but he hadn't built up enough courage yet. Maybe after Friday night's game, he thought, after I score a couple of touchdowns. A grin creased his face as he followed Sarah to the Maid-Rite booth.

The black Ford pickup slowly turned the corner of Chautauqua Park Drive and eased up the street towards Main Street, but that was blocked off and filled with people. Jimmy pulled over and scanned the crowd ahead, looking for the girl with the long blonde hair. He spotted the black-and-gold cheerleader outfit and followed her with his eyes until she was out of sight. A crooked smile creased his face as he got out of the truck, pulled his red cap low over his face, and began to walk towards the crowd. He wanted to get close to her, smell her young sweaty body, maybe touch her in some way. He stopped before he reached the crowd of people, realizing that she was lost to him that night and he'd have to find a different treasure. The cheerleader would have to wait, but she would be his eventually.

Jimmy got back into his pickup and drove out of Acorn towards another small Iowa town where the treasures were also young and numerous.

CHAPTER 3

Nick sat on the wooden bench in the locker room, elbows on his knees, his eyes closed. He didn't hear a word the local preacher was saying during the team prayer, concentrating instead on what it would be like to run out onto the Acorn football field in his gold pants and black jersey with the number twenty-five, with the crowd screaming and Sarah Rogers jumping up and down in her cheerleader outfit. He smiled at the thought just as the preacher said "Amen."

All thirty-five Acorn High Oaks players stood up and huddled together in a moving circle, hands extended, shouting "Mighty Oaks! Mighty Oaks! Mighty Oaks!", then broke up and ran for the locker room door, cleats clicking and sliding against the cement floor. As Captain, senior quarterback Allen Neal led the team out onto the field, with Nick and Tim somewhere in the middle of the pack. The cheers were getting louder as they reached the area behind the south goal post. A large circular hoop with a picture of an oak tree was held by two cheerleaders and Allen Neal rushed forward, breaking the paper picture, leading the Acorn Mighty Oaks onto the field. Nick rushed through the large hoop, the adrenalin pumping through his veins as he spotted Sarah Rogers off to the left, jumping and twirling her pompoms. He ran to the sideline, took his black helmet off and looked back at Sarah, who was staring at him and smiling.

The team ran onto the field and began doing calisthenics and stretching, getting their tight muscles loose. After ten minutes Coach Davis ordered them to the sidelines.

"Okay, stretch out your legs while Neal goes out for the coin toss," Assistant Coach Walters yelled. "Everybody get your head into the game." He looked at Nick, who was looking at Sarah. "That means you, Paxton."

Nick felt his face grow red. He stretched his legs and looked at the assistant coach. Walters was tall, dark-haired, with a jaw that jutted out like solid granite.

"Paxton, over here," Walters said.

Nick ran to the coach's side, looking up because Walters was at least eight inches taller than he was. "Yeah, coach?"

"Get your helmet on, son," Walters said, "and listen up. If we get the ball, Coach Davis wants to start with eighty-eight reverse. They won't be expecting it, thinking we'll run something into the middle. You get ready to turn those jets on, okay?"

Nick's heart was pounding. "Got it, coach!"

Walters grabbed Nick's face guard and pulled him close. "And don't even think about fumbling, you got that?"

Nick nodded. "Yeah, got it, coach."

"Okay, stretch out those legs and get loose, son."

Nick ran back and began some serious stretching, his heart felt like it was about to beat out of his chest at the thought of running the first play of the season. He looked up as he saw Allen Neal running back to the sideline, smiling broadly.

"Receiving team, on the field!" Coach Davis yelled.

Nick was one of two kick returners on the receiving team, so clapped his hands and ran as fast as he could onto the field, stopping near the five-yard line close to the south goal post. He looked up at the home town stands, looking for his parents and brothers but couldn't find them. He swung his gaze to the six cheerleaders in front of the stands and saw Sarah kicking up her right leg, her hands on her hips. The Acorn High band was blaring out a fight song. Nick grinned as he looked over at Mike Thomas, the other kick returner .

"Here we go, Mike," Nick said. "Let's take it all the way!"

Mike clapped his hands. "Yeah, baby!"

Nick heard the referee's whistle blow and stared up into the Friday night sky, waiting for a football to come floating down to him end over end. Instead it was shanked to the right and went out of bounds at the Oaks forty-yard line. Disappointed, Nick ran up to the Oaks huddle and listened to Allen Neal bark the play.

"Eighty-eight reverse," he said, glancing at Nick. "Let's give Nick some blocks. On two."

Nick took his position on the right side of the T-formation. Mike Thomas was in the middle at fullback, and another speedster, Tommy Jensen, was at left halfback. Nick listened for the count and when Neal barked out the second 'hut,' he turned and ran to his left as Neal ran backwards, faking a handoff to Thompson who ran into the middle. Neal placed the ball firmly into Nick's gut as he ran by. Nick followed the left halfback, Jensen, around the left end and searched for an opening. Jensen laid a nice block on the defensive end and then Nick was on his own. He spotted an open lane, made a nice cut and was ten yards downfield before the other team knew what hit them. Nick sprinted down the sideline towards the north goal post. He crossed the twenty-yard line with no one around him and coasted into the end zone untouched. He stopped and turned around and saw his entire offense running towards him. Before he knew it he was on the bottom of a pile of delirious teammates.

"It's gonna be a great year, Nick baby!" Allen Neal shouted into his ear.

Nick climbed out of the pile and stood up, looking for one person on the side line. He spotted her at the same time she spotted him. He raised his arm high, holding the football. Sarah waved back and blew him a kiss. "Yep, a great year, Allen!"

CHAPTER 4

The Frosty Freeze on State Highway Six, on the west edge of town, was the hangout after football games, having the biggest parking lot in Acorn. There were at least twenty cars in the lot when Nick arrived with his parents and two brothers.

"Remember," Nick's dad, Clint, said, "home by eleven thirty. Okay?"

"Okay, Dad." Nick nodded, scanning the crowd for Sarah. "Thanks for the lift."

"Great game, son. Great game." Clint had a proud smile on his face.

"Can I stay with you, Nick?" Bo said, pleading with his eyes. "I promise I won't be a clown."

Nick's mom, Eloise, an attractive, brown-haired woman in her early forties, grabbed Bo by the arm. "Let's let Nicky enjoy tonight with his friends, Bo. Come on, we'll get some ice cream and go home and watch Bonanza."

"Yeah, little Bo watching Little Joe, should be fun," Nick said, softly hitting his little brother on the arm. "See you at home, little man."

"Nicky."

Nick turned and saw Ethan, his little hands reaching out for him. Nick took his 3-year old brother in his arms and hugged him.

"It's past your bedtime, little guy," Nick said. "You want to grow up to be a football player like me, you need to get your sleep."

"Yeah, a football player, like Nicky!"

Nick kissed him on the cheek and passed him off to his mom. "I'll be home by eleven thirty. Bye."

11

Nick walked through the crowd of teenagers, people slapping him on the back and offering congratulations. His smile turned into a grin when he saw her standing next to Tim Preston and Susie Daniels, licking a soft vanilla ice cream cone. He walked up to Sarah and touched her on the shoulder. She turned and smiled. He laughed when he saw the ice cream on her upper lip.

He pointed at her lip. "You have some, uh, ice cream …"

Sarah wiped her mouth with her napkin and pulled Nick into her and hugged him tightly. Shocked, Nick looked at Tim, whose eyes were wide, just like his grin. Sarah had never hugged him before, never really touched him at all.

Sarah released him, showering him with her smile and blue eyes. "You were so good, Nicky! Three touchdowns!"

"Don't give him a bigger head than he's already got," Tim said.

A small crowd of people began forming around them, slapping Nick's back and yelling "Great game!" Nick, shy by nature, began to tire of all the attention. He kept staring at Sarah, wanting nothing more than to hug her again. He looked at Tim and nodded his head to the left. Nick grabbed Sarah's hand and guided her through the growing crowd to a quiet, dark part of the parking lot, with Tim and Susie following.

Nick leaned against a shiny, red '56 Chevrolet, shaking his head.

"What's wrong, Nicky?" Sarah had a worried look on her face.

"Ah, nothing, just don't like all the attention and stuff."

"Well, then you shouldn't have scored three touchdowns," Tim said, laughing.

Nick chuckled, hitting his best friend on the shoulder softly. "You didn't do so bad yourself, Timmy. How many tackles you get, along with that interception?"

"A few." Tim smiled at Susie. "It was a pretty easy game, so let's not make a big deal out of it."

"Forty-nine to nothing, I'd say it was an easy game," Susie exclaimed. "Sarah and I were exhausted from all the jumping and screaming tonight."

Everyone laughed.

"Next week we play Wilson High from Council Bluffs, so it won't be anything like tonight," Nick said. "They're a big city team and we're just a bunch of small-town hicks."

"Ah, heck, Nicky, that doesn't mean anything," Tim said. "The way we beat up on Hanford tonight, we can beat anybody."

Nick looked at his best friend, shaking his head. "Sure hope you're right."

Sarah leaned in close to Nick and took his hand. He felt the electricity run through him as she kissed him on the cheek.

"Tonight is all that matters. You're the hero tonight, Nicky."

Nick felt his face heat up as he glanced at Tim and Susie, shuffling his feet. "Uh, thanks." He hung his head. *What a putz.*

They leaned on the red Chevy, talking and laughing until an older, much bigger boy walked up to them, followed by several other boys. He had black, slicked-back hair, a two-day growth of beard on his face, and wore a leather car club jacket that said "Ring of Fire."

"What the hell you doin' on my car, asshole?" he said, looking at Nick. "You scratch it, you're dead."

Nick stood up and moved away from the Chevy, looking at Tim, then Sarah. "Sorry, I don't think we hurt it."

The boy rubbed his hand on the car, checking for scratches. The other boys stood in front of Nick and Tim, their fists clenched.

"I found a scratch, kid," the older boy said. "How you gonna pay me for that?"

Nick and Tim looked at each other, eyes growing wide.

"Somebody's gotta pay for that scratch," the boy said, pushing Nick in the chest as he glanced at Sarah. "Maybe I'll just take this pretty little thing for a drive and call it even."

Sarah leaned into Nick, grabbing his arm.

Nick cleared his throat, trying to sound brave. "Show me the scratch."

The boy leaned close to Nick. "You callin' me a liar?" He poked Nick in the chest.

"Uh, no, just, uh, show me the scratch."

"I said it was scratched, you scrawny piece of—"

"Hey, Nick, you okay?"

Nick turned and saw Allen Neal and several other football players walking towards them.

"Hey, Allen," Nick said. "We're just talking about this guy's car."

Allen and several large boys, linemen on the football team, stood next to them. Allen looked at the car and back at Nick. "This guy giving you any trouble?"

The older boy took a step back. "Hey, you're Neal, the quarterback, right?"

Allen nodded. "Yeah. So are you bothering my friends here?"

"Naw, just talkin', that's all." The boy patted Nick on the shoulder. "You see, they was leanin' on my car and I don't like people leanin' on my car."

"We said we were sorry," Nick said. "Didn't mean any harm."

Allen stood next to Nick and looked at the older boy, waiting for a response.

The older boy smiled and backed away. "Hey, no problem, man. It's cool." He reached out his hand to Nick. "My name's Rocky. I graduated two years ago. Didn't play any football, but I saw lots of action, if you know what I mean." He looked at Sarah and winked.

"Nice to meet you, Rocky. See you around. Thanks, Allen." Nick grabbed Sarah's hand and hurriedly walked past the three boys to the crowd in front of the Frosty Freeze, Tim and Susie following.

"What a creep," Sarah said.

"My older brother went to school with him," Tim said. "He's in trouble all the time. Breaking and entering, petty theft, that kind of stuff. He's a member of some car club. Best to stay away from that guy."

"I will, don't worry." Nick looked at Sarah. "I'm glad Allen was around."

Sarah nodded. "Me, too, but you handled yourself okay, Nicky."

Nick felt his neck getting red. "I have to be home at eleven thirty, so I better get going. Tim, can you give me a ride home?"

"Sure. You girls need a ride home?"

"My mom's picking me and Susie up in a few minutes, but thanks," Sarah said, standing on her tiptoes and giving Nick a peck on his cheek. "Mr. Hero." She gazed into his eyes and smiled.

"Okay, but no walking through the woods at night, you promise?"

She smiled and squeezed his hand. "I promise."

Nick said goodbye to everyone as he and Tim walked towards Tim's pickup. "I wanted to ask Sarah if I could walk her home. Sure wish I had my driver's license, you lucky dog."

"Aw, you'll have yours soon enough," Tim said. "I guess being held back in third grade's paying off now, huh?"

Nick smiled, remembering Tim's long battle with pneumonia in the third grade, forcing him to be held back a year. "And it put us in the same grade, so it all worked out."

They climbed into the red pickup and pulled out of the parking lot. Nick saw Rocky and his friends staring at them.

"I don't think we've seen the last of Rocky," Nick said.

"Yeah, I think you're right, Nicky. Hope Neal's around the next time, too."

Nick glanced back at the lights of the Frosty Freeze as they pulled out onto Highway Six, but Sarah was lost in the crowd. He touched his cheek where she'd kissed him and felt like he could float home.

CHAPTER 5

As Nick climbed the steps he looked up at Acorn Public School, a big, red-brick two-story building that included both the Acorn Elementary and High School. It was an imposing-looking facility on the outside, with wide concrete steps leading to the front double doors. Nick walked the four blocks from his house to the school with his two little brothers every day. Bo was in second grade and little Ethan in a special pre-school, set up to help working mothers. The boys' mom worked mornings from six to noon as the town's telephone switchboard operator and their father worked in Council Bluffs as an insurance adjuster, leaving home at six thirty in the morning every day, so Nick had to get his brothers cleaned up, dressed, fed, and ready for school each morning. Ethan was no problem, but Bo was a daily pain in the butt.

Nick climbed the last few steps with Bo and Ethan on either side, helping Ethan up the last step, pulling him into the air.

"Wheee!" Ethan yelled. "Do it again, Nicky."

"Nope, time for school, little man."

Bo ran through the double doors and rushed off to his classroom. Nick shook his head as he walked Ethan down the hallway, stopping every few feet to accept congratulations from teachers and parents.

"Great game, Nick!"

"What a blowout, Nick!"

"Way to kick butt, Nick!"

Nick smiled broadly as Ethan kept looking up at him with his big eyes. They came to the pre-school classroom on the first floor, which was the Elementary part of the building. Nick bent down and straightened his little brother's shirt, tucking it into his jeans.

"You have fun today, little man," he said, hugging his brother.

"Okay, Nicky. Why does everybody like you so much?"

"Aw, I don't know. Because I can run fast, I guess. Go on, get inside. Mom will pick you and Bo up this afternoon."

Ethan turned and ran into the classroom, immediately heading for the toy box.

Nick waved at the pretty twenty-something teacher's aide, Miss Hastings.

"Nice game Friday night, Nick," she said, waving back.

Nick smiled as he continued down the hallway, dodging kids, reaching the wide staircase that led to the high school classrooms on the second floor. The bell began to ring, so he bounded up the stairs two at a time and reached his classroom just as Mr. Walters was closing the door.

"Glad you weren't this slow on Friday night," Walters said, a slight smirk on his face.

Nick walked back to his desk in the last row, looking around the room and spotting Sarah. She was grinning at him as he sat down.

Mr. Walters cleared his throat, the signal that class was starting. The laughter and chit-chatting stopped.

"I hope everyone had a good weekend," Walters said. "I know a couple of boys in this room had a pretty good Friday night."

This was the signal to begin the clapping and cheering, all eyes on Nick, Tim and several other players in the room.

"Okay, okay, we got that out of our system, so let's get back to world history. Open your books to chapter two. I assume you all read the assignment over the weekend," Walters said, a smile on his face.

Everyone groaned.

Nick looked over at Sarah, who was looking back at him. She was two rows over from Nick, and several desks in front. He couldn't keep his eyes off of her, thinking about Friday night.

"Nick, since you made a little history of your own on Friday night, why don't you do the honors by starting us off and reading the first chapter." Walters grinned.

Another round of clapping ensued as Nick felt his face grow red. He cleared his throat and glanced up at Mr. Walters.

"Anytime, son, and don't you even think about fumbling it." Walters chuckled.

Everyone broke out in laughter, even Nick. He shook his head as he began reading.

CHAPTER 6

At twilight, Jimmy pulled the truck up to the edge of the cornfield, out of sight of the farmhouse where his father lived. He had arrived from his cross-country trip two weeks before and found his father living on this bleak patch of Iowa farmland, alone and demented. After reconnecting with his estranged father, Jimmy learned that he had been fired as a teacher due to some issues with young boys. Jimmy remembered his mother talking, ranting actually, about his father and his penchant for boys. His father rarely left the old farmhouse now, the farm falling into disrepair, the fields lying fallow, except for the one cornfield. The old man kept the cornfield alive and fertile for some reason, and now Jimmy knew why.

He got out of the truck and walked to the corner of the field, gazing back at the old farmhouse. He saw a light on in the kitchen but no other activity. He walked back to the pickup and opened the passenger door, lifting the young girl out of the seat and throwing her over his shoulder. The smell of the chloroform was still strong, so he lifted his handkerchief to his nose and began walking through the cornfield, swiping the brown cornstalks away from his face.

It took him ten minutes to reach the clearing in the middle of the field. He slowly dropped the girl to the ground, standing over her and staring for several seconds, his eye twitching. She was a brunette, short and stocky, but with a pretty face. He bent down and moved her hair away from her face, seeing the smooth skin. He took off his glove and caressed her face, like his mother used to do to him. He looked at her legs, covered by the pleated skirt.

He lifted the skirt and rubbed her legs, from her knees to her private parts, closing his eyes when he felt her fleshy thighs. He opened his eyes, covered her exposed legs, and stood up. He would enjoy this one when she awoke from the chloroform-induced sleep. She had fought him, scratched and clawed until the chloroform kicked in, then went limp, just like all the rest.

He walked to a pile of dead cornstalks and began removing them until he saw the underground cellar door. He took out a key, opened the padlock, and lifted the heavy door up, pushing it to the ground with a thump. He checked the girl, then took his flashlight and pointed it at the steep concrete stairs. He peered into the blackness of the fallout shelter below and began descending carefully, a step at a time, until he came to another door at the bottom. He unlocked the padlock and opened it slowly, smelling the dank, musty air immediately as it wafted out of the dark room. He reached down and picked up a kerosene lantern and lit it, illuminating the dark room. He held his handkerchief to his nose as he slowly walked to the far wall. His last treasure was lying lifeless against the wall on a thin mattress, curled up in a ball. He knelt down and felt for a pulse and found none. After unlocking her ankle from the shackles, he put a canvas tarp on the ground, picked up the dead girl and placed her on it. He then began rolling her into the tarp until she was completely covered. He picked her up, threw her over his shoulder and walked out of the cold room and up the steep stairs. He was out of breath when he reached the top, He placed her on the cold ground and took several deep breaths, smiling as he looked down at his new treasure.

Jimmy picked the new girl up and carried her down the steps and placed her in the same spot next to the wall. He attached the shackles to her ankle and locked them in place, then walked to the far corner of the room and brought back an empty bucket, toilet paper, and a thermos of water, placing them next to the girl. He took a candy bar out of his jacket pocket and laid it next to the thermos. He then got a blanket from the corner and covered her head to foot, making sure she was lying in a comfortable position. He always took care of them in the beginning, until he tired of them. He would be back later to enjoy his new treasure, but right now he had to dispose of the old one. He turned on the electric space heater and waited until the room was warm and toasty, then closed the door, locked it, placed the kerosene lamp next to the door after turning it off, and climbed back up the steep concrete stairs into the cold night air.

CHAPTER 7

Nick and Tim stood on the sidelines of Woodrow Wilson High's football field and watched in awe as the green-and-white-clad Wilson High Warriors came bursting onto the field. They ran to the center of the field, gathered into a big circle and began chanting.

"Warriors! Warriors! Warriors!"

"Damn, they're big." Tim stared, mouth open.

Nick watched the green and white circle begin to move left to right, then right to left before they broke up. "Uh huh."

Coach Davis began marching up and down the sideline, yelling at the Acorn players. "Get your heads up, boys! They aren't any bigger or better than you, they just sound tough. You boys go out there and show 'em what tough is."

Allen Neal yelled, "Mighty Oaks!"

The entire team followed his lead. "Mighty Oaks, Mighty Oaks, Mighty Oaks!"

That got everyone excited and ready to play. Nick stretched his legs as Neal went to the center of the field for the coin toss. After Neal came back to the sideline, the coach gathered the team around him.

"Kick-off team, on the field. Let's show these big city boys how we play football in the country!"

"Mighty Oaks!" was heard up and down the sideline as the kick-off team ran onto the field.

"Go get 'em, Timmy!" Nick slapped him on the shoulder pads.

Tim grinned and ran onto the field and took his position near the side-line, several yards behind the teed-up football. The kicker raised his hand, got the go-ahead, and took several steps and kicked the ball high in the air, end-over-end, to the Wilson twenty yard line. The Wilson receiver caught it cleanly and cut to his left across the field where he handed it off to another player, their speedster named Monroe.

"Reverse!" Nick heard Coach Davis yell. "Right side! Right side!"

It was too late. The Acorn players were caught off guard and Monroe had a clear field down the right sideline, directly in front of the Acorn bench. He waltzed into the end zone untouched. Tim Preston made a last-ditch effort to tackle him but fell yards short.

"Darn, that guy's got some jets," Nick said to the player next to him.

After Wilson kicked the extra-point, making the score seven to zero, Coach Davis gathered his receiving team around him. "Let's run the same thing back at them," he said. "Thomas, you receive the kick-off and hand it off to Paxton on the reverse. Everybody, and I mean everybody, knock somebody down. Let's go!"

Nick felt someone grab his arm. It was Walters.

"Just like last week, Nick. Turn on those jets, son."

Nick nodded to his coach and ran onto the field. *This doesn't feel anything like last week.*

The reverse didn't fool Wilson High as Nick was tackled on the Acorn ten-yard line. From there it got worse. The Oaks lost five more yards on two plays into the middle, putting them close to their own goal line.

Allen Neal leaned into the huddle, looking directly at Nick. "Nick, get us out of here, just like last week. Eighty-eight reverse, on one."

The Oaks broke the huddle and Nick took his position on the right side. Neal barked out the signals, the ball was snapped and Nick started in motion to the left, waiting for Neal to hand him the ball, but Neal never made it. The middle linebacker of the Warriors blitzed through the line and caught him just as he was faking the handoff to Thomas. The ball was knocked free and bounded into the Oaks end zone, where the middle linebacker pounced on it, resulting in another touchdown for Wilson.

Nick sat on the metal bench in the visitor's locker room, holding his black helmet in his hands as he stared down at the floor. He had blood on his gold jersey from a hit to the nose and felt his ankle swelling up after he had twisted it in the third quarter. He was just as dejected as he had been happy the week before. Acorn had lost the game forty-two to seven, with the second team playing most of the fourth quarter. Mike Thomas scored the Oaks only touchdown on a two-yard run in the third quarter. Nick had twenty-seven yards rushing the entire game.

Coach Davis walked into the locker room and slammed his clipboard to the floor, making a loud crack. Everyone looked up.

"Well, we sure taught them about country toughness, didn't we?" he yelled. "You guys had your heads up your ass all night, probably thinking about how great you were last week. Well, last week was a joke, just like tonight was a joke."

The coach looked at Nick. "Where was the big hero tonight, Paxton? You looked like you had cement in your cleats all night."

Nick lowered his head.

"And Neal, where was the leadership out there? You looked like you were playing a pick-up game on the sandlot, for God's sake!"

Coach Davis scanned the room, looking at every player, walking around, a scowl crossing his face. "Mighty Oaks, my ass! More like little twigs, blowing in the wind. You get your heads straight before next Friday night. Coach Walters and I will have something to help you come next Monday. You'll be running your butts off until your damn cows come home!"

Coach Davis picked up his clipboard and walked out of the room, slamming the door behind him.

Coach Walters stared around the room at the terrified and defeated football players. "They were better than us, but not thirty-five points better. You guys quit, surrendered. You were beat the minute they ran onto the field. I'm disappointed in every damn one of you."

Walters walked towards Nick. "And I know you have more inside of you than you showed tonight." He slapped Nick on the shoulder pads. "And it's up to you, every one of you, to prove it next Friday against Walnut Hills. They're our first league game, so every game counts from now on. Shake this one off and get your minds ready for next week. Grab your gear and get on the bus—now!"

CHAPTER 8

The mood at Acorn High was dark on Monday morning. No backslaps, no congratulations, just shaking of heads as Nick walked the halls. *From penthouse to outhouse in one week.*

He walked into Mr. Walter's history class a few minutes early, hoping to see Sarah. He hadn't seen her all weekend and wasn't sure why. He had called her several times, but no one answered. He even rode his bike to her house on Sunday and knocked on the door, but still no answer.

He looked around the half-empty class room, sat down at his desk and laid his head in his hands.

A group of students walked in, talking loudly, so Nick looked up. They stared at him, one pointing to his face.

"What happened to your face?" a boy said.

Nick blinked, and then remembered the white tape on his broken nose. His mom made him wear it to help the healing but he hated it.

"Broke my nose Friday night." Nick felt his face turning red.

The boy laughed. "It looks like you broke more than your nose."

The others in his group snickered, taking their seats when Mr. Walters walked in. Walters put some books on his desk and looked back at Nick. "How's the nose, Nick?"

Nick shifted in his seat. "Okay."

Walters looked at the clock, which read seven fifty-eight, two minutes before the bell. He walked down to Nick's desk and put his arm on his shoulder. "And the ankle, the swelling go down yet?"

"Yeah, it's okay." Nick looked around in embarrassment.

"Good. We need you Friday night." Walters smiled and patted him on the shoulder.

The bell rang and the last few students ran into the room and took their seats. Nick glanced over at Sarah's empty desk. Now he was getting worried.

"Okay, let's settle down everyone," Walters said. "Anyone know where Miss Rogers is?"

Just then the door opened and Sarah rushed in, her blonde hair tied up in a ponytail. "Sorry, Mr. Walters." She was out of breath as she walked to her desk, briefly looking at Nick.

"Nice of you to join us, Sarah," Walters said. "Okay, class, let's open our book to chapter three, The Byzantine Empire."

A groan went up as everyone opened their world history book.

"History isn't always fun or relevant," Walters said, "but it's always important. Sarah, you want to start us off?"

Sarah nodded, glanced back at Nick and smiled.

Nick suddenly felt better, just seeing her smile. The pain in his nose and ankle didn't feel so bad now. Life was returning to normal.

After class, Sarah, in a pretty green plaid dress and white mohair sweater, sidled up next to Nick at a hallway water fountain.

Nick turned towards her and felt a jolt of electricity run through his body once again.

"How's the nose?" she said, reaching up to touch it.

"It's okay," he said, putting his hand on hers. "I missed you this weekend."

"I know, me too. My parents decided to drive up to Sioux City to see my older brother. He's going to college up there."

"Oh, wish I had known. I was a little, uh, worried." Nick wished he hadn't said anything.

"Oh, why?" She tilted her head, a smile on her face.

"Uh, just thought that maybe, you know, we could, uh . . ."

She smiled and touched his arm. "Really? Oh, I'm sorry, Nicky. It was last minute and I didn't have your phone number, and, well . . . I'm sorry."

Nick chuckled. "All you have to do is call the operator, who's my mother."

Sarah laughed. "I know, I didn't think about that."

When the bell rang, they said goodbye and hurried off to their next class: Nick to English, Sarah to Home Economics. Nick looked back as he entered his classroom and saw Sarah smiling at him at the end of the hall. They exchanged waves before she disappeared into the classroom.

CHAPTER 9

Walnut Hills was only fifteen miles from Acorn and similar in size, around twelve hundred people. They were usually the patsy of the league, at least in football, but were a powerhouse in wrestling, winning the conference championship almost every year. Tim Preston was a wrestler after football season was over and had several friends who lived in Walnut Hills.

"You think Walnut Hills will be the team to beat again this year in wrestling?" Nick looked at Tim, who sat next to him on the team bus.

"Yeah, no question. Most of their wrestlers don't play football, just work out all year long. It takes a whole different set of muscles and stamina to wrestle."

"What weight are you gonna wrestle at this year?"

"Don't know, probably one thirty-three, if I can't make weight at one twenty-eight. I weigh around one forty right now, so I'll have some work to do after football."

"You think I'd be a good wrestler?" Nick said.

Tim looked Nick up and down. "I don't think you'd have the stamina, old buddy. Plus, you're too good at basketball. Walters would never let you wrestle."

"What do you mean I don't have the stamina? I can run for miles without getting tired."

"It's a different kind of stamina. I wrestle all-out for six minutes, with every muscle in my body stretched to the limit and my heart rate at maximum. It's just a different sport, and I don't think you'd like it."

Nick nodded his head. "Guess I'll stick to basketball, anyway."

Coach Walters, sitting two rows away, turned and looked at Nick and Tim. "You both better get your minds on football or you can start practicing those other sports right now."

Nick, feeling the heat on his neck, nodded to his coach. "Damn, he has good ears," he whispered to Tim.

Three hours later the Acorn Oaks were back on the bus, feeling satisfied with a twenty-seven to six win over Walnut Hills. Nick had run a kick-off back for a touchdown to start the second half and ran for another touchdown on an end-around sweep in the third quarter. He was sitting next to Tim, gingerly touching his tender nose, when Coach Walters walked back to the boys.

"You finally got your head in the game in the second half, Paxton. Nice game. How's the nose and ankle?"

Nick smiled at his coach. "Nose is a little tender, but not bad. The ankle held up pretty good, but not a hundred percent yet."

Walters patted him on the shoulder. "Well, good game. We need you one hundred percent next week against Lynn, so stay off that ankle and protect that nose."

"Okay, coach."

"Preston, nice interception and good tackling tonight, for a wrestler," Walters smiled.

Tim grinned. "Thanks, coach!"

When they got off the bus at the high school, a large group of people greeted them, something they hadn't gotten after the game against Wilson the week before. Nick looked out the window and saw the cheerleaders bouncing up and down, leading cheers for the crowd.

"Mighty Oaks! Mighty Oaks!" they screamed as the players stepped off the bus one at a time. When Nick stepped off the bus, a cheer went up from the back of the crowd.

"Must be my family," he said to Tim.

Sarah came running up to him, a big grin on her face. "Mr. Hero again," she said, planting a kiss on his cheek. "How's the nose?"

Nick grinned. "Nose is okay. You going to Frosty's later?"

"Sure, we'll all be there after you take a shower," she said, holding her nose. "You'd better hurry before I change my mind."

Nick laughed and headed for the locker room in the basement of the school. He turned and watched Sarah do her cheerleading thing for several seconds and then ducked into the dark tunnel leading to the locker room.

CHAPTER 10

Sunday night was family night at the Paxton house, usually spent watching television or doing homework. Tonight the whole family was gathered around the black-and-white TV. Little Ethan was lying on the floor playing with toy army soldiers, with Bo next to him knocking them over when their mother wasn't looking. Nick sat on the sofa next to his mother, staring at the fuzzy images on the screen. Clint Paxton sat in his easy chair puffing on a pipe filled with an aromatic cherry-flavored tobacco.

"Nicky, can you wiggle the rabbit ears a little to see if we can get a better picture?" Eloise said.

Nick got up and walked to the TV, moving the two antennas around until the picture cleared up.

"Thanks, Nicky."

They watched as Walter Cronkite leaned on his desk, his grandfatherly face peering out at them.

"President Kennedy received the letter from Soviet Premier Khrushchev today, which stated that the young President should be under no illusions. An American attack on Cuba would bring retaliatory action against Berlin."

"What does he mean, retali . . . retali . . ." Bo asked, looking at his dad.

"Retaliatory. It means the Commies will strike us back if we do anything in Cuba," Nick said, glancing at his father. "Right, Dad?"

Clint Paxton continued watching the TV, nodding his head as he puffed on his pipe. "That's right, Nicky. Those damn Russians are testing us, testing President Kennedy to see how far they can push him."

"Why are the Commies so mad? They're the ones with all the bombs and stuff in Cuba." Bo said, standing up. "Where's Cuba?"

Nick shook his head. "What do they teach you in school, knucklehead? Cuba is off the coast of Florida, not very far away."

"I knew that," Bo said. "Why does President Kennedy say 'Cuber' instead of Cuba?"

Nick reached over and punched his younger brother in the arm. "'Cause he's from Boston, they all talk weird."

"Khrushchev is going to push us until we have no other choice but to retaliate," Clint said. "Mark my words, this is going to escalate until someone pushes the damn button."

Clint got up and changed the channel on the TV, then raised his hand to shush the boys.

"And in local news, two counties in southwestern Iowa, Walnut and Adams, are dealing with their own crisis. A teenage girl from Walnut Hills was reported as missing on Friday morning. This makes the third teenage girl reported missing in the last three weeks, the first two from Adams County. The families are distraught as law enforcement officials frantically look for the girls. So far they have no clues to the three girl's disappearance. Residents of surrounding counties are urged to keep a watchful eye out for the girls, pictured on your screen, and contact your local police or sheriff's office if you see or hear anything. And a final word to the parents in southwest Iowa. Keep your doors locked and your children close until this crisis is resolved."

Clint got up and turned off the TV, took the pipe out of his mouth, and exhaled one last puff of smoke. "The last girl is from Walnut County, right next to us. You know any of these girls, Nick?"

Nick shook his head. "No, but we just played Walnut Hills on Friday."

Eloise Paxton stood up and walked quickly to the front door and locked it. "Bo, go lock the back door, please."

"I don't think there is a lock on the back door, Mom," Bo said, standing up. "But I'll go check."

Eloise looked sternly at her husband. "Clint, I want you to go to the hardware store tomorrow morning and get us a lock for the back door."

Clint put his hands out, palms down, and slowly moved them up and down. "Let's settle down here," he said. "Panic isn't going to accomplish anything."

Eloise continued to stare at her husband as Nick and wide-eyed Ethan stared up at her.

"Okay, okay, I'll buy a lock in the morning," Clint said, looking at the two boys.

"What about tonight?" Eloise asked.

"It's okay, Mom," Bo said, walking back into the living room. "We have a hook lock so I locked it. I didn't even know we had one."

Clint smiled at his middle son, letting out a chuckle. "Neither did I."

"Are there bad men outside?" Little Ethan looked at his mother.

Eloise reached down and picked the three-year old up, cradling him to her chest. "No, we're just being careful, sweetie. Nothing to worry about."

Bo came running back into the living room carrying his little league bat. "I'll break his legs if he tries to get into our house!"

Nick reached for the bat and grabbed it from Bo. "Hold on, slugger, nobody's getting into our house. Besides, it sounds like whoever is doing this only wants girls. We're all boys in this family—except Mom, of course."

Clint and Eloise laughed, with little Ethan giggling along with them. "Yeah, we're boys!"

Nick slowly lost his grin when he thought about Sarah. *But Sarah's a girl, and a pretty one. I need to talk to her tomorrow at school about this.*

"I think we need to be just as worried about the Russians," Clint said, puffing on his pipe again. "Things look like they're starting to heat up in Cuba."

"That's Cuber, Dad," Bo said with a big grin.

Everyone in the Paxton family laughed, except Nick.

CHAPTER 11

Jimmy pulled his red cap tighter as he walked through the chilly evening air, adjusting the bag on his shoulder. He began pushing his way through the rows of corn, slapping away the long, sharp leaves, keeping his flashlight trained on the ground in front of him, looking for the markers that would lead him to his treasure. As the sun finally set in the west, he broke out into a clearing in the middle of the cornfield.

He shined his flashlight on the pile of dead corn stalks in the middle of the clearing and began moving them to one side. When the last corn stalk was moved, he bent down and unlocked the padlock on the latch. Putting the key and the padlock in his overalls, he slowly opened the door, the rusted hinges creaking loudly. He laid the heavy door on the ground and shined his flashlight into the blackness. He took the steps one at a time, his heart pounding with each step. Knowing what was at the bottom of this pit excited him, making his left eye twitch. As he came to the bottom, he took out another key and unlocked the padlock and slowly opened the creaking door to more blackness. The familiar smell of urine and feces almost made him gag. He took a step into the pitch black darkness and felt for the Kerosene lantern next to the door. He turned the knob on the lamp and lit it, peering into the musty, dank room. He felt the warmth of the space heater as he peered around the room. His heart was hammering, his eye twitching uncontrollably as he saw his newest treasure against the far wall, dressed in her cheerleader outfit, curled up in a ball. A crooked smile crossed his face as he slowly walked towards the terrified girl.

Jimmy set the bag down on the floor next to the girl and took out some bread and a tin of soup, placing them next to her. "Here you go, eat."

The girl turned to look at him. Her eyes were bloodshot and had dark circles around them from the smeared makeup. She shook her head, turning back to the wall.

Jimmy grabbed her arm and turned her around. "You need to eat something, pretty one. Come on, open your mouth."

He took the lid off the tin and scooped some hot soup into a spoon. "Open up."

The girl was shaking, but opened her mouth. He poured the spoonful of soup into her mouth slowly. He did this until the soup was all gone, then broke off a piece of bread and gave it to her.

"Are you warm enough, pretty one?"

She nodded, pulling the blanket up to her chin.

"Do you remember my name?" Jimmy smiled at the frightened girl.

She nodded again.

"What is it? I want to hear you say it."

She licked her dry, cracked lips. "Ji . . . Jimmy."

Jimmy grinned. "Yes, very good. What's your name, pretty one?"

She stared at him, not speaking.

"That's okay. We can get to know each other later. But right now, I need to make sure you're healthy and clean. Are you clean?"

She shook her head.

"Then let's clean you up."

Jimmy slowly pulled the blanket off of her and looked at the sweater with the 'WH' on the front, the pleated red-and-white skirt that he pulled up, exposing her milky thighs. He looked into her tear-filled eyes and smiled his crooked smile. "My sweet treasure."

CHAPTER 12

After dropping Ethan off at his pre-school classroom, Nick bounded up the steps to the second floor, where high school students scrambled to get to their classrooms. He looked up and down the hallway for Sarah but didn't see her. Several boys walked by and slapped him on the shoulder.

"Great game, Nicky."

"What a run back, Nick!"

"Way to go, Nick!"

Nick waded through the crowd of kids in the hallway and entered his World History classroom. Mr. Walters wasn't at his desk yet, but he saw Sarah in the corner talking with some other girls. She wore a blue poodle skirt and a light blue sweater. Her hair was down below her shoulders, shimmering in the light. Nick felt his heart skip a beat as he walked to her.

"Hi, Sarah."

Sarah turned and smiled. "Hi, Nicky."

The other girls giggled as they walked to their desks.

"How, uh, was your weekend?" Nick asked.

Sarah reached out and laced her fingers through his. "Same stuff, mostly chores and homework. You?"

He coughed. "Yeah, same stuff, I guess. I, uh, need to talk to you after class. Did you see the news—" Nick stopped when he heard the door open.

"Alright, let's settle down and take your seats," Mr. Walters said as he entered the room and walked to his desk.

"After class," Nick said, releasing Sarah's hand.

She nodded and walked quickly to her desk.

"Nick, you going to stand up all class or sit down?" Walters said, staring at him.

Nick felt his face burn as he walked to his desk.

"Good choice, Mr. Paxton." Walters smiled. "How's that nose, by the way?"

Nick instinctively reached up and touched his sore nose. "Uh, it's okay, Coach, er, Mr. Walters."

Nick heard giggles around him as he stared at the top of his desk.

"Good. I hope everyone had a nice weekend and, more importantly, everyone read the assignment?" Walters looked around the room. "We have one piece of important business to take care of before we jump back into the Byzantine Empire."

Everyone in the room sat quietly in anticipation, staring at Mr. Walters.

Walters held up a mimeographed piece of paper and waved it. "A directive from the principal's office that I need to read to everyone.

> From Principal Hayes to the student body of Acorn High School. There have been some apparent kidnappings in several nearby counties, specifically Adams and Walnut counties, where three teenage girls have gone missing over the last three weeks.

Walters looked up to make sure everyone was paying attention then looked down at the memo.

> It is not known at this time what happened, but we need to take precautions at Acorn High to ensure nothing like this happens here. Until such time as the girls are found or the perpetrator captured, every student, male or female, will walk in pairs to and from school and while at school.

Walters heard some whispering and looked up from the memo. He glanced around the room before continuing.

> While we don't want to alarm you, please be very alert and watchful for any stranger, male or female, on or

close to the school grounds. If you notice anyone act-
ing strangely, or if they are unfamiliar to you, contact
my office immediately. We have brought in security
personnel to stand watch at the front entrance and the
side entrance that leads to the playground and rec area.

Walters looked up and saw several hands in the air. "Hold your questions
until I've finished." He cleared his throat.

We are sending memos with each one of you to give to
your parents, to make sure they are aware of the potential danger that exists in our area. Above all, be calm,
but cautious. Principal Leonard Hayes.

Walters began passing out copies of the memo for students to give to the
their parents. "Questions?"

Half the class put their hands in the air and the room began to grow
louder from the whispering and mumbling.

"Okay, one at a time, and no talking. Everyone listen up." Walters pointed
to a girl in the front row. "Becky."

"Mr. Walters, how old were the girls?"

"Teenagers, all approximately fifteen or sixteen, according to accounts."
He pointed to a boy in the second row. "Dwayne."

"Uh, did they just disappear without anyone seeing anything?"

"Apparently, yes. It's not known where the girls were when they disappeared, but it could have been as they were walking home from school, in
the rec area, at the ice cream parlor. No one knows at this point." He noticed
the fear creeping into the student's eyes. "One more question, then we need
to get back to work." He pointed towards the back of the room. "Sarah."

"I know one of the girls, the one from Walnut County. She's a cheerleader
at Walnut Hills and we attended cheerleader camp together last summer.
Her name is Debbie. I talked to a couple of the other cheerleaders over there
last Friday and they said she always walked home through some wooded
area next to the school. She's been missing since last Thursday."

Nick stared at Sarah. *You knew about this?*

"Did you or the kids from Walnut Hills inform the sheriff of this?" Walters said.

"I didn't, but they probably have. I don't know." Sarah glanced around the room.

The room suddenly got very noisy with everyone talking at once.

"Okay, quiet down," Walters said. "Sarah, let's you and I walk down to Mr. Hayes' office and tell him what you told us. Everyone, turn to the assignment on page seventy-one and begin reading—silently. Sarah and I will be back in a couple of minutes."

Nick watched Sarah walk out of the room with Mr. Walters and stared at the door for several seconds.

"Nick, did Sarah tell you about that?" Tim Preston was looking back at him from his desk.

"No, didn't say a word on Friday night," Nick said. "What's going on in her head?"

"She probably didn't think it had anything to do with us, so she forgot about it." Susie Daniels was looking at Nick. "How could they just vanish like that, without anyone seeing anything?"

Nick's mind was going in a hundred different directions. *Why didn't Sarah tell me?*

CHAPTER 13

The rest of the school day was like a blur to Nick, with people whispering, gossiping, the fear in their eyes palpable. He saw girls walking together holding hands, glancing around at everyone. He went down to Ethan's room at lunch time to check on him, saw that he was okay, then went to check on Bo.

"How's everything going, little man," Nick said to his younger brother.

"Nicky, everybody is going bonkers! Even my teacher looks scared. I'm not scared, though, Nick."

Nick smiled. "Just be careful and keep looking for anyone you don't know or that might look suspicious. That what your teacher said?"

Bo was excited. "No, Principal Hayes came to talk to us. He told us not to leave the school grounds without a parent or guardian. Guess that's you, Nicky."

Nick clapped him on the shoulder softly. "Mom will pick you up after school because I have football practice. Make sure you hold Ethan's hand the entire time until Mom gets here, okay?"

"Okay, Nicky. I'll protect him." Bo gave a karate chop and a kick in the air.

Nick laughed. "Good man, Bo. Just don't take any chances. See you later."

"Later, gator," Bo said.

Nick walked back up the stairs to the second floor and saw Sarah talking to a group of girls. He walked up to her and tapped her on the shoulder.

When she turned around he noticed that her eyes were red.

"What's wrong, Sarah?"

Sarah pulled him to her and put her face in his shoulder. When he heard her sniffle he pushed her back and stared at her. "What is it?"

"Principal Hayes just announced that the first two girls have been found. Nick, they're *dead*."

Nick felt the blood drain from his face, felt his muscles tighten. "Oh no."

"A fisherman on the Pottawattamie River over in Adams County found them in some bushes on the banks of the river," she said, wiping her nose with a handkerchief. "They were naked."

Nick couldn't get any words out, so he pulled Sarah to him and hugged her. He looked down the hallway and small groups of students were huddled together doing the same thing.

Nick finally found his voice. "The girl from Walnut Hills, did they..."

Sarah shook her head. "I haven't heard anything yet." She stared at Nick. "Nicky, I'm so scared."

A voice over the loudspeaker got everyone's attention. "All students and faculty are to go directly to the auditorium for an assembly. Sit in your designated spots with your grade level. Please do so quickly, but quietly."

Nick looked at Sarah, wiping away another tear. "Let's go."

They followed everyone down the stairs to the basketball gym, which served double duty as the assembly auditorium. Nick and Sarah slid into a seat in the bleachers, Sarah resting her head on Nick's shoulder. Tim and Susie Daniels slid in next to them. Nick looked across the basketball floor at the elementary children filing in, class by class. He spotted Bo, who saw him and waved. Then he spotted Ethan walking in, holding hands with a little girl, following their teacher to their sitting area.

Principal Leonard Hayes walked to a microphone in the middle of the auditorium, followed by another man in a uniform.

After tapping the microphone to make sure it was on, Principal Hayes began speaking. "By now, you have all been told about what happened today. Over in Adams County, two of the missing girls were discovered on the banks of the Pottawattamie River." Hayes cleared his throat. "They were both . . ." He hesitated, glancing at the other man. "They were both dead."

A hush fell over the auditorium as the fear engulfed every single student and teacher in attendance.

"The girl from Walnut County is still missing," Hayes continued. "Sheriff Logan, the Sheriff of Acorn County, will give us some instructions on how to deal with this news, and what will happen here in Acorn over the next few days. Sheriff Logan."

Kenny Logan, a middle-aged man with grayish hair, stepped to the microphone.

"This is a terrible shock to southwest Iowa, as you all know. We are taking every precaution to make sure this does not happen to anyone here in Acorn. I am adding reserve deputies to my staff and we will also be assisted by the police from Council Bluffs and surrounding counties. We are closing the school until these murders are investigated fully. We are calling all of your parents to come pick you up within the next hour. You will not be allowed to leave school property without a parent or responsible adult escorting you. Everyone will sign out before you leave to ensure that all students are safely home. You are to remain here in the auditorium until your parents or a responsible adult comes to pick you up. Please remain calm and orderly as you leave. Principal Hayes has another announcement."

Principal Hayes stepped to the microphone. "We have established a hot line, through Sheriff Logan's office, for any information regarding suspicious people or strangers in Acorn or the surrounding area. Sheriff Logan and his deputies will be handing out some flyers to your parents when you are picked up. Please stay calm, but vigilant, and keep a watchful eye out for anyone or anything that may look suspicious. We are hoping that the perpetrator of these horrible acts will be caught soon so that Acorn can get back to normal. God bless you . . . and be safe."

Nick and Sarah sat silently, watching the scene in front of them. Sarah had Nick's hand in a death grip.

"Sarah, easy, I need this hand Friday night." He smiled at her, trying to ease the tension. It didn't work.

"How can you think of football right now? Nick, those girls are dead and the person, or animal, that did it is walking around, maybe right here in Acorn."

Nick put his arm around her, but she pushed it away. "Is this a big joke to you? What if that was me next to that river?"

"Hey, easy Sarah. What's gotten into you?"

She stared at him for several seconds before the tears began to flow. She buried her face in his shoulder, the tears turning into sobs.

Nick stroked her hair, not knowing what to say. "What's going on, Sarah?"

She slowly moved away from him and wiped her eyes. "I should have told someone about the Walnut Hills girl. I just didn't think that it would be like this. I feel so guilty, Nick."

"It's not your fault, the girl had already been kidnapped. What could you have done?"

"I could have gone to Principal Hayes, or the Sheriff, or at least told my parents, or you."

Nick saw the guilt and sadness in her eyes. "It's okay, Sarah. Nobody knew that it would end up like this. Now everyone knows and we can protect ourselves. It's not your fault."

Sarah stared at him with a look of pure fear in her eyes. "I think I might have seen him."

Nick's eyes grew wide. "Seen who?"

"The man, the . . . the kidnapper."

Nick blinked and shook his head. "What? When?"

"The day of the Fall Festival, when I was late getting to the parade. I ran out of the house and saw this black pickup truck on the street with a man sitting behind the wheel, watching me."

Nick's breathing became short, his heart beating through his chest. "What happened? Why didn't you tell me, or somebody?"

"I was embarrassed, and I didn't know who he was. I just ran through the woods until I saw you at the parade. He scared me."

"Why did he scare you?"

"When I ran out of the house and started running down the street, he started following me in his pickup. He got within a few feet of me when I started to run across the street. He stopped right in front of me and stared at me, and then I ran into the woods. I was so scared that he was going to come after me, I ran as fast as I could."

Nick sat still, stunned at what she was saying. "Can you describe the truck, his face?"

She nodded. "It was an older, black pickup . . ."

"What model, what make?"

"I don't know. It was black. But his face . . . his face."

Nick was beginning to freak out. "What about his face."

Sarah stared at him, absolute terror in her eyes. "It was evil, like the devil himself was looking at me."

CHAPTER 14

Nick walked Sarah down to the auditorium floor, holding her around the waist. They walked up to Sheriff Logan, who was talking to Principal Hayes.

Nick cleared his throat. "Uh, excuse me, can we talk to you, Sheriff?"

"Sure, in just a minute son."

Nick raised his voice slightly. "This is important, Sheriff."

Sheriff Logan and Principal Hayes turned to look at Nick. "What's so important, Mr. Paxton?" Hayes said.

"You're Nick Paxton?" Logan asked.

"Yes sir, I am," Nick said. "Sarah has something she has to tell you, Sheriff."

The sheriff turned his attention to Sarah, who was dabbing her eyes with her handkerchief. "What is it, Sarah?"

Sarah told the sheriff and Principal Hayes all about her encounter on the day of the Fall Festival. They stood speechless, glancing at each other.

"Why didn't you tell anyone about this when it happened, Sarah?" Principal Hayes said. "That was three weeks ago."

Sarah blinked back more tears. "I was embarrassed and not even sure what happened, it all happened so fast. I didn't know about the other girls . . ."

Sheriff Logan and Principal Hayes looked knowingly at each other. Sheriff Logan was the first to speak.

"That was Monday, the tenth, the same day the first girl from Adams County disappeared. Exactly three weeks ago today," Sheriff Logan said. "What time did you see him in Acorn, Sarah?"

"I think it was just after two o'clock in the afternoon. The parade started at two and I was late."

"Then it couldn't have been him, Sheriff," Nick said. "Adams County is forty miles away, so how could he—"

"The first girl disappeared that evening, around seven o'clock," the Sheriff said. "Plenty of time for someone to drive from Acorn to Adams County."

Sarah suddenly became limp. Nick caught her before she fell to the floor. "Sarah!"

Sheriff Logan and Principal Hayes exchanged glances.

"If it was the same guy, Sarah's lucky that wasn't her on the banks of the river," the Sheriff said.

Nick looked up at them and then back at Sarah. "Sarah . . ."

"Nick, I need to get more information from Sarah. Meet us in Principal Hayes' office in ten minutes. Okay, son?" Sheriff Logan was leaning down, his hand on Nick's shoulder.

Nick nodded, trying but failing to keep the fear from his eyes. "Okay, Sheriff."

"Let's get Sarah to the nurse's office first, Nick. She doesn't look too good," Hayes said.

Principal Hayes waved Tim Preston over, who had been watching and listening to the conversation nearby. "Tim, help Nick take Sarah to the nurse's office, will you?"

Tim nodded and helped Nick pick Sarah up, who was conscious but obviously distraught. They put her arms around their shoulders and walked her slowly out of the auditorium. Students stared at them, whispering to each other.

Once outside the auditorium, Nick and Tim quickly walked her to the nurse's office down the hall. Inside, they gently sat her in a chair.

"Sarah, you okay?" Nick said.

She looked up at him, glassy-eyed. "Can I have some water?"

"I'll get it," Tim said as he walked into the next room.

Nick brushed her hair out of her eyes. "You scared me, Sarah."

Sarah stared straight ahead, not saying a word.

The school nurse, Miss Jackson, walked into the office and immediately knelt down to look into Sarah's eyes. Tim brought a cup of water and handed it to the nurse, who helped Sarah slowly drink it.

"Sarah, how are you feeling?" Nurse Jackson said.

Sarah blinked several times, looking up at Nick and Tim. "I'm okay, just a little woozy."

"Tim, can you get her some more water?" the nurse said.

When Tim was gone, the nurse turned to Nick. "What happened, Nick?"

Nick glanced down at Sarah. "She sort of fainted, I guess."

"Fainted? Why?"

Nick cleared his throat as he held Sarah's hand. "She got emotional about the dead girls, that's all."

Sarah looked at him and smiled weakly.

"We have to go to the principal's office now," he said.

"Okay, but let her drink some more water. Are you okay now, Sarah?"

Tim walked back into the room and handed the water to Sarah.

Sarah drank it all. "Yes, I'm okay now. Thank you."

"Can you walk on your own, Sarah?" Nick said.

She nodded, stood up and grabbed his hand. "But I need you by my side."

"I'm here." They walked out of the nurse's office holding hands and headed towards the principal's office, with Tim following behind.

CHAPTER 15

The Paxton family had a subdued dinner that evening, with even young Bo being quiet. The events of the day had put everyone's nerves on edge. Conversation around the dinner table was sporadic.

"How was work today?" Eloise Paxton asked her husband.

Clint Paxton looked up from his fried chicken and mashed potatoes. "Not bad, until I got home and heard the news."

"Mom, you must have been pretty busy, with all the phone calls from the school and stuff," Nick said. "Did you have any help?"

Eloise put her fork down on her plate and took a deep breath. "I was going a million miles an hour on that switchboard today. I finally had to call Mabel Hawkins to come in and help me. I've never seen anything like it."

Bo and Ethan stared at their mother while chewing their chicken. Nick had his head down, moving his food back and forth but not eating anything.

"What's wrong, Nicky? You've hardly eaten a bite," Eloise said, putting her hand on her oldest son's arm.

Nick looked at her. "Just a long day, Mom. Sarah and I spent an hour with the sheriff and Principal Hayes. The sheriff was kinda tough on Sarah for, you know, not telling anybody."

Clint stopped eating and looked at Nick. "Not telling anybody what?"

Nick put his fork down and let out a big sigh. "She thinks she might've seen the kidnapper three weeks ago, the day of the Fall Festival."

Everyone at the table stared at Nick. "What? You didn't tell me about that," Eloise said. "Tell us what happened."

46

Nick described the school assembly and how emotional Sarah had gotten. He glanced at his two brothers when he mentioned the dead girls. Ethan just stared at him with big, wide eyes. Bo was unusually quiet.

"She told me about being late for the parade and running out of her house and a truck following her and stopping in the street and—"

"Whoa, son. Back it up. What truck?" Clint was leaning forward.

Nick took a deep breath. "A black pickup was sitting on her street when she ran out of the house. It started following her down the street, but then Sarah ran into the street and it slammed on its brakes right in front of her, almost hit her."

Bo and Ethan sat still, mouths open, eyes wide.

"Did she know the driver?" Eloise asked.

"No, and she'd never seen the truck before. But she, uh . . ."

Clint and Eloise leaned over their plates, staring at their son. "Nicky?" His mom had a worried look on her face.

"She stared at him for what she said was a long time, and . . ."

Everyone at the table was staring at Nick, waiting for him to continue.

"She said his face was evil, like the devil himself was looking at her."

Eloise raised her napkin to her mouth, suppressing a gasp. Clint blinked several times. Bo and Ethan continued to stare with their mouths wide open.

"The . . . the thing is, the first girl from Adams County was kidnapped that same night. One of the," he looked at Ethan, "dead girls."

"Oh, my God," Eloise gasped.

Ethan and Bo looked at their mother, a single tear forming in Ethan's eye. "What's wrong, mommy?"

"Nothing, sweetheart. Eat your dinner. You too, Bo."

"So Sarah thinks that the man she saw may have been the one that . . ." Clint stopped and looked at his two youngest sons. "You know."

Nick nodded. "And so does Sheriff Logan."

The Paxton's were silent for several minutes, eating their chicken and mashed potatoes, each with their own thoughts. Bo and Ethan stared at Nick, then at their mother, then at their father. Nick looked down at his plate and played with his food some more.

"Nicky, eat your dinner," his mother said quietly. "And Clint, I want a real lock on that damned back door."

CHAPTER 16

On Tuesday morning at nine o'clock the phone rang at the Paxton home. Eloise Paxton, who had stayed home from work that day, dried her hands and answered it in the kitchen.

"Hello?" she said.

After several seconds, she covered the phone with her hand and yelled, "Nicky, it's for you!"

Nick was still in bed, but wide awake. He bounced out of bed and ran to the phone in his underwear.

"Nicky, put some pants on," his mother said.

Nick ran back to his bedroom, threw on a pair of jeans and ran back to the phone. "Who is it?"

"I think it's your coach."

Nick took the phone from his mother. "Hello?" He listened for several minutes, not saying a word. "Okay, coach. Bye."

Eloise was standing at the sink, drying breakfast dishes. "What did your coach want?"

"He said the principal has approved football practice for this afternoon."

Eloise raised her eyebrows. "With everything going on, they're going to have practice?"

Nick nodded. "Life goes on, he said, and we have a big game on Friday."

Eloise shook her head and went back to her dishes. "Who do you play on Friday?"

Nick didn't answer immediately. He stood staring at his mother.

"Nicky, who do play on Friday?"

"Lynn."

Eloise dropped a coffee cup into the sink. "Oh, no."

Nick shuffled his feet. "And it's over there, in Lynn."

After the fourth wind sprint, Coach Davis blew his whistle. "Water break! Make it quick."

Nick stood with his hands on his knees, breathing heavily. Tim Preston patted him on the back.

"Let's get some water," Tim said between deep breaths. "Coach is being a prick today."

Nick walked slowly behind the rest of the team to the water jugs on the sideline, Tim walking next to him.

"I think he's trying to get our minds off the other stuff," Nick said.

After drinking as much water as he could hold, Nick walked back out on the field. Coach Walters walked up next to him.

"You doing okay, Nick?"

"Yeah, guess so, Coach."

"I heard about Sarah and Sheriff Logan. How's she holding up?"

Nick shook his head. "I don't know, she won't talk to me. I've called her several times and her mom says she doesn't want to talk." Nick looked at Walters. "I'm worried about her, Coach."

Walters put his hand on Nick's shoulder pads. "She'll be fine, just needs some time. Right now, let's think about football, okay, son?"

Nick nodded and ran to join his teammates.

Coach Davis stood in front of his team. "Everyone take a knee."

Nick and the rest of the team dropped to one knee, staring at their coach.

"We're playing Lynn on Friday, on their field. You all know what happened over there the past few weeks, and days. I've been talking to the Lynn coach and he's telling me that the town leaders might cancel the game."

A loud groan went up from the players.

"If that happens, there's nothing we can do about it. Under the circumstances, it wouldn't surprise me if they cancel," Davis said. "However, we're going to continue to practice and get ready for them, just in case. Lynn is good this year, undefeated so far. They have a damn good defense that's allowed only one touchdown in three games."

Nick turned and looked at Allen Neal. They exchanged knowing glances, as if to say *We'll change that!*

Davis continued. "But they haven't played us yet. They haven't seen our running game. We're better on offense than they are on defense, so what say we run them into the ground Friday?"

Everyone raised their helmets above their heads and yelled, "Mighty Oaks!"

Davis smiled. "Okay, line up for more wind sprints. Let's go!"

Another loud groan went up.

That evening the Paxton family gathered around their television set to watch the local news. Clint had just installed a new deadbolt on the back door and reinforced the lock on the front door. He said the hardware store had just about run out of locks and had to order more from Omaha.

The local news, broadcast from Omaha on WOMA, talked about more nuclear missile buildup threats in Cuba, and showed images of massive military parades in Russia. President Kennedy was to have a national news conference the next evening to explain to the American people what was happening.

"Those damn Communists," Clint exhaled a puff of pipe smoke.

"Clint, your language," Eloise said, frowning at him.

"Shhh, here it comes," Nick was lying on the floor with Bo and Ethan.

"In local news, the two murdered teenage girls from Lynn, Iowa, in Adams County, were autopsied by specialists from the FBI Omaha office. They are searching for any clues that may lead to the perpetrator and his whereabouts. The third girl, identified as Debbie Nordquist, of Walnut Hills, in Walnut County, remains missing. Reporters in the southwest Iowa communities of Lynn, Walnut Hills, and Acorn, in Oak County, remain on strict lockdown by authorities. Schools in all three communities are closed until further notice. Reports of local hardware stores running out of door and window locks are coming in, as everyone in the three-county area is on high alert. A new development from the Sheriff's Office of Oak County has evidence of a possible sighting of the kidnapper and his vehicle prior to the actual kidnappings, but has not been confirmed. Again, this news has not been confirmed, but the lead is being investigated thoroughly."

Nick laid his head on his arms and closed his eyes. *They don't believe Sarah.*

"Nicky, are you okay?" Eloise had a look of concern on her face.

Nick nodded but didn't raise his head. "They don't believe her."

Clint took the pipe out of his mouth, blew a puff of smoke up in the air, and leaned forward in his chair. "The law has to make sure before they spread the news about who this man might be or the car he drives. They can't run the chance of targeting the wrong man on just a teenage girl's statement that she 'thinks it's the kidnapper.' The law just doesn't work that way, son."

"I know, Dad, but Sarah is all alone, and now people are talking about her, whispering behind her back, saying things like 'why didn't she tell anyone.' I just want to be with her through this."

"Honey, she'll let you know when the time is right. She probably just wants to be with her family right now," Eloise said. "Be patient, Nicky."

Nick stood up and wiped his eyes. "I'm going into my room and study."

Bo sprang up from the floor. "Study? There's no school, dummy!"

Nick reached over and knocked his little brother to the floor. "Don't you call me dummy, you little freak!"

Clint quickly got between the two boys and separated them. "That's enough. Nick, go on into your room. Bo, we don't call people names, especially people in this family. You got it?"

Bo nodded his head and rubbed his arm where Nick had hit him. "But there's no *school.*"

Nick shook his head, waved his little brother away, and walked into his bedroom and slammed the door.

CHAPTER 17

The Paxton's got the call from Acorn school officials Tuesday night. Both elementary and high school would resume on Wednesday morning. Nick's mother had told him on Tuesday night and said that their father would drive them to school Wednesday morning rather than them walking the four blocks. Nick protested, but she was firm. No walking until they were sure everything was safe.

Clint pulled up in front of the main steps of the school at seven fifty Wednesday morning after waiting in line all the way down the street. Nick helped Ethan out of the car and waved to his father, who then drove off. The three Paxton brothers walked up the wide steps to the main entrance hand-in-hand, with Ethan struggling on each step.

"You can do it, little man, just two more," Nick said, as he wrestled with Bo, who wanted to run alone to the entrance. "Hold on, slugger. You're with me until we get inside." Nick had to pull him back several times, which infuriated the seven-year-old.

"I don't need you to hold my hand, let go!" Bo said, straining against his older brother's grip.

They finally reached the entrance and Nick let go of Bo's hand. "Remember, stay inside unless you're with an adult," Nick said, as Bo took off like a shot.

Nick dropped Ethan off at his pre-school classroom, chatted with the teacher for a few seconds, then walked to the stairs. Several kids greeted him as he climbed the stairs to the high school floor. The mood was subdued, quieter than usual, everyone unsure of what was happening.

"Only one day off," said one pimple-faced boy racing by Nick. "I thought we'd be off all week, dang it."

Nick took his time going up the two flights of stairs, finally reaching the second floor as the bell rang. He walked quickly to his World History classroom and opened the door. The room was buzzing, with everyone talking at the same time.

"I heard they put Sarah in jail."

"Naw, they didn't put her in jail, the sheriff grilled her for hours, though."

"She saw the guy who killed those girls. He was here in Acorn."

Nick listened to the gossip as he sat down at his desk, glancing over at Sarah's empty desk.

"Hey, buddy, how you doing?" Tim Preston walked up next to Nick. "Seen Sarah yet?"

Nick shook his head. "Hi, Tim. No, haven't seen her since Monday, haven't even talked to her. She wouldn't answer my calls."

The room got eerily quiet when Sarah walked into the room and strode to her desk, sitting down without looking at anyone, even Nick.

Nick stared at her and wanted to go over and talk, but he wasn't sure it was the right thing to do at the moment. Finally, Sarah looked back at him just as Mr. Walters entered the room. No smile, no greeting.

"Good morning, everyone," Walters said. "What a quiet group this morning."

No one said a word.

"Okay, silence is golden. Let's get started. Open your books to page ninety-two."

Nick continued to stare at Sarah, who kept her head down in her book. A girl in the front row raised her hand.

"What is it, Becky?" Walters said.

"Mr. Walters, have you heard any news about the . . . you know."

Walters closed his book and walked around his desk and sat on the edge, looking at the class. "Okay, we've all been through a difficult time the last few days, some more than others." He looked at Sarah. "But it's time to try to get things back to normal, as much as we can. I haven't heard anything that you haven't heard, so we're all in the same boat. As far as I know, they haven't found the girl from Walnut Hills, and there have been no accounts of anyone else gone missing in the area, so let's get to work. Tim, you want to start us off on page ninety-two?"

Nick never took his eyes off of Sarah until he noticed Mr. Walters looking at him. He looked down at his history book, occasionally looking out of the corner of his eye at Sarah. *Why won't she look at me? At least acknowledge me? What did I do?*

Throughout the entire day, Nick tried to talk to Sarah but she would always walk away before he could speak. At two thirty he walked down the steps to the football locker room and began to dress for practice. Tim Preston was at the locker next to his.

"She won't talk to me, Tim. Won't even look at me. I don't know what I did to upset her so much."

Tim was pulling his football pants over his hip pads. "She's been through an ordeal, Nicky. Probably really embarrassed and frightened. Give her some time, buddy."

Nick pulled his shoulder pads down over his head and tied them in front. "But we're a couple, or at least I thought we were. I want to comfort her but she won't even let me get close. It's frustrating, Tim."

Tim was bending over tying his cleats. "Well, take your frustration out on the football field. Hit somebody, just not me." He smiled up at Nick.

Nick smiled back. "Yeah, good idea, but it might be you."

The two boys grabbed their football helmets and walked out of the locker room and up the steps to daylight.

CHAPTER 18

Thursday was another unusually quiet day at school. All the students went about their business as though a fog hung in the air, blocking out the sunlight. It was eerily silent in the hallways between classes, with whispers instead of shouts, frowns instead of laughter. Nick was becoming more and more depressed because Sarah wouldn't talk to him.

Nick and Tim were having lunch in the cafeteria when Sarah walked up to them carrying her tray.

"Can I sit here?" she said, a blank expression on her face.

Nick slid over to make room, but she sat next to Tim on the other side of the table.

Nick picked at his corn, looking up at Sarah. Both were silent.

Tim kicked Nick under the table and motioned with his head towards Sarah. Nick looked up, but went back to moving his corn around his plate.

"So how've you been, Sarah?" Tim said, looking at Nick. "We haven't talked to you much this week."

Sarah looked up from her food at Tim, smiled weakly, and looked back down at her plate. "I'm okay, Tim. Thanks."

"It's been a rough few days, huh?" Tim tried to keep the conversation going.

Sarah nodded. "Yes, it has."

Nick had had enough. He dropped his fork onto his plate, clanking loudly. He stared at Sarah until she raised her head and looked at him. "What's going on, Sarah? You haven't talked to me since Monday. Why the cold shoulder? What did I do?"

Sarah stared at him and chewed her food, but Nick saw her eyes becoming moist.

"Please, Sarah, talk to me. Please."

She lowered her fork, placed it on her plate and wiped her mouth with her napkin. "We're moving."

Nick's eyes opened wide as he tried to digest the news. "Moving, like to another house?"

Sarah's eyes filled with tears. "Moving, as away from Acorn."

Nick looked at Tim, then back at Sarah. "Because of what happened the last few weeks?"

Sarah dried her eyes with her napkin, looking around the cafeteria. "My parents said they want to move to Sioux City, to be close to my brother, but I know why they really want to," she said. "They're afraid the man might come to our house because he knows where we live. They're moving because of me."

Nick blinked. "But you've lived here all your life. You grew up in your house, and you're just going to pick up and move, just like that?"

Her eyes flashed. "What would you do, Nick? I stared into the face of a deranged, evil man who knows where I live. I'm convinced he's the man who killed those three girls, so do I just sit still until he grabs me some night while I'm walking home from school?" Her eyes were wide open, tears beginning to run down her cheek.

Nick was sick inside, wanting to hold and comfort her. He reached out and put his hand on hers. She pulled her hand back.

"Sarah, I want to help you but you've shut me out. Why?"

Her lips began to tremble as she put the napkin to her eyes. "You can't help me. No one can help me, not even the Sheriff. He doesn't believe me, that I saw the devil that afternoon. What can you do to help me?"

Nick stumbled over his words. "I can, I can . . . I don't know, talk to you, hold you—just be there for you, dammit!"

Sarah began to cry softly, hiding her face in her napkin. Nick moved around the table and slid in next to her, putting his arm around her shoulders. She laid her head on his shoulder and cried silently. Tim, who had moved to the other side of the table, sat silently and watched the drama unfold.

"Sarah, I . . . I love you, and I'm here for you," Nick said, moving the napkin away from her face. Her eyes were wet, red and swollen. "We can get through this together. You're not alone. I believe you and will protect you."

Sarah blinked while she wiped away the last tear. She grabbed Nick around his neck and held him tightly to her. "I'm so sorry, Nicky. I didn't know what to do, I felt so alone."

"You're not alone. We're a couple, we're—you're my girlfriend."

Sarah moved her head back, staring at Nick. "I'm your girlfriend? When . . . when did this happen?"

Nick felt the familiar heat on his neck and knew his face was turning red. "It happened the first time I ever saw you, when we were in first grade. I knew we'd be together someday."

She smiled and put her hand on his red face. "Nicky, you never said anything."

"He did to me," Tim said, "lots of times. Loottts of times." He was smiling as wide as his mouth would stretch.

Nick grinned at Tim. "Yeah, I mentioned it a few times to Timmy, I guess."

"A few times? How about ten times a day," Tim laughed.

Sarah laughed for the first time in days. "I'm your girlfriend?" she said again.

Nick nodded as he brushed her blonde hair out of her eyes. "Forever."

They hugged tightly and then Sarah stood up and looked around the cafeteria. She bent down and kissed Nick on the cheek. "I'm going to go tell my friends. I'm Nicky Paxton's girlfriend." She ran out of the cafeteria, forgetting her books and lunch tray.

Tim was still laughing. "Way to go, Nicky. You just created a tornado named Sarah."

Nick sat staring at the cafeteria door, his mouth hanging open. "Yeah. She took it well."

Tim burst out laughing again. "That's the understatement of the century."

CHAPTER 19

It was dusk when Jimmy left the farmhouse and walked to the edge of the cornfield. Before entering he looked back at the house and saw his father watching him through the kitchen window. They had had an argument about the fallout shelter, about his using it for 'unsavory' reasons. Evidently the old man had seen him carry things, big things, through the cornfield to the shelter, and went out to look for himself. When he found the shelter padlocked, the old man went berserk, accusing his son of everything from building bombs to keeping children locked up inside. And he knew about the chloroform, finding a carton of the drug in the barn, hidden behind some hay bales.

Jimmy thought back to the day he had arrived at his estranged father's farm. He'd been driving for three days with little or no sleep, staying awake on pills and coffee, and the thought of the treasures that awaited him in Iowa. He hadn't seen his father's farm since his mother had spirited him away in the middle of the night when he was only ten years old. He was now thirty-five so it had been nearly twenty-five years since he had lived there. Seeing the old man was a shock in itself—the haggard face, the white hair and the deep set eyes set within dark circles. His father hadn't received him with open arms and, in fact, told him to go away. But Jimmy was convincing after showing the old man the scrapbook that his mother had kept about him and his oldest son, Johnny. His father softened and allowed him to stay for a week, but only a week. It was now into the fourth week.

Jimmy raised his middle finger at the old man in the window. *Screw you, you old bastard. At least I don't get off on young boys, you perverted asshole.* He knew then that he would have to take care of the situation before the old man went to the police. He'd had his latest treasure, the cheerleader from Walnut Hills, for a week and was becoming bored with her. He had to do something soon, before his perverted old man ruined everything. But he had to have his treasure one more time before disposing of her. He turned on his flashlight and entered the cornfield.

CHAPTER 20

Nick arrived at football practice feeling like he was walking on air. He had a permanent smile on his face as he ran out onto the field, Tim by his side.

"How you feeling now, Nicky?" Tim said, running next to him.

Nick glanced at his best friend. "On top of the world, Timmy. On top of the world."

The two boys reached the other players, who were gathered around Coaches Davis and Walters. They dropped to one knee, like everyone else.

"We got the word from Lynn High," Coach Davis said. "We're on for tomorrow night."

A loud cheer went up from the players, and then the chant of "Mighty Oaks" began and went on until Coach Davis raised his hands.

"Okay, settle down, boys," he said. "It will be different over there in Lynn tomorrow night. Number one, the game's been moved up to six o'clock instead of seven thirty. Second, there will be lots of security around the field and in the stands. It might be a little intimidating at first."

Nick and Tim looked at each other, the grin gone from their faces.

"So, our buses will be leaving school at three thirty tomorrow, to give us plenty of time to drive to Lynn, get dressed, and have a good warm up. Tell your parents and friends that a convoy will be organized to leave at three thirty, with an escort from the sheriff's office. Any questions?"

Mike Thomas, the big fullback, raised his hand. "Yeah, Coach. Will the cheerleaders be riding with the team? Paxton wants to know."

The entire team laughed and looked at Nick, who was shaking his head. *Tornado Sarah must have told everyone at school.*

Even the two coaches laughed at the question. "As a matter of fact, they will be in the second bus, with the equipment, not the players." Coach Davis looked at Nick. "Sorry, Paxton."

After everyone laughed, Coach Walters held up his hands. "Okay, enough fun. Let's get to work. Offense with me, defense with Coach Davis." He clapped his hands together. "Let's go!"

Nick patted Tim on the shoulder pads and ran off with the offense towards Coach Walters. Mike Thomas ran by and slapped Nick on the helmet, a big smile on his face.

That night at dinner, Nick told his parents and brothers about what happened at school with Sarah. He was embarrassed, but a huge smile crossed his face.

"Oh, Nicky. That's wonderful," said Eloise.

"I knew it!" Bo said, standing up and doing his swivel-hip dance. "Nicky's in love, Nicky's in love."

Clint laughed at Bo and then told him to sit down. "I always thought you two were already boyfriend and girlfriend," he said. "Ever since you were little kids, about Bo's age, you've been smitten with her."

Eloise laughed. "That's true. Every Valentine's Day you'd get her a special card, not just one of those generic 'Be My Valentine' things. I always knew you two would be a couple someday."

Nick couldn't get the smile off of his face. "Yeah, that's what I told her today. She went and told just about everybody in school about it and I took some heat at football practice."

Clint reared his head back and laughed. "Ha! I bet you did. Bet your teammates razzed you the entire practice, right?"

"Nicky's in love," Bo said, moving back and forth in his chair.

Little Ethan just stared at everyone as he pumped mashed potatoes and corn into his mouth.

"What do you boys do these days when you have a steady girlfriend?" Clint asked. "You don't have a class ring to give her yet. That's what we would do, and the girl would hang it around her neck, or put tape on it to make it fit on her finger."

Nick stopped smiling. "I didn't think about that, it happened so fast. What should I do?"

Eloise stood up, wiping her mouth. "I think I have just the thing. Be right back."

Nick watched his mother walk out of the kitchen, then turned and saw his father smiling.

"What?" Nick looked at his dad.

"I think I know what she's getting." He winked.

Eloise brought out a gold ring, with white tape still wrapped around the bottom. "This is the ring Clint gave me in high school. It has a black onyx stone with a tiny diamond in the middle. He got it from his father." She handed it to Nick.

Nick held it in his hand and tried it on his middle finger. "This is a man's ring, too big. It won't fit Sarah."

"That's what the tape is for, or she can put it on a necklace and wear it around her neck," Eloise said. "This could do until you get your class ring in a year or two."

"Are they getting married or something?" Bo said, looking at Nick. "He's still in high school."

Everyone laughed, including Nick.

"Thanks, Mom and Dad, but I think I'll do something on my own, something special just between Sarah and me." Nick handed the ring back to his mother.

"Well, okay, but if you change your mind, let me know. Congratulations, Nicky. She's a lovely girl."

"Is she doing better after her ordeal with the sheriff on Monday?" Clint asked.

Nick shook his head. "She was really shaken up and wouldn't even talk to me for a couple of days. She said that her parents are thinking about moving to Sioux City."

Eloise raised her eyebrows. "Sioux City? Why? That's two hundred miles away."

"They said because they want to live closer to their son, who's in college up there. But Sarah thinks it's because the man she saw might come back. He knows where Sarah lives."

Eloise looked at Clint, who nodded. "That's pretty drastic, isn't it? I mean, they don't even know for sure if he's the, uh, you know . . ." She glanced at Bo and Ethan.

"Sarah's convinced it's him, or at least that he's a really bad man. It really freaked her out."

"Why is she so convinced?" asked Clint.

Nick glanced at his two brothers and then looked at his mother.

"Bo, why don't you and Ethan go into the backyard and play before the sun goes down. But stay in the back yard where we can see you," Eloise said.

Bo bounded off his chair and ran to the back door, with Ethan struggling to keep up. Once they heard the back door slam shut, Nick looked at his parents.

"She is convinced that he's the devil, a really evil person," he said.

"Why does she feel so strongly about him?" Clint was leaning on his elbows as he lit his pipe.

"She said it's because of his eyes. He has evil, dark eyes."

"How could she see him that well?" Clint said, puffing on his pipe.

"He slammed on his brakes right in front of her while she was crossing the street. She said they stared at each other for a long time and she got cold chills when she looked into his eyes."

Eloise shook her shoulders, as if shaking off her own chill. "Well, I sure hope she's wrong. But sometimes your gut knows, it just knows."

"Do you really think they would move?"

"I don't know, Dad, but it scares me to think about it."

Clint continued to puff on his pipe while Eloise cleared the dinner dishes.

"Oh, yeah, I almost forgot," Nick said as he helped his mother with the dishes. "The game's on for tomorrow night at Lynn."

Eloise turned from the sink and looked at her husband, who was leaning back in his chair in a cloud of pipe smoke.

"I thought they would cancel it because of the two girls," she said. "That's going to be a difficult situation over in Lynn. I hope they thought this through."

"Coach said there would be lots of security and stuff, and the game's been moved up to six o'clock, so a convoy is leaving school at three thirty. Can you guys make it?"

"I can pick the boys up from school at three. Clint, can you make it back from Council Bluffs by three thirty?" Eloise said, drying a dish.

Another cloud of smoke. "I think I can get off a little early. I'll be there and we can all drive together."

"Except for me," Nick said. "I'll be on the player's bus."

Eloise had a worried look on her face. "What about Sarah? Is she going?"

"Sure, she's a cheerleader. Why?"

"Think about it, Nick," Eloise said. "The man may be there. What if she sees him again—or worse, what if he sees her again?"

Nick stopped drying dishes and stared at his mother. "I hope she does see him over there, because there'll be lots of police and security around. If they catch the guy, she won't have to move."

Eloise nodded. "Just make sure she's always with somebody, at all times."

Nick smiled weakly at his mother. "I'll talk to her tomorrow, Mom."

CHAPTER 21

The atmosphere at Acorn High on Friday was electric, with everyone buzzing about the big game in Lynn that night. When Nick walked up the stairs to the second floor after dropping off Ethan, all eyes were on him. Some kids smiled, some stared, but everyone looked. He swiveled his head around, wondering why they were all looking at him, then saw Sarah at the top of the stairs. She was wearing her cheerleader outfit, had her blonde hair in a ponytail, and was grinning from ear to ear.

"Hi, Sarah," Nick said as he reached the top, "you look, uh, happy."

Sarah, knowing that everyone was staring at them, gave him a hug. "Hi, Nicky."

The two held hands and walked down the hall to their World History class, Sarah still smiling ear to ear.

"A lot of people seem to know about our, uh, relationship." Nick felt the heat on his neck. "Even my coach knew about it. Who did you tell yesterday?"

She giggled. "Just my friends, and anyone else that wanted to listen. It's a small school, Nicky, and you can't keep big news like this quiet for long."

Nick smiled and shook his head. "I guess not—not that I'm complaining, but I feel like a celebrity or something."

"You are, dear boyfriend." She stopped outside of the classroom and gave him a peck on the cheek. "Boyfriend. I like how that sounds." She giggled again and strolled into the classroom to her desk.

Nick stood outside for a moment as others filed into the classroom, trying to wrap his mind around the last twenty-four hours. He felt his cheek and grinned. *I like the sound of girlfriend, too.*

Nick walked quickly to his desk as Mr. Walters came in, closed the door, and put his books on his desk. He walked around to the front of the desk and sat on the edge, facing the students, holding up his hands for quiet.

"As your homeroom teacher, I have some news I need to discuss with you before starting class." He cleared his throat and looked around the room. "As most of you already know, our game with Lynn High is back on for tonight at six o'clock." He waited for the buzz to die down. "And we are going to take every precaution we can, in light of the events of the past week or so. We will have a convoy of our school buses and private cars, led by Sheriff Logan, leaving the school parking lot at exactly three thirty today. We encourage everyone, especially you students, to be part of this convoy, for security reasons, not for school spirit reasons." He paused as he looked around the classroom. All eyes were on him and it was totally quiet. "But school spirit is encouraged," he said, smiling.

The classroom erupted in laughter and cheers. He held up his hands again. "Sheriff Logan will have several deputies in the parking lot making sure everyone has a ride and no stragglers are left behind." His eyes narrowed. "Folks, there is a killer out there and we don't know who he is, what he looks like, and when or if he will strike again." He looked at Sarah and then at Nick. "We need everyone to remain on high alert for any stranger or strange activity, especially this afternoon and evening. Questions?"

Several hands went up. "Donny," Walters said, pointing to a brown-haired boy in the second row.

"What are they going to do at the game, Mr. Walters? I mean, that's where the first two girls lived, so . . ."

Walters nodded his head. "There will be plenty of sheriff's deputies, from both Lynn and Acorn, at the game, watching the crowd and parking lots. But you have to be very careful if you go and do not walk anywhere alone, even to the bathroom. Stay away from dark or isolated places, and remain with the crowd. Just use common sense."

Walters pointed to a girl sitting next to Nick. "Laura."

Laura was a slender redhead with freckles covering her thin face. "My father wants to take his twenty-two to the game. Will guns be allowed?"

Walters scratched his head. "Good question, but that will have to be answered by Sheriff Logan. We don't want a bunch of vigilantes roaming around looking for trouble, especially if they're carrying guns. However, if it's only for protection, it probably will be allowed. Have your father call the sheriff's office, Laura, and anyone else here that plans on carrying a firearm. One more question, then back to history."

Sarah raised her hand.

Walters hesitated. "Sarah."

"Mr. Walters, do you know if there will be a memorial or some kind of ceremony for the . . . the girls that died? My parents would like to bring flowers if it's okay."

Walters nodded his head. "Good question, and thank you for asking it, Sarah. Yes, there will be a short memorial prior to the start of the game and I'm told that there will be an area in front of the Lynn stands where people can place flowers."

The class got quiet.

"The Romans! Let's talk about the Romans," Walters said. "Turn your books to page one thirty-five. Who wants to read for us today?"

Several hands went up, including the skinny, freckled-faced redhead next to Nick.

"Laura, go ahead."

After class, while walking to their next class, Nick told Sarah what his mother had said the previous night.

"I hope I do see him, Nick," she said, "so I can point him out to the sheriff."

"But what if you don't see him but he sees you?"

She stopped walking and stared at him. "He can see me any time he wants, Nick. He knows where I live."

Nick nodded and squeezed her hand. "Good point. We'll get through this, Sarah."

She kissed him on the cheek and walked quickly to her next class. He watched her enter her classroom before continuing on to his English class.

CHAPTER 22

Nick and Tim walked up the concrete steps from the locker room to the parking lot in full uniform, their metal cleats clicking on the hard cement. When they reached daylight their mouths dropped open at the sight in front of them. Dozens of people were mingling around the school buses, including several sheriff's deputies in uniform. They saw many more cars lined up in the street next to the parking lot, waiting for the convoy to begin. Nick searched the crowd and spotted the black-and-gold cheerleader pompoms behind the group of people.

"I'll meet you on the bus, Timmy," Nick slapped Tim on the pads.

"Okay, I'll save you a seat."

Nick walked through the crowd, several people slapping him on his shoulder pads, until he came to the group of cheerleaders. He didn't see Sarah and began to panic. He spotted Susie Daniels and walked quickly to her.

"Susie, where's Sarah?"

"She had to go to the bathroom inside the school," she said. "It's okay, someone's with her." Susie had a big grin on her face. "I'm so excited and happy about you two. Sarah's on cloud nine, Nicky."

Nick forced a weak smile as he scanned the crowd of people. He was looking for Sarah, but also was looking for the dark-haired man. He recognized most of the people in the crowd and then saw Sarah coming through the double doors of the gymnasium, another girl walking next to her. His smile grew larger as she approached.

"Hey, you had me worried," he said as she stood next to him. "I thought of the Fall Festival all over again."

Sarah's grin radiated happiness. "I'm glad you worry about me, but don't, Nicky. I'll be fine."

Nick glanced around one more time. "I've been searching the crowd, for, uh, you know . . . him."

The smile faded from Sarah's face. "He won't be in the crowd, he'll be in his black pickup, waiting and watching. Keep your eye out for an old black pickup, Nicky."

Nick looked down at her, his cleats making him look much taller than normal. "I will, but your face will be on my mind."

Sarah tilted her head and took his hand. "Aw, that's so sweet."

"Gotta go." Nick spotted Coach Walters looking in his direction. "See you in Lynn." He started to walk away but stopped.

Sarah reached up and kissed him on the lips, squeezing his hand tightly. "Score a touchdown for me."

"Two." He squeezed her hand. "Later."

He quickly walked through the crowd to the player's bus, avoiding Walters' glare.

"Sorry, Coach." Nick climbed up the steps.

"Get your mind on football, Paxton," Walters said, slapping Nick's shoulder pads.

"Gotcha, Coach."

Nick walked down the narrow aisle and found Tim sitting in the back next to the window. He sat down and put his helmet on the floor and looked out the window at the street next to the school parking lot. He searched the waiting cars for a black pickup, but didn't see one.

"Man, you are really in love, pal," Tim said. "You got it bad."

Nick smiled. "Yeah, I think you're right, Timmy." He glanced through the opposite window and saw the black-and-gold pompoms. "Wish they were riding with us."

"She'll be fine. There's lots of security with everyone."

Nick nodded. "Be on the lookout for an old black pickup on the way to Lynn."

Tim looked at his friend. "What kind—Ford, Chevy, International, what?"

"Don't know, just an old, black pickup, with the devil himself behind the wheel."

CHAPTER 23

Jimmy carried the heavy sack through the cornfield, being careful not to break any cornstalks along the way. It was a slow, tedious walk but he finally reached the edge of the field. Dropping the sack, he peered out into the open area, spotting his black truck behind a grove of trees about seventy feet away. He looked in all directions, making sure there was no one around, and finally looked at the farmhouse in the distance, seeing a light on in the kitchen but no face staring out at him through the window. It was just about twilight, around five thirty in the afternoon, so if anyone happened to be close they could spot him. He would wait until dusk before loading the sack into the pickup bed, covering it with a tarp, just like the last time. He sat on the ground on the edge of the cornfield and stared at the burlap sack next to him.

Now what do I do? My last treasure is gone, used up. She was a feisty one, a fighter. I want another one just like her, one that will kick and scream and show some life.

Jimmy closed his eyes and thought about the cheerleader in Acorn, the pretty one with the long, blonde hair. He hadn't been to Acorn in over a week since he'd had the little dark-haired cheerleader from Walnut Hills to keep him company. Now she was dead and he had to dispose of her like the first two. He knew he couldn't take her to the river bank because of the publicity and too many people watching. But he'd found a new place, somewhere they wouldn't think to look. He didn't want to get everyone riled up again like the last time, it was too dangerous. The new place would be deserted tonight because of the football game. He'd wait until six o'clock, when everyone from Acorn was in Lynn, and drive over to Acorn and dispose of her way back in the woods, where the pretty blonde cheerleader liked to walk. Yes, that would be ironic, even poetic. Then he could concentrate on the blonde, his next and greatest treasure.

CHAPTER 24

The Mighty Oaks from Acorn slowly walked off the field after the pre-game warm ups and stood on the sideline as the Lynn High School marching band came onto the field playing "Onward Christian Soldiers." They marched to the center of the field, directly in front of the Lynn High bleachers, turned to face the completely-filled seats, and stopped. A flatbed truck drove from the south end zone to the area in front of the Lynn bleachers. It was filled with flower arrangements and a large sign that said "In remembrance of Kimmie and Delores." Two men got out of the flatbed and began removing the flowers, placing them in front of the bleachers. The band played "Amazing Grace," with a haunting solo by a talented trumpet player that brought tears to everyone's eyes, including Nick and Tim. After the flatbed truck drove away, the front of the Lynn bleachers were covered with wreaths of roses and all sorts of flowers. Nick got choked up watching the proceedings, but almost lost it when the parents of the dead girls came walking out onto the field, with the help of several Lynn High football players. They stood in front of the flowers next to a man with a microphone.

"Ladies and gentlemen, please let us have a moment of silence for our dearly departed daughters, Kimberly Albertson and Delores Sundstrum."

After a minute of complete silence, the man with the microphone began talking.

"Kimberly, known affectionately as Kimmie, was a straight A student at Lynn High School, the only child of Randall and Ann Albertson of Lynn. She was a member of the Math Club and the Honor Society, was a junior at Lynn High, and had a huge desire to go to college at Northwestern, in Chicago. Kimmie wanted to be a lawyer and help poor people. May she rest in peace."

After several seconds, the man continued. "Delores was a farmer's daughter from outside of Lynn who raised prize calves and pigs in her 4H Club. She was one of three daughters of Martin and Helen Sundstrum and was a sophomore at Lynn High and wanted to be a farmer's wife, just like her mother. Her nickname was Dell Bell. May she rest in peace."

The Lynn football players escorted the parents off the field as the band played "Just A Closer Walk With Thee." Nick wiped his eyes and noticed most of his teammates doing the same thing. As the band marched off the field, Coach Davis gathered his team around him.

"Take a knee," he said, as the entire team kneeled on one knee. "We knew this would be an emotional night, for the people of Lynn and for us. But it's time to put the emotions behind us and turn to our job, football. Lynn is going to want to win this game very badly, for the two girls and for the town. Our job, like it or not, is to not let them win. It's a game, gentlemen, and one that you guys are very good at. Lynn is undefeated, but they haven't played anyone like us yet. I want you to get fired up and ready for some smash-mouth football. Are you ready?"

"Yes!" The whole team held their helmets in the air.

"Are you ready?" Coach Davis yelled.

"Yes!"

"Who are we?"

"Mighty Oaks!"

"Again!"

"Mighty Oaks! Mighty Oaks! Mighty Oaks!" The team jumped up and down in a circle, their helmets raised high.

Coach Davis held out his hands to quiet them down. "Receiving team on the field. Let's go!"

Nick looked back at the Acorn cheerleaders before he ran out onto the field to the five-yard line. He slapped hands with Mike Thomas and grinned. "Time for a butt-kicking!"

"Yeah, baby!" Mike said, smiling.

The referee's whistle pierced the cold night and Nick watched the ball sail end-over-end directly towards him. He caught it at the ten-yard line and cut right, following his blockers. One red-clad Lynn tackler missed him and another was blocked cleanly by Mike Thomas. Nick saw an opening down the right sideline and turned on the jets. Blocker after blocker leveled the Lynn players, leaving thirty yards of open field in front of Nick to the goal line. He glanced to his left, saw nothing, and sped into the end zone untouched. He turned around as his teammates swallowed him up.

As Nick trotted back to the sideline, still holding the ball, he saw Sarah doing her cheerleader dance in front of the visitor's bleachers. He felt like his heart could burst open at any time. Coach Walters greeted him on the sideline and slapped him hard on the helmet.

"That's getting your head into the football game, Nick! Way to go, son!"

Tim jumped on him as he headed out onto the field for the kick-off. "Quite a week for you, old buddy!"

Nick grinned as wide as his mouth would allow. "Kick some ass, Timmy!" He turned and looked for Sarah. She was bouncing up and down, as usual, her blonde hair flailing in the cold night air. He scanned the crowd for a dark-haired man but no one fit the description. He turned back to the field and watched Tim tackle the kick returner at the Lynn fifteen yard line.

In spite of the pre-game emotion and ceremony, the Acorn High Mighty Oaks destroyed the Lynn High Lancers thirty-five to nothing. Nick had another touchdown in the third quarter before being taken out in the fourth quarter to let the second string play. Once on the bench he took his helmet off and glanced behind him. Sarah was smiling and blowing him a kiss. He turned back around and smiled. *Life can't get any better than this.*

As the school bus pulled into the Acorn High parking lot, Nick peered out the window and saw hundreds of people standing and cheering, with Sarah and the other cheerleaders in front, leading the cheers of victory. Nick couldn't keep his eyes off Sarah as she kicked her legs up and bounced around, pompoms flying everywhere.

"This is the best, Timmy." Nick grinned at his best friend.

"This is our time, Nicky. Our time."

The players walked single-file out of the bus, each one receiving a cheer from the crowd. When Nick walked off the bus, the noise level rose dramatically. Sarah was there to greet him with a long, wet kiss on the lips.

"My hero returns," she whispered in his ear. "But you need a shower."

Nick laughed, smelled his jersey and scrunched up his nose. "Be right back."

He walked down the driveway towards the locker room, Tim by his side. He glanced to his left when something caught his eye. He thought he saw a black pickup drive down the street, disappearing around a corner. He stopped and peered into the darkness, the lights of the parking lot distracting his view. He blinked several times but didn't see anything. He turned and searched for Sarah, saw her talking to some students, then let out a sigh.

"You okay, Nicky?" Tim said.

"Yeah, yeah. Let's get showered so we can reap our rewards."

"Sounds like a plan, buddy."

Nick gave one last glance at the street before heading down the steps to the locker room.

Jimmy slowed the black pickup as he turned the corner and made a U-turn. He drove back up the side street next to the high school parking lot, driving slowly, watching the crowd begin to thin out. He stopped under the limbs of a large oak tree, away from the street lights, and searched for the black and gold pompoms. He'd gotten rid of his latest treasure in the darkness, just a hundred yards from the home of his next conquest. He'd miss the little dark-haired cheerleader, but began salivating when he saw the long blonde hair with the black and gold pompoms, jumping up and down, so full of energy. His left eye began its incessant twitching as he watched her from the darkness of the oak tree. His next treasure was there for the taking.

CHAPTER 25

Nick woke up on Saturday morning stiff and sore. Even though he'd scored two touchdowns the night before, the Lynn Lancers were a tough bunch and very good tacklers. He stretched out his sore muscles as he sat up in bed. He thought about the night before, after everyone had returned to Acorn and after his shower. He'd met with Sarah only briefly before her parents drove her home. There was no gathering at Frosty Freeze, no celebrations. The entire town went to their homes, locked the doors and pulled their curtains shut. Nick's parents, along with Bo and Ethan, picked him up at the high school and drove straight home. His mother had warmed up some leftovers for the family and they sat in the living room, watching Bonanza on television. Nick couldn't stop thinking about Sarah until he finally fell asleep around eleven thirty. He smiled as he sat up in bed now, yawning and thinking about her long blonde hair and her big blue eyes.

"Nicky, breakfast," he heard his mother yell. He smelled the bacon frying and he was starving so he bounded out of bed, threw on a pair of jeans and a tee shirt, and rushed to the kitchen.

"Wash your hands, Nicky. You too, Bo," his mother said as she picked the bacon strips out of the frying pan and placed them on a plate. Ethan was already sitting at the table, staring at the bacon and potatoes, waiting quietly for his brothers.

Nick and Bo came out of the bathroom and sat down quickly, waiting for their mother to serve them bacon, eggs and fried potatoes. Once the greasy food was on their plates they stared at it while Eloise said a prayer.

"Okay, dig in," she said.

The three boys started shoveling the food into their mouths as though they hadn't eaten in days.

"Where's Dad?" Nick looked at his Mom.

"He had to go into work to make up the time he lost yesterday. He'll be home around noon."

"Nicky," Bo said with a mouth full of potatoes, "great game last night. That kick-off return was awesome."

Nick softly punched his brother's shoulder. "Thanks, little man. It felt great."

"That was a nice ceremony over in Lynn," Eloise said. "Short but very poignant."

Ethan stared at his mother, waiting to swallow his food. "What's ponant mean, Mommy?"

Eloise laughed. "Poignant. It means meaningful, special."

"That band had the whole football team wiping away tears," Nick said. "Especially the trumpet player when he did a solo of 'Amazing Grace.'"

"Oh, my goodness," Eloise sat back in her chair, "that was beautiful."

"And ponant," Ethan grinned, bits of food falling out of his mouth.

"Ethan, don't talk with your mouth full, honey." Eloise wiped his mouth.

"It was too mushy for me," Bo said. "Why didn't they play something fast?"

Nick shook his head. "It was a memorial service, twerp. Have some respect."

Bo made a face at his big brother so Nick punched him in the arm.

"Boys, not at the table. Eat your breakfast. Nick, what are your plans today?"

"Same as every Saturday morning. Going downtown to sweep up the sidewalks in front of the hardware store and stuff. I get paid today so I'm going to look for something for Sarah."

"Like a promise ring?" Eloise smiled.

"I don't know, maybe." Nick glanced at his brothers. "Don't say it, Bo, or I'll clock you."

Bo stood up and did his swivel-hip dance. "Nicky's in love, Nicky's in—"

"Shut up," Nick said, staring at his younger brother. "That's getting old, you clown."

Eloise put her fork down and stared at Bo. "Bo, don't tease your brother. Someday you'll like a girl and you won't want Ethan making fun of you, will you?"

Bo turned to look at Ethan, who looked like a chipmunk with both cheeks full of food. "I'll cream the little twerp if he does. Besides, I'll never like a girl, they're creepy."

Eloise and Nick looked at each other and started laughing. "We'll see, little man, we'll see," Nick said, still laughing.

After Nick spent two hours sweeping the Main Street sidewalks in front of the downtown merchant's stores, he went to see Mr. Krause at the hardware store to get paid.

"All done, Mr. Krause," Nick said, wiping his forehead.

"Nice job, Nick." Mr. Krause opened his cash register. He pulled out a twenty-dollar bill and handed it to Nick. "Here you go, for last Saturday and today. See you next week."

"Thanks, Mr. Krause." Nick put the twenty-dollar bill in his jeans. "You want me to shovel the sidewalks this winter like last year?"

"Sure do, son. Don't know what we merchants would do without you. By the way, how'd you boys do last night against Lynn?"

Nick smiled broadly. "We smacked 'em thirty-five to zip."

Krause whistled. "Whoa. You score any touchdowns?"

Nick, the smile even wider, said, "Yeah, two, including a kick-off return."

"Well, we have a real star working for us. Congratulations, son."

"Thanks, Mr. Krause. I gotta go over to the jewelry store now. See you next week."

"Jewelry store? Something for your mom?"

Nick nodded. "Yeah, for my mom. Bye."

"Bye, Nick."

Nick walked out of Krause's Hardware Store and walked three stores down to Bennett's Jewelry. The bell clinked when he walked through the door.

"Hi, Nick," the owner, Mr. Bennett, said. "Nice job on the sidewalks, as always."

"Thanks, Mr. Bennett. Can I look at some, uh, rings? Not the expensive ones, but something like, uh, a promise ring?"

Mr. Bennett's eyebrows rose. "Oh, for someone special? You have a special girl, Nick?"

Nick felt the heat crawling up his neck once again. "Yeah, for my, uh, girlfriend."

Mr. Bennett smiled. "Who's the lucky girl?"

Nick looked around nervously. "Sarah Rogers."

"Oh, Larry Rogers' daughter, the cheerleader. Lovely young girl. Let me get those rings for you."

"I don't have much. Could I put something down and pay over time?"

Mr. Bennett came back with a rack of inexpensive rings. "I think we can work something out, Nick. After all, I see you every week. These are popular as friendship rings or promise rings. Most of them are around thirty or forty dollars. Anything strike your fancy?"

Nick looked them over and picked a silver one with a small blue stone. "How much is this one?"

"Excellent selection, sterling silver band. It's forty dollars, plus tax."

Nick pulled out his twenty-dollar bill. "Can I give you twenty dollars now and then the rest in two weeks when I get paid by Mr. Krause?"

Mr. Bennett put his hand to his chin and rubbed it. "I'll tell you what, Nick. Because you do such a great job on our sidewalks, summer and winter, I'll let you have it for just twenty dollars. But don't tell my wife."

That brought a big smile to Nick's face. "Thanks, I'll take it. And mum's the word."

"A deal. You want it sized? You can always have Miss Rogers come in and we can size it for her."

"Uh, okay, I'll take it as is and tell her to come in if it doesn't fit."

Mr. Bennett reached down and picked out a small gray box and put the ring inside. "Here you go, Nick. Congratulations, son, I think Miss Rogers will love it."

"Thanks, Mr. Bennett." Nick put the box in his jeans. "See you next week."

Nick walked out of the store, got on his bike and whistled as he began the ride home. As he turned right off Main Street, a black pickup passed him. He jerked his head around so fast he crashed the bike into a wisteria bush. He scrambled up and stared at the pickup as it turned down Main Street. He quickly picked up his bike and turned around and pedaled after it. He saw the pickup pull into a parking space in front of Krause's hardware store, so he rode down the opposite sidewalk, keeping his eye on the driver, almost running into a farmer and his wife. After apologizing, he looked back at the black pickup, but the driver was not in the truck. Nick leaned his bike against the Lincoln Nickel and Dime store and crossed the street. He put his hands around his eyes and peered into Krause's hardware store. He saw Mr. Krause behind the counter talking to a woman, so he scanned the rest of the store but didn't see anyone. He took a deep breath and walked into the store, waved at Mr. Krause, and looked down the first aisle, which was empty. He walked to the second aisle and saw a man in farmer's overalls looking at shovels, his back to Nick. Nick turned and acted like he was looking at pruning shears, watching the man out of the corner of his eye. He couldn't see the man's face yet, but he had a red cap on, pulled down low over his face.

Nick jerked when he felt a hand on his shoulder. He turned and saw Mr. Krause standing next to him.

"Hello again, Nick. You buying some pruning shears with the twenty dollars? I thought you'd have something more personal to buy your mother with your money."

"Uh, no, no. My dad wanted me to look at them to get a price. He'll, uh, probably come down later today to buy them." Nick looked down the aisle but the man in the red cap was gone.

"Oh, okay. These are six ninety-nine, plus tax. Nice shears, but not top of the line. Do you want—"

"Sorry, Mr. Krause, I have to go. Sorry."

Nick walked quickly out of the store just as the black pickup was backing out of the parking space. He saw the driver, wearing the red cap, but could only see his chin. The pickup started moving forward so Nick walked down the sidewalk parallel to the truck, trying to get a look at the man's face. The black pickup increased its speed as it rounded the corner onto Chatauqua Park Drive, so Nick began jogging. As he turned the corner he started running as fast as he could, but the pickup was pulling away from him. Nick stopped when he saw the man turn around and look at him, but couldn't get a good look at his face.

Nick walked back up to Main Street to his bike, deep in thought. It was probably nothing, but the man seemed so nervous. *Why did he look back at me? Could it have been him?*

Nick pedaled down Main Street and turned right at the Deep Rock gas station, looking back at Main Street one more time.

CHAPTER 26

After the Paxtons returned from church, Nick changed into his jeans and an Iowa State University sweatshirt. After a quick lunch, he pulled the lawn mower out of the garage and began mowing the front yard, figuring this would be the last time until the next spring. His mind was on Sarah, the ring, and the black pickup. He couldn't wait to give the ring to Sarah, but her family had driven to Sioux City on Saturday and wouldn't be home until Sunday evening. Sarah had told him that they would be looking at homes while in Sioux City, which made Nick sick to his stomach. *She can't leave now, not now.*

After mowing the side and back yards, Nick emptied the grass catcher into a trash can, cleaned and returned the lawnmower to the garage. He walked into the house, drank a full glass of water, and washed his hands.

"All done, son?" his father asked.

"Yeah,"

"By the way, I was in the hardware store yesterday afternoon and Mr. Krause said you were looking at pruning shears. What was that all about? We have two sets in the garage."

Nick dried his hands and looked at his Dad. "I saw a black pickup yesterday while I was downtown. I followed it to Krause's and went inside to get a look at the driver, but Mr. Krause surprised me. I told him you wanted me to price some pruning shears. I didn't know what else to say."

"Well, other than being disappointed that you lied to Mr. Krause, what happened with the black pickup? Did you see the driver?"

"I didn't get a good look at his face because he had a red cap pulled down low over it. He was wearing overalls, like all the farmers around here do. Then he took off too fast and I couldn't catch him."

"Do you think it was him?"

Nick threw his hands in the air. "I don't know, Dad. But he took off awfully fast and he looked back at me when he was driving away, down Chatauqua Park Drive."

"Did you get a license plate number?"

"No, it happened too fast."

"What kind of truck was it?"

Nick shook his head. "A Ford, I think, but I'm not sure. I was so intent on seeing his face, I didn't notice anything else."

"What was he looking at in the hardware store?"

Nick's eyes grew big. "Shovels. He was looking at shovels."

Clint raised his eyebrows. "Really? Did he buy one?"

"No, he left the store really fast. I think he knew I was looking at him or something."

"Was he tall, skinny, heavyset, anything?"

"Well, the overalls kind of hid his body, but he wasn't heavyset. But he did have dark hair, and he had a good tan, kind of like a farmer's tan."

"Did Sarah say anything about dark hair?"

"I think so, Dad. I'll ask her when she gets home."

"Her family left town this weekend?"

Nick hung his head. "They drove up to Sioux City for the weekend."

Clint put his hand on his son's shoulder. "Well, maybe they just wanted to visit their son at college."

Nick shook his head. "Sarah told me they were going to be looking at some homes up there."

Clint put his arm around Nick's shoulders. "Sorry, Nick. Maybe they'll change their mind."

Nick nodded. "Yeah, maybe. I'm gonna ride my bike before dinner, okay?"

"Okay, but don't go too far. Are you going to be looking for a black pickup?"

"Yeah, maybe. Can't get anything by you, can I Dad?"

"You want to me to drive you around, take a look around town?"

"Naw, thanks, Dad, I just want to ride my bike and think some."

"Okay, son. Be careful, and if you see anything, notice the license plate number and make of the truck, and that's it. Don't take any chances. You promise?"

Nick nodded. "Promise, Dad."

Clint clapped him on the shoulder. "Be home by five, okay?"

"Okay."

The Paxton house was only four blocks from the school, so Nick rode his bike there, looking at any cars parked on the street. He saw nothing unusual and no black pickup. He decided to ride to Sarah's house, another five blocks from the school, on the outskirts of Acorn in an area called Palmer's Woods, one of the more exclusive areas of Acorn. One side of her street had large houses with big lawns and the other side was a huge wooded area that separated the homes on Sarah's street from the homes on the other side of the woods. Acorn kids had played in Palmer's Woods for years and sometimes it was used as a shortcut to walk to downtown Acorn, as Sarah did on Fall Festival day.

Nick grew winded riding up the hill to Sarah's house. It was a fairly gradual incline and her house was the third from the end, where the street dead-ended. He stopped pedaling at the corner and looked up the street. He noticed one car parked in the street, but it wasn't a black pickup. There were large oak trees on the woods side of the street, providing a dark hiding place for someone who wanted to go unnoticed. He began pedaling again, climbing the hill until he was in front of Sarah's house. It was a two-story gray house with white trim, a well-manicured yard with rose bushes on either side of the large covered porch. Nick got off his bike and laid it on the ground next to the street, turning in a full circle, looking at the homes and lawns surrounding the Rogers' house.

He walked across the street and peered into the dark woods, remembering when he and his friends used to play army there. He had a good friend who lived on the other side of the woods whom he had known since grade school. He had walked the well-worn path from one side to the other many times, but not in several years. He remembered Sarah saying she ran through the woods the day of the Fall Festival, so he walked down the street to the entrance to the pathway. He turned and looked back, imagining the black pickup driving slowly down towards Sarah, who was standing about where he was now. How scared she must have felt, looking into the eyes of the man in the black pickup, knowing that the neighborhood was deserted, and that the only option she had was the dark, foreboding woods. A cold shiver ran up his spine at the thought. He now had a better idea of why Sarah was so upset and scared. She could have been his first victim, but instead she used the woods as a getaway that may have saved her life.

Nick slowly walked back up the street to his bike, picked it up and began the long coast down the hill. He passed several side streets before he came to the bottom of the hill, which was a block from the high school, but saw no black pickup. He was relieved as he pedaled back home.

Jimmy stood watching from the shadows of the big oak tree at the end of the street next to the woods as the teenage boy rode his bicycle up the hill, stopping in front of the cheerleader's house. Jimmy recognized him as the football player that the cheerleader had kissed. He watched the kid walk down to where the path into the woods began, saw him look around and stare back up the street, as though he was calculating something. Jimmy slid behind the oak tree, thinking back to the first day he saw the cheerleader, when she ran out of the gray two-story house and into the street right in front of him. It happened exactly where the kid was standing now. What did he know?

The cheerleader didn't seem to be home, so Jimmy decided to follow the kid. He waited until the boy was on his bicycle, headed down the hill, before he walked quickly to his truck, parked on a side street a block away. He drove down the street until he saw the kid at the bottom of the hill. He followed, several blocks behind, pulling his red cap low over his face, his left eye twitching.

CHAPTER 27

Nick walked his bike into the garage and closed the heavy door. As he was walking to the house, out of the corner of his eye he saw a black truck quickly pass by his driveway. The Paxtons had a long gravel driveway, so it took him several seconds to run to the street. By the time he got there the black truck was gone. He didn't know if it was the same black pickup he had seen the day before, but it made him think. He stared down the street for several seconds but there was no sign of the truck. He walked into the house through the front door and locked it behind him.

"Why wasn't the front door locked?" he said, peering out of the front bay window, looking up and down the street.

"What?" Eloise asked, walking into the living room while mixing something in a bowl.

"The front door wasn't locked. What good is a lock if we don't use it?"

His mother frowned. "We only lock it at night, when we go to bed. You know that, Nicky."

"Well, we should keep it locked all the time, that's all."

"Nicky, what's wrong? What happened?" She stopped mixing.

"Did you see him?" Clint walked into the room.

Eloise turned to look at her husband. "See who? What's going on here?"

Clint let out a sigh as he picked up his pipe and began to pack it with tobacco. "Let's sit down while Bo and Ethan are in their rooms. We need to talk."

Nick was still at the window, looking up and down the street.

"Nicky, come sit down next to me," Eloise said. "Why are you so nervous?"

Nick took one last look and then sat down next to his mother. "I'm not nervous, nothing happened."

Clint finished packing his pipe and lit it, sucking in deeply several times until the tobacco glowed bright orange. He blew out a large cloud of smoke. "Nick thinks he saw the black pickup downtown yesterday."

Eloise had a confused look on her face as she stared at Nick. "Why didn't I know about this?"

Nick felt the heat on his neck. "I didn't want to worry you, I guess. I just told Dad this afternoon."

Eloise glanced from Nick to Clint and back. "Well, someone better start explaining now."

Nick told her about the incident in the hardware store yesterday, how he ran after the truck and the driver looked back at him.

Eloise was slowly mixing her batter as she listened to Nick. She stopped and looked at him. "What makes you think it was the same pickup that Sarah saw?"

Nick shrugged his shoulders. "I don't know, just a gut feeling. The guy took off really fast when he saw me and drove out of town." Nick rubbed his eyes. "And he looked back at me."

Clint was puffing away on his pipe, filling the room with the smell of cherry-flavored tobacco. "He was looking at shovels."

"Well, did you get a good look at him? At his face?" she asked.

"No, he had his cap pulled down too low and it happened really fast. He was wearing farmer's overalls and had a red cap on."

"Did Sarah mention he had a red cap on the day she saw him?"

Nick glanced at his mother. "No."

Eloise put her mixing bowl down and looked sternly at both her son and her husband. "Then what makes you think this man, wearing farmer's overalls in a farming town, wearing a red baseball cap that Sarah didn't see, driving a black pickup, one of probably thirty in the county, was the same man that Sarah saw?"

Clint cleared his throat as he blew out another smoke cloud. "Well, he was looking at shovels, Eloise."

Eloise stood up, grabbed her mixing bowl, and glared at her husband. "A farmer looking at shovels, what a surprise! Call Sheriff Logan and give him that nugget of evidence." She walked back into the kitchen shaking her head. "And they say women are paranoid."

Clint watched her leave then turned to Nick. "She makes some good points, son."

"Dad, do you know if anyone on our street drives a black pickup?"

Clint stopped puffing. "No . . . no, I don't recall seeing one, but like mother just said, there are lots of them in the county."

"I just saw one that looked a lot like the one from yesterday drive right in front of our house."

"Did you get a look at the driver?"

"No. I was closing the garage door so it was too far away, but it looked like the same one."

Clint leaned forward in his easy chair. "Son, I think you're over-thinking this now. How would he even know where we live?"

"I don't know, maybe he followed me yesterday from downtown. Dad, it's too much of a coincidence."

"Maybe, but let's try to be realistic here, son. Even if he did know where we live, why would he care? He doesn't know who you are, or that you and Sarah know each other."

"But maybe he does. Maybe he's been watching us at school or at football games. We've made our relationship pretty public lately, Dad."

Clint sat back and took a long drag on his pipe, blowing the smoke cloud out slowly. "Well, I think it's time to call Sheriff Logan and fill him in on everything. He'll probably call us crazy, or paranoid, but at least he'll know. If it isn't the same man, then no harm done. But if it is, he and his deputies can be on the lookout for him." He took another drag and blew it out. "Better safe than sorry."

Nick nodded. "Okay, let's call him now."

Clint held his hand out. "Slow down, Tiger. I'll call him in the morning, during working hours. No need to interrupt his Sunday over this."

Nick thought about protesting, but nodded. "I need to let Sarah know he's in Acorn."

Clint sat back and thought about this. "I don't know if that's such a good idea, Nick. She and her family are already very upset about this. I don't think you want to upset them any more right now."

"But they need to know that he's in Acorn!"

"Well, we don't know that for a fact. All you saw was a man in a black pickup that was looking at shovels and acted a little nervous. Nothing to prove he's the same man that Sarah saw."

Nick stood up. "Well, I'm telling Sarah tomorrow when I see her. It's like you said, Dad, better safe than sorry."

CHAPTER 28

As Nick came out of the shower after football practice, Allen Neal stood next to him, drying off.

"What was with you today, Nick? You weren't with us, man, you were somewhere else."

"Yeah, I know. Sorry, Allen, I just have a lot on my mind."

"Well, Coach Walters wants to see you in his office. Hope you have a good excuse, man."

Nick dressed and combed his hair then walked over and knocked on Coach Walter's door.

"Come in, Nick. Sit down," Walters said from behind his desk.

Nick sat down in a wooden chair in front of Walters, head down.

Walters got up and closed the door to his office. "Nick, I know the last couple of weeks have been a roller coaster ride for you and I don't blame you for spacing out every now and then, but you've got to fight it. We're counting on you, son. You have any more practices like today, Coach Davis will kick you down to the second string. You understand that?"

Nick nodded. "Yeah, I understand Coach. I had a bad weekend and with Sarah not at school today, I . . ."

Walters leaned forward on his desk. "I know what's going on, Nick. You two are getting pretty serious and sometimes that causes problems. And with her encounter a few weeks ago, it has to be weighing on her, and you."

"You don't know the half of it, Coach." Nick let it spill out about buying a ring for Sarah, about his encounter at the hardware store on Saturday, about seeing the black pickup on Sunday, and about Sarah's family looking at houses in Sioux City.

"When she didn't come to school today, I just felt crushed, Coach. I'll be okay tomorrow, I promise. I'm going to call her tonight, maybe go over to her house."

Walters stood up and walked around the desk, sitting on the front edge next to Nick. "That's a lot of negative stuff you're keeping in your head. Falling in love is not easy, but it should be a fun time in your life, but circumstances have robbed that from you, it seems. It would really suck if Sarah moved to Sioux City, I understand that. But her parents are doing what they think they need to do to protect her from potential danger. There may be better ways of doing that, but it's their choice."

"I know, Coach. I don't blame them, but everyone is scared. Nothing like this has ever happened in Acorn before, so people react in different ways. I want to protect her and try to find the guy, and I'll keep trying. Her parents want to run, to go hide somewhere. It just doesn't seem fair."

"Fair is relative, Nick. What's fair to you may not seem fair to them when their daughter is in danger. I'm not a parent, but I can understand how they must feel about their daughter, even though it seems drastic to us. The man Sarah saw in that black pickup that day may not be the killer. It could be an innocent man that just looks like a bad guy. After all, no one has gone missing in Acorn yet. It's all been in other counties. Paranoia can spread like wildfire sometimes."

"Thanks, Coach. It helps to talk to someone about all this stuff."

"My door is open all the time, son. Anytime you want to talk, whether at school or out on the practice field, I'm here. But just try to separate football from all the other stuff, for a couple hours a day at least. We need you, Nick."

After dinner, Nick asked his mother if he could call Sarah.

"Sure, honey, but don't be too long. It's a school night."

He picked up the phone in the kitchen and dialed zero for the operator. Agnes Harris was the evening switchboard operator.

"How may I direct your call?"

"Hi, Agnes, it's Nick Paxton."

"Oh, hi, Nick. You're having quite a season so far. Your mother brags about you all the time."

"Uh, thanks. Can you connect me with the Rogers house?"

"Sure, hon, just a sec."

After a few clicks, a man answered the phone. "Hello, Rogers residence."

"Uh, hello Mr. Rogers." Nick tried to hide his nervousness. "This is Nick Paxton, could I speak with Sarah?"

"Oh, hello, Nick. She hasn't been feeling well but let me see if she's able to come to the phone. Hold on."

Nick shuffled his feet nervously. Several seconds later Sarah was on the phone.

"Hi, Nicky, how are you?"

"Hi, Sarah. It's so good to hear your voice. How are you feeling?"

"I'm better, just a slight cold, I guess. I'll be at school tomorrow."

Nick smiled. "I can't wait to see you. I have something I want to give you."

"Oh, what is it?" she said, excitement in her voice.

"I, uh, don't want to tell you on the phone. Let's have lunch together tomorrow and I'll give it to you then."

"Nicky, don't tease me," she said, giggling. "Is it what I think it is?"

"Maybe, I don't know what you think it is." He was smiling from ear to ear.

"I have some news for you, too."

"Really? Good news, I hope." Nick could hear the excitement in her voice.

"Better than good—great news. We're not moving!"

Nick almost dropped the phone. He turned around in a circle, pumping his fist in the air. "Oh, wow, that's the best news I've heard . . . ever!" He quieted down. "What made your parents change their minds?"

"Well, we had a long talk on the drive to and from Sioux City, and we talked with my brother up there. We all decided as a family that we need to stay in Acorn and ride this thing out. Oh, and you were part of the discussion."

"Me? How so?"

Sarah giggled. "I told them that I . . . that I love you and didn't want to leave you."

Nick felt elated. She had never told him that she loved him before. He couldn't speak for several seconds.

"Nicky, did you hear me?"

"Yes, yes, I heard you. I . . . I love you, too, Sarah."

"Nicky, we can show the world that we're a couple now."

Nick wiped the tear from his eye. "I wish I could come over right now and see you and give you my gift."

"Oh, I do too, but it's probably not best. I haven't showered and I look a mess from this cold. Tomorrow will be here soon."

"Okay, I guess I can wait." Nick thought about telling her what happened over the weekend but decided not to ruin the moment. "I love you, Sarah Rogers."

"I love you, Nicky Paxton."

Nick hung up the phone and did a little dance in the kitchen. He ran to his bedroom and got the gray box with the ring inside. He wanted to show it to his parents and let them know the news.

Clint puffed on his pipe, the cherry tobacco smoke already filling the living room. Eloise sat on the couch knitting something and watching a comedy on television, with Bo and Ethan at her side.

"Hey, Nick, come watch TV with us," Eloise said.

"Okay, but I want to show you and Dad something first, and tell you the news." A big smile creased Nick's face.

Clint got up and turned the television set off. "What is it, son?"

"Hey, why'd you turn the TV off, Dad?" Bo yelled.

"Daddy, the TV," Ethan chimed in.

"In a minute, boys. Your brother has something to show us and tell us. Nick?"

Nick took the gray box out of his pocket and opened it in front of his mother. "I bought this for Sarah on Saturday."

Eloise picked up the ring and looked closely at it. "Oh, this is beautiful, Nicky. She'll love it."

Clint looked at the silver band and blue stone. "What did that cost you, Nick? It looks kind of expensive."

"Let me see, let me see," Bo said, jumping up and down.

"Me too!" Ethan tugged at Nick's jeans.

Eloise showed the ring to the two younger boys. "Nicky got this for his girlfriend, Sarah."

Bo wrinkled his nose. "A ring? What the heck for?"

Nick ignored him and looked at his father. "Mr. Bennett gave it to me for twenty dollars. It normally would cost forty."

Clint whistled. "Pretty nice, Nick. Mr. Bennett doesn't do that very often."

Nick's chest swelled with pride. "They all like me downtown, said I do a great job on the sidewalks."

"What's the news, Nicky?" Eloise said.

Nick's grin stretched wider. "Sarah's family isn't going to move to Sioux City. They're staying in Acorn."

Eloise stood up and hugged her son tightly. "Oh, that's wonderful, Nicky. You were so worried."

"Yuck, how boring," Bo said. "Can we watch TV now?"

Clint chuckled as he reached over and turned the television set back on. He clapped Nick on the shoulder as he walked back to his recliner, grabbing his pipe. "Great news, son."

"Nick, get out of the way!" Bo yelled. "I can't see."

Nick stepped to his left so Bo could see. "I'm giving the ring to her tomorrow at lunch."

"She'll love it, Nicky," Eloise said, already turning her attention to the TV set.

Nick realized his moment was over so walked back into his room and closed the door, but he couldn't get the smile off his face. *Sarah loves me!*

CHAPTER 29

It was all Nick could do to hold down his excitement about seeing Sarah. The smile on his face was there the moment he woke up Tuesday morning and was still there when he and Ethan walked through the big double doors of Acorn Public School. As usual, Bo had run ahead and was already in his classroom. Nick deposited Ethan in his pre-school classroom, said goodbye, and walked towards the stairs, his heart pounding. He had five minutes before class started and he hoped that Sarah would be there early too. As he put his foot on the first step leading to the second floor he heard someone cough behind him. He turned and saw Sarah standing there in a yellow dress and white sweater, her blonde hair tied up in a ponytail. She had an ear-to-ear grin on her face as their eyes connected.

"Hi, Nicky."

Nick grabbed her hand and led her to the area underneath the stairs, an empty alcove where no one could see them.

"Hi." He held both of her hands. "You look . . . amazing."

She tilted her head, her ponytail falling to one side. "I feel amazing."

Nick pulled her to him and they kissed. He almost fainted at her smell, a sweetness that he had missed. She put her right hand behind his neck and kissed him again, this time lingering longer than ever before.

"I missed you so much, Nicky." She was breathing heavily.

Before they could kiss again, a janitor came through the maintenance door directly behind them. They moved out of the dark alcove and, holding hands, walked up the steps to their World History class. Nick opened the

94

door and they walked into the room holding hands, a confirmed couple. Mr. Walters was sitting behind his desk when he looked up, saw them together, and smiled.

"Good morning, you two. What a beautiful morning, huh?"

Nick grinned at him. "You got that right, Mr. Walters."

Nick walked Sarah to her desk, reluctantly let go of her hand, and walked back to his own desk. All eyes were on them, including Mr. Walters'. Nick met Tim's gaze and grinned even wider. Tim nodded his head up and down and smiled back at his friend.

The eight o'clock bell rang as Mr. Walters stood up and sat on the front edge of his desk, as usual. "Good morning, everyone. Nice to see Miss Rogers back. I assume you're feeling better?"

Sarah grinned and looked at Nick.

"No announcements this morning, but I did want to take a couple of minutes to talk about what is going on in Cuba. Who can tell me, in summary, what's happening down there?"

Four hands went up, including Nick's.

"Nick, enlighten us," Walters said.

"Well, uh, the Russians—"

"You mean the Soviet Union."

"Yes, the Soviet Union has been bringing missiles into Cuba, along with lots of other military equipment, and President Kennedy is getting really anxious about it."

Walters smiled. "'Anxious about it' is an understatement, Nick. Top government officials, including the top brass at the Pentagon, are talking about a pre-emptive strike against the missile sites in Cuba. Why would they be so nervous? Anyone?"

Tim raised his hand.

"Tim, why do you think they want to strike against Cuba?"

"Because the missiles are medium and intermediate range ballistic missiles that have a range of a thousand miles. Cuba is only ninety miles off the coast of Florida, so the missiles could reach most of the eastern seaboard within minutes."

"And why is that such an issue?" Walters said.

"Well, if they're nuclear missiles, it could pretty much wipe out the east coast of the U.S., including Washington D.C."

Walters smiled. "Not just a dumb jock after all, Mr. Preston. Well said. Yes, our military is quite nervous about having nuclear warheads so close to the United States. And the Soviet Union continues to bring in more and more missiles, stockpiling them a mere ninety miles from our eastern seaboard, as Tim said." Walters gave the students a minute to think about that statement. "And who can guess what would happen if we, the United States, invaded Cuba and destroyed those missile sites?"

Laura, the freckle-faced redhead, raised her hand.

"Laura."

"Retaliation from the Soviet Union, probably with nuclear weapons."

"You invade us, we invade you, and so on and so on," Walters said. "Or in this case, you fire missiles at us, we fire missiles at you."

"World War three," Tim said.

"Maybe, if there is a world left to wage war." Walters stood up. "This is a serious and dangerous time we're living in, folks. President Kennedy will have some very difficult decisions to make in the coming days and weeks. I advise you and your parents to keep a close eye on the developments, as I'm sure the entire world will be doing. Any questions?"

Sarah raised her hand.

"Yes, Sarah."

"Why is the Soviet Union doing this? I mean, they have to know that we will do something to protect our country. Why take the chance?"

"Very good question. Who wants to answer Sarah's question?"

Nick raised his hand quickly.

Walters smiled. "Go ahead, Nick."

"Because we have nukes in Europe and Turkey and they feel threatened. They want to have nukes somewhere close to us to be a deter . . . deter—"

"Deterrent," Walters interrupted. "Absolutely right, Nick. The USSR and the U.S. are waging cold war, with the threat of nuclear war being used as a weapon. Unfortunately, all it takes to turn this into a real, live war is one or the other pulling the trigger."

Walters walked back around his desk. "Someday students in the future will be talking about this time in history just as we talk about the Roman Empire or World War II. See, world history can be pretty exciting. Speaking of the Roman Empire, turn your books to page one fifty."

CHAPTER 30

Nick waited nervously outside the cafeteria, holding the little gray box in his pocket. As students filed in for lunch they smiled and some snickered at Nick. Word had spread about what was about to happen and in a small school like Acorn, it was big news. Star athlete and pretty cheerleader making it official that they were a couple.

Nick saw Sarah walking down the hall, carrying her books and chatting with another girl, her ponytail bobbing from side to side. He felt the ever-present heat on his neck, felt his stomach tighten, felt the sweat on his hands. She stopped ten feet away from him and stared, a smile growing on her luminous face. She walked slowly towards him, the smile growing into a grin.

"Hi, Nicky."

Nick looked around at the other students. He and Sarah were the center of attention that day. "Hi. Let's get a table in the corner, okay?"

Sarah grabbed his hand. "Okay."

They walked into the cafeteria and headed for a table in the far corner. Two trays of food were already sitting there, with a single flower in the middle sticking out of a milk bottle. Nick glanced at Tim, who had his thumb up and a huge grin on his face. Nick mouthed the words 'thank you' to him.

Nick and Sarah sat down next to each other, with their backs to the rest of the cafeteria. Nick knew that everyone was watching because you could hear a pin drop in the usually noisy cafeteria. He heard Tim say "Okay everybody, let's eat lunch and leave the lovebirds alone." *Good old Timmy.* The usual noise returned immediately, but many eyes were still on Nick and Sarah.

Sarah had turned her chair towards Nick and was now facing him, her hands in her lap, her head tilted to one side. "I can't wait, Nicky."

Nick cleared his throat, reached into his pocket and pulled out the little gray box. He opened it and put it in front of Sarah. "Will you be my girl-friend, for now and forever?"

Sarah put her hand to her face and stared at the silver ring with the blue stone. She slowly took it out of the box and stared at it some more. "It's beau-tiful, Nicky. Will you put it on my finger?"

"Uh, sure, okay. Which one?" He was a nervous wreck.

She held out her left hand and pointed to her ring finger. "That one."

He stared into her blue eyes and grinned as wide as his mouth would stretch. He slid the ring on her finger as he leaned over and kissed her.

Sarah reached behind his neck and pulled him to her and kissed him again, longer this time.

The cafeteria erupted in cheering, clapping and yelling. Tim led the cheers several feet away.

"Yay, Nicky and Sarah!"

"Way to go, Nicky!"

"Attaboy, Nick!"

Sarah held her hand out in front of her and admired the ring and then turned around and showed it to everyone in the cafeteria. They cheered again, louder this time. She turned and looked at Nick, who was turning red, but grinning. "I love you, Nicky."

Nick looked at their 'audience' before saying, "I love you, Sarah."

After one more loud cheer, the normal sounds of clanking dishes and glasses, talking and laughing ensued. Nick and Sarah didn't touch their food. They stared at each other until Tim came over and said "congratulations."

"You guys better hurry up and eat lunch before the bell rings."

"Join us, Timmy," Sarah said.

"Naw, I'm already finished. I've got to get some last minute cramming in for a Geometry test. I'm happy for you guys."

They watched Tim walk out of the cafeteria and then went back to star-ing at each other until the bell rang for their next class.

That afternoon at football practice, Nick was focused and back to his old self. He broke off several long runs during a scrimmage against the defense, including stiff-arming Tim on his way to a touchdown.

"Take five and get some water," Coach Davis yelled. "Good scrimmage."

Nick was breathing hard from his last touchdown run as Coach Walters walked up to him, putting his arm on his shoulder pads. "Nice bounce back, Nick. I think Coach Davis is pleased."

Nick grinned. "Thanks, coach. What a difference a day makes, huh?"

Walters slapped him on the helmet. "You're having a pretty good day, Paxton. It has nothing to do with Sarah, right?"

Nick laughed. "A little."

Walters slapped him on the helmet again. "Keep it up, son."

The rest of practice was going over offensive plays for the game against their arch rivals, Taylor Falls, who were unbeaten. They weren't far from Council Bluffs and recruited players from the city, so were bigger and stronger than most of the teams in the conference. Acorn had to get through Taylor Falls every year if they wanted to win the conference title.

Coach Davis blew his whistle. "Bring it in, take a knee."

The team circled around the two coaches and knelt on one knee, waiting for their words of wisdom.

"Friday night is our toughest game of the year," Coach Davis said. "We all know how good Taylor Falls is, and they're better this year than last. They have a middle linebacker that likes to hit and hit hard. His name is Grant, and he's a bull, and just as mean. We're going to run Thomas right at him, pound it up the middle and make him prove how good he is. And then when we've softened them up, we'll run Paxton and Jansen around the ends. We're in better shape than they are and we want it more. Right?"

"Right!"

"Come on, girls, I didn't hear you. Right?"

"Right!"

"Who are we?" Coach Davis yelled.

"Might Oaks!"

"Who?"

"Mighty Oaks! Mighty Oaks! Mighty Oaks!" The entire team stood, raising their helmets above their heads.

"From tiny acorns do mighty oaks grow," Davis said. "That's us on Friday night, gentlemen. From tiny Acorn, Mighty Oaks will grow! Good practice, see you tomorrow."

CHAPTER 31

Nick and Sarah were inseparable after Tuesday. Sarah had shown her promise ring to all of her friends and the word had spread throughout school about the couple. They found privacy wherever they could, which wasn't easy in a crowded school, and kissed and held hands until they had to go to their next class. Several times at football practice on Wednesday and Thursday Nick was caught daydreaming and forced to run laps around the field until he got his head in the game. Coach Walters kept pushing him harder than the other players, trying to get Nick to focus.

Sitting in front of his locker at six thirty Friday night, Nick was once again thinking about Sarah instead of the most important football game of the season. A small smile creased his face as he thought about meeting her after the game. Suddenly he was brought out of his daydream by a slap on the shoulder pads.

"Paxton, Coach Walters wants to see you in his office." Allen Neal was standing over him. "Damn, Nick, we need you to get your head into this game. This is the big one, man."

Nick felt the heat rising on his neck as he walked to Walters' office, dressed in his uniform and carrying his helmet. He knocked on the coach's door.

Walters looked up from his playbook and waved him in. Nick walked in and sat in the wooden chair in front of Walters.

"I was just going over our play sequence for tonight, Nick, and I want to inject a couple of plays that we didn't practice. Have a seat."

"Okay, coach." Nick had a quizzical look on his face as he sat down.

"We've been practicing running Thomas up the middle to soften up their defense and to wear down the middle linebacker, Grant, right?"

Nick shifted nervously in the chair. "Right, so . . . ?"

"So I talked to Coach Davis and we want to run you into the middle a few times. Once they get used to Thomas' power, they'll be keying in on that. If we run you at them, with your speed, they won't be ready for it. Everyone but Grant, anyway. We think you can break off a couple good gains if you can get by Grant."

Nick nodded. "Sounds like a good plan."

Walters leaned on his desk, putting his face closer to Nick's. "Grant is a bull, Nick, and he's smart. You can't run right at him, you have to use your quickness to cut and make sure he doesn't get a direct bead on you. Understand?"

"Got it, Coach. I'm ready for him."

"Don't let him get a direct shot at you, Nick."

Nick nodded his head. "Okay."

Walters sat back in his chair. "One more thing. As of right now, you have to keep your head in this game, from start to finish. I don't want you looking over at the sideline at your girlfriend, I don't want you blowing her kisses, I want you looking out at the field even when we're on defense. No distractions, Nick, it's too important, and," Walters stopped and leaned forward, "you could get hurt if you're not one hundred percent into this game. Grant has ended the football careers of more than one running back. He's no joke, he's the real deal. They say he already has scholarship offers to every major college in the country. Don't screw around out there Nick. You were zoned-out at practice the last couple days and it can't happen on that field tonight. I'll take you out of the game the first time I see you look over at the cheerleaders or see you daydreaming. Do you understand?"

Nick felt his face getting red. "I understand, coach. You can count on me."

Walters stood up and walked around the desk. "I'm happy for you and Sarah, Nick, but now is the time to focus on one thing and one thing only. Focus on getting by Grant, nothing else." He slapped Nick on the shoulder pads. "Go get ready, son."

Nick walked out of the office just as the team was gathering around Coach Davis. He squeezed in next to Tim.

"Tonight is our toughest game of the year, gentlemen." Davis was standing on a bench so everyone could see him. "They are going to be ready for us and will be hitting us hard and fast. Our linemen have to block and hold your blocks. Our backs need to be aware *at all times* where number fifty-two is. Grant is a man among boys, and he's not only big and fast, but he's smart. Don't run right at him, run slants to take away his power. We'll be running Thomas and Paxton up the middle in the first half, hopefully wearing Grant down. Do *not* let up out there. We need everyone—*everyone*—to play their best game tonight. And if you do, we'll win, and our road to the conference championship will be a lot easier."

Tim nudged Nick in his side when Davis mentioned him running up the middle. "When did that happen?" he whispered.

"Just now," Nick whispered back.

"Who are we?" Davis yelled.

"Mighty Oaks!"

"What are we gonna do?"

"Win!"

"Okay, let's get out on that field and show those boys from Taylor Falls what we're made of. Let's go!"

Allen Neal led the charge out of the locker room and onto the field to the cheers of the home crowd. The stands were full on both sides, the Acorn band was playing the school fight song, and the cheerleaders were dancing and prancing in front of the home bleachers. Nick felt a rush of adrenalin as he reached the sideline. He was tempted to look for Sarah, but fought it off.

As Allen Neal ran out to the center of the field, Walters gathered the receiving team around him. "If we get the ball, I want Thomas to receive it, but hand it off to Paxton on a reverse. Nick, you find your lane and turn on those jets, son."

"Okay, Coach." Nick began jumping up and down to get loose.

"And Nick, don't even think about—"

"Fumbling. I know coach."

Neal ran back to the sideline and went straight to Nick. "Turn on the burners, Nicky, and give us a lead."

"Receiving team, on the field!" Coach Davis yelled.

Nick fought the urge to look at Sarah as he ran to the south goal post. He took his position opposite Mike Thomas, stretching his legs and arms.

"Be ready, Nick, if I get the ball," Thomas yelled. "Let's burn these guys!"

Nick smiled as he blew out some air from his lungs. He heard the whistle and waited for the ball to fall out of the sky, end over end.

"It's coming my way," Thomas yelled.

Nick watched Thomas catch the ball on the fifteen yard line and began running to his left, towards him. Thomas was running right and placed the ball in Nick's stomach as he passed by. Nick looked up the field and saw an opening on the sideline, but a big blur was bearing down on him fast. He ran as fast as he could but the red jersey, number fifty-two, slammed into him chest high, knocking the air out of Nick's lungs as he fell backwards. The ball popped out on the seventeen yard line and the red-jersey-clad Taylor Falls Titans recovered it. Nick was lying on the field, gasping for air. He thought he was going to die, unable to get air into his lungs. He saw number fifty-two standing over him, grinning. Grant had just sent him a message.

Coach Walters and Tim picked Nick up, once he could finally breathe, and helped him to the sideline. Nick avoided looking at the stands or the cheerleaders, wanting to get to the bench and catch his breath.

"Looks like you met Grant earlier than we thought," Walters said. "You feel pain anywhere?"

"Yeah, everywhere," Nick said, holding his ribs.

"Your ribs hurt?"

"Yeah, a little."

"Shake it off and let me know when you're ready to go."

Nick sat on the bench, hunched over while he tried to get his breathing back to normal. Allen Neal came over and asked him if he was okay. Nick nodded, not very convincingly.

A groan rose up from the Acorn stands as a Taylor Falls halfback broke free and ran seventeen yards for a touchdown. Less than a minute gone and Acorn was already down seven to zero.

Walters bent down and looked Nick in the eyes. "You okay, Nick, or do you want Jansen to return the kickoff?"

Nick stood up, took two deep breaths, and nodded. "I'm okay, Coach."

Coach Davis walked over and said something to Walters.

"Coach Davis wants you to sit this one out, Nick. He's sending Jansen in to receive the kickoff. Rest up and be ready to go in on the first play."

Nick took a couple more deep breaths, felt his sore ribs, and began stretching again. He watched as Thomas took the kickoff, ran it back ten yards to the Acorn twenty-two yard line.

"Offense on the field," Walters yelled. "You too, Paxton."

Nick put his helmet on and ran onto the field, ducking into the huddle.

"Ram 48 slant, on two," Allen Neal said.

They broke the huddle, Nick taking his usual spot in the backfield on the right side. Neal took the ball from center and took two steps backwards and handed it off to Thomas, who was met at the line of scrimmage by number fifty-two for no gain.

They huddled up again. "Eighty-four slant, on two," Neal said, glancing at Nick. "You okay, Nicky?"

Nick nodded as they broke the huddle. Neal took the ball from center, ran to his right and put the ball in Nick's stomach as he ran a slant over the right guard. The guard made a good block on his man but number fifty-two was waiting for Nick and slammed him to the ground after a two-yard gain. Nick felt his ribs burn, but he held onto the ball. He felt Grant slap him on the helmet as the linebacker climbed off him.

"Give it up, twenty-five," Grant said. "You ain't going anywhere tonight."

Nick limped back to the huddle, his breathing labored.

"You okay, Nick?" Neal said. "He stuck you pretty good."

"I'm okay. Call the play." Nick held his ribs.

"Eighty-eight left, on three." Neal glanced at Nick. "Burn 'em, Nicky!"

Nick took a deep breath and took his position. Neal barked out the signals and took the ball from center, took a step back as he faked a handoff to Thomas running into the middle, then took another step as he placed the ball in Nick's stomach as he ran to the left. Grant had taken the fake and tackled Thomas, leaving Nick with room to run on the left side. He cut the corner, turned up field, dodged a defensive back and ran down the left sideline with a clear field ahead. He jogged into the end zone untouched, his ribs burning like crazy.

The cheers from the Acorn stands were deafening as Nick ran to the sideline. Tim was the first one to greet him.

"Grant took it, hook, line and sinker. Nice run, Nicky!"

Walters slapped Nick on the helmet and grabbed his single-bar facemask. "That's what we were hoping for, Nick. Get Grant to plug the middle and send you on an end-around. Way to execute, son!"

Nick was out of breath from the long touchdown run and from the blow to the ribs by number fifty-two. He sat on the bench, fighting the urge to look at Sarah. He slowed his breathing, rubbing his ribs as players came up, slapping him on the shoulder pads.

We fooled Grant this time, but what about the next time? I don't know if I can take many more runs up the middle. It's going to be a long night.

Nick stood up and turned his head slightly to look at the Acorn cheerleaders. Sarah was looking his way and gave him a smile. Nick turned back and saw Walters staring at him, shaking his head.

CHAPTER 32

The game against Taylor Falls ended in a seven-to-seven tie. Nick didn't play the rest of the game after Walters caught him looking at Sarah. Nick was disappointed and angry, but couldn't do anything about it. The Acorn defense tightened up and held Taylor Falls in check the rest of the game. Without Nick's speed, Acorn resorted to running up the middle, gaining little if any yardage against Grant. They sent Tommy Jansen around the ends a couple of times, but he didn't have Nick's speed or cutting ability. Allen Neal tried a few passes, but Grant caught him in the backfield several times so the coaches gave up on that strategy.

Nick showered and dressed, his sore ribs making any movement difficult. As he was about leave the locker room, Coach Walters waved him into his office.

"Sit down, Nick. How do those ribs feel?"

"Pretty sore, Coach, but they'll be okay."

"I wanted to make sure you knew why we didn't play you anymore after you scored the touchdown," Walters said. "Coach Davis and I didn't want to risk further injury to your ribs, with Grant obviously targeting you. I don't know if you heard him, but Grant was yelling at us to put you back in. He wanted another shot at you, and we weren't going to give it to him."

Nick hung his head. "I thought it was because you caught me looking at Sarah."

"Yeah, I saw that. No, I wouldn't hold you out of a game like this for something like that, especially after you saved our bacon with that seventy-six yard touchdown run. That was a thing of beauty, Nick."

Nick smiled. "Thanks, Coach. Sure glad Grant went after Thomas instead of me."

Walters chuckled. "So am I. I want you to get those ribs checked out this weekend if they continue to hurt. We don't want to take any chances with them. Okay?"

Nick nodded. "Coach, I could've played, even with the ribs. I could've run around the ends and returned punts. I just don't know if I could've handled those slants into the middle, with that gorilla waiting for me."

Walters smiled. "I know you could have, but we have four more games to go and we're tied with Taylor Falls for first. If we win out and they win out, we'll have to play them again. We need you for our last four games. By the way, you think you feel bad, did you talk to Mike?"

"Thomas? Yeah, he was really banged up. He took a beating inside against Grant."

"I guarantee you he'll spend the weekend soaking in the hot tub," Walters said. "He's a tough nut, Thomas."

Nick nodded. "Thanks for talking to me, Coach."

"Go have fun at Frosty Freeze. I think you have someone waiting for you."

Nick grinned. "Thanks, Coach. See you on Monday."

Nick walked out of Walter's office feeling much better about things. He met his parents outside and they drove him to Frosty Freeze, where the crowd wasn't as big as most nights. The autumn winds were bringing a chill to the air, and most people went straight home after the game. Nick got out of the car and said goodbye to his parents and two brothers, agreeing to be home by eleven thirty. He looked into the crowd and saw the blonde hair and the black-and-gold cheerleader's outfit. He walked quickly to Sarah, who had her back turned, and gave her a peck on the cheek.

Sarah turned around and smiled, showing her perfect white teeth. "Hi, Nicky, we were just talking about you."

Tim was there with Susie Daniels. Tim shook his head at Nick.

"Man, am I glad I was on defense. That Grant is one big, tough mother. How do your ribs feel?"

Nick rubbed his left side. "Pretty darn sore. He hit me so hard on that kickoff return, I thought I was gonna die. I couldn't catch my breath."

Sarah put her hand on his face. "Poor Nicky." She gave him a kiss. "Now do they feel better?"

Nick laughed. "No, but do that a few more times and they might."

Tim and Susie laughed. Sarah gave him two more quick kisses.

"I'm starting to feel better already." Nick kissed Sarah one more time.

"Okay, you two, this is getting sickening," Tim said.

Several people came up to Nick and congratulated him on the touchdown and asked about his ribs. After three or four of these encounters, Nick grabbed Sarah's hand and guided her to a darker spot in the Frosty Freeze parking lot, making sure not to lean on any cars. Tim and Susie didn't follow, letting the lovebirds have some time alone.

When they were alone, Nick pulled Sarah to him and gave her a long kiss. "I've been waiting for this all day."

Sarah kept her eyes closed and put her hand on his neck and kissed him until he had to come up for air.

"Whoa, have you been saving that one up?"

Sarah nodded. "You bet I have, and I have a few more left. You interested?"

Nick grinned. "Heck, yeah."

Out of the corner of his eye, Nick saw a black pickup drive by on Highway 6, going slow in front of the Frosty Freeze. The driver was wearing a red cap. Nick's muscles tightened and his heart started beating faster.

"Sarah, a black pickup just drove by . . . and the driver was wearing a red cap."

Sarah jerked her head around to look up and down the highway. "Where is he? I don't see a black pickup."

Nick grabbed her hand and walked back to the well-lit front of the Frosty Freeze and stood next to Tim and Susie.

"I just saw a black pickup pass by." He looked at Tim. "And the driver had a red cap on."

Nick and Tim walked to the edge of the highway and looked in both directions, but there was no sign of the pickup.

"There are lots of black pickups around, Nicky, and red caps are fairly common, too."

"Yeah, I guess, but it seems like quite a coincidence. I'd better get Sarah home, just in case."

Sarah heard his comment. "I don't want to leave yet, Nick. We're safe here at Frosty Freeze, in the light."

"Do you have a ride home?"

"Well, no, not yet," Sarah said. "My parents are in Omaha tonight at a dinner or something. My house isn't that far, so I can walk home."

"No way you're walking home alone." Nick looked at Tim and Susie. "Tim, do you have your truck tonight?"

"Sorry, but my dad's coming to get me in the pickup, with my mom. Sarah would have to sit on someone's lap."

"Susie, how about you?" Nick asked.

"Sorry, my mom's picking me up at eleven, too" Susie said, "but we're driving to Council Bluffs tonight to spend the night with my grandmother. I don't think we'll have room."

"How about you, Nick. Your parents are picking you up, right?" Tim said.

"No, they were going to take Bo and Ethan over to some friend's house and play cards for a while, so I was going to walk home."

"Nicky, maybe you could walk me home," Sarah said. "It's not that far to your house from my house."

"Are you home alone tonight?" Nick held her hand.

"Well, yeah, until my parents get home around midnight. I'm home alone all the time since Randy went off to college."

Nick craned his neck to look up and down the highway.

"Nicky, you're freaking me out here," Tim said. "It's probably not the same guy that Sarah saw, anyway. A girl hasn't gone missing in nearly three weeks. The kidnapper probably got nervous from all the news and stuff."

"I know, but I'm not letting Sarah stay home alone tonight." Nick looked at Sarah. "Can I come over and stay until your parents get home?"

"Yes, I'd love that, Nicky, but I don't know about my parents. I mean, well, you know. My dad can drive you home once they get back."

"Sure, sounds good. I'll explain when they get there." He reached for her hand. "I'm walking you home."

"Okay, we should probably go now because it will take us about half an hour."

"I'd come with you but my parents have probably already left and I have no way to get hold of them," Tim said.

"That's okay, Timmy, stay here with Susie and have a good time. We'll be okay as long as we're together," Nick said. "Assuming it's okay with Sarah."

Sarah grabbed his hand and kissed him. "It's more than all right. It's romantic."

Nick finally smiled. "Okay, let's go. Bye, guys." He waved to Tim and Susie.

"Be careful, and keep your eyes open," Tim said.

Nick and Sarah began walking down Highway Six, away from Frosty Freeze. He held Sarah's hand tightly, holding her close to him, every now and then glancing backwards.

"We're finally all alone, Nicky."

They turned onto Oak Street and walked towards Sarah's neighborhood, which was ten blocks away. After walking two blocks, Sarah stopped in a dimly lit part of the street and put her hand on Nick's neck.

"I love you, Nicky." She kissed him softly.

"I love you, too." Nick put his arm around her. "It's getting cold, so let's pick up the pace." He looked back down the street but no cars were coming.

"Nicky, we can take the shortcut through Palmer Woods. It would save us fifteen minutes."

Nick stared at her, shaking his head. "No, Sarah, no. We can't walk through those woods at night."

"But I've done it lots of times when I had to walk home from school. I know those woods like the back of my hand."

Nick glanced down the street and back at Sarah. "I don't know, Sarah."

"He's not around and if he is, he won't know we took the shortcut. We'll be easier targets walking on the street." Sarah squeezed his hand. "Let's do it."

Nick rubbed his eyes and looked down the street one more time, seeing nothing. "Okay, but let's hurry."

They walked quickly through the dark streets toward Palmer Woods. Nick had an uneasy feeling, as if they were tempting fate.

"Don't worry, Nicky. I have a flashlight in my purse." Sarah kissed him as they approached the entrance to the dark woods.

CHAPTER 33

The black pickup was parked in the dark, empty parking lot of the bowling alley across the highway from Frosty Freeze. Jimmy watched intently as the football player and the cheerleader began walking up the highway. He smiled as he rolled the chloroform bottle in his hand, his left eye already twitching. *Everything is falling into place. Tonight's the night.* He turned on the ignition and slowly pulled out of the parking lot onto the highway.

He turned his headlights off when he turned onto Oak Street and stopped when he saw the young couple up ahead. He stayed far enough away to remain unseen, always parking in a dimly lit part of the street, headlights off. There were few cars on the residential streets at that time of night, so he continued following them very slowly. He stopped when he saw the two kids stop. He peered through the darkness, barely able to make out their silhouettes. They were talking or arguing and then they began walking quickly and took a side street. Jimmy picked up speed and turned onto the same street that they had turned on, his lights still off. He saw the high school at the end of the street, less than two blocks away. He rubbed his chin, wondering where they we going. Then it hit him. *The woods. They're going to take the shortcut through the woods.* He grinned as he made a U-turn and sped back down towards the highway. He would be on the other side when they came out. His eye began twitching as he realized that his elusive treasure would soon be his.

The black pickup turned onto Sarah's street, headlights off, moving slowly. Jimmy planned how to take both of them when they emerged from the woods without making any noise that would wake up the neighbors. He rummaged through his glove compartment for an extra rag. He would soak two rags with chloroform, hide in the thick brush and hit the football player with a tire iron from behind, then use the chloroform on the girl, who would succumb as easily as all the others. Then use the second rag on the football player in case he wasn't knocked out.

He parked the truck under the large oak tree at the end of the street, gathered his chloroform bottle, rags, and tire iron and walked quickly to the path that the cheerleader had taken the day of the Fall Festival. He found some thick brush near the end of the path and knelt down, listening for any sounds coming from the woods. He heard voices in the distance, and they were getting closer. He smiled and quickly took off the cap to the chloroform bottle and soaked each rag. He had done it many times and knew exactly how much to use. He added a little extra for the football player, just in case. The voices were getting closer so he stood up and peered over the large bush at the dark path. He saw movement and a small light about fifty feet down the path, coming towards him, the voices growing louder. He crouched back down and waited. He would take them just before they emerged from the woods, the football player first, then the cheerleader.

When they were ten feet away, almost on top of him, Jimmy grabbed the tire iron and got ready to pounce. Suddenly, he saw headlights coming up the street towards him. He slowly backed into the brush, his tire iron ready. The headlights stopped in the middle of the street just as the two teenagers passed by him, emerging from the woods. Jimmy crouched lower, almost on his belly, as he heard the teenagers talk to whoever was in the car. He was five feet from them, within striking distance. His heart pounded as he watched the two get into the car and drive away. He stood up and watched as they pulled into the cheerleader's driveway and got out. He continued to watch as a large man got out on the driver's side of the car and walked with them towards the house.

Jimmy slumped down in frustration. They had been so close. He rubbed his forehead and suddenly jerked his head up when he remembered his truck at the end of the street. He had to move it before they saw it. He stood up quickly, grabbed the chloroform bottle, and slowly walked along the edge of the woods, watching intently as he passed the gray house. He reached his truck, got in and put it in neutral and slowly began rolling down the street, the gradual incline helping him pick up speed. When he passed the gray house he glanced over and was shocked to see the football player and the big man running towards him with something in their hands. He quickly turned the engine on, put the truck in gear and hit the accelerator. The man and boy were only five feet behind him, yelling for him to stop. Jimmy turned the corner and stomped on the accelerator again, putting distance between him and the two people running behind him. He watched in his rearview mirror as they grew smaller and smaller. He turned onto another street as they disappeared from view.

Jimmy pounded his steering wheel as the anger and frustration boiled over. He had been so close, his treasure within his grasp. Who was the tall man in the car and why did he stop at that spot and not drive to the house? Jimmy jerked his head up as he remembered the two rags and the tire iron, still under the bushes. He thought about going back for them but decided it was too dangerous. They were hidden in the brush and the chloroform would dissipate overnight. No one would find them.

He relaxed and thought about what to do. He needed a new treasure to replace the little cheerleader from Walnut Hills.

Jimmy drove out of Acorn, heading south.

CHAPTER 34

Nick walked out the back door, crouched down low and moved quickly up the driveway to the edge of the gray house. He had a baseball bat in his hands as he looked up and down the dark street. He heard Mr. Walters behind him, breathing hard.

"See anything?" Walters whispered.

"No, not yet. Wait . . . there he is!"

They saw the black pickup slowly rolling down the street with its engine off, and ran out into the street, yelling and holding their baseball bats in the air. They were five feet away when its engine started and the truck began pulling away. They ran as fast as they could, shouting for the truck to stop, but it picked up speed and turned the corner. They stopped running and watched it pull away.

Walters had his hands on his knees, his breathing labored. Nick was breathing hard and was holding his ribs.

"Did you get a look at him?" Walters said between deep breaths.

"No, it was too dark and he had the red cap pulled low on his face," Nick answered. "But I got a look at the license plate."

Walters stood up and put his arm around Nick's shoulders. "Good, good. Let's get back to Sarah and call the Sheriff."

They walked up the street, seeing lights come on and window shades open in the houses along the street.

"Looks like we woke up the neighborhood," Walters said.

"Wait, let's check the bushes near the entrance to the woods," Nick said. "I smelled something weird when Sarah and I were talking to you in the car."

"You think he was in the bushes?"

"I don't know. Let's check."

They walked across the street to the entrance to the woods and the smell hit them immediately.

"You smell that, Mr. Walters?"

Walters held his nose. "Yes, and I think I know what it is."

"What?"

"Chloroform. Let's check the bushes over there."

They followed the smell and found the two chloroform-soaked rags. Walters held them up, away from him, and pinched his nose. "He was waiting here for you and Sarah."

Nick held his nose as his eyes grew wide. "How did he know we were walking through the woods?"

Walters looked at him. "We're dealing with someone with a diabolical mind, Nick. How does he know anything? Let's go call the Sheriff before Sarah has a heart attack."

"Wait! There's something else in the bushes." Nick bent down and picked up the tire iron. "What was he going to do with this?"

Walters shook his head. "I'm afraid he was going to use that on you, Nick, and finish you off with the chloroform. Try not to touch it too much. Maybe the Sheriff can run his prints. Come on, let's go."

As they walked up the front steps of the gray house, Sarah opened the door. Her eyes were wet and red.

"Oh, my God," she said, hugging Nick. "I saw you running down the street screaming like a madman."

Nick hugged her tight, his breathing finally back to normal. "We almost caught him."

"Nick, get Sarah some water while I find the phone," Walters said.

Nick led Sarah to the sofa. "Sit down, I'll get some water."

Walters found the phone in the kitchen and dialed zero for the operator.

"How may I direct your call?" the operator said.

"Acorn Sheriff's office, please."

"I'll try, but there probably won't be anyone there this time of night."

"That's fine, thank you."

After five or six rings, the operator came back on the line. "I'm sorry, sir, but there is no answer. Do you want me to try Sheriff Logan's home phone?"

"Yes, this is an emergency."

"Oh, my, just one moment, sir."

Walters listened to the phone ring and finally a man answered. "Hello, Logan."

"Sheriff, this is John Walters."

"Hi, John. Nice game tonight."

"Sheriff, I'm at Sarah Rogers' house. There was an attempted kidnapping just a few minutes ago. I think you need to get over here immediately."

"Kidnapping? Sarah?"

"Yes, Sarah and Nick Paxton, but the kidnapper drove away before he could . . . grab them. They're both here now."

"I'll be there in ten minutes. Are Sarah's folks home?"

"No, I'll stay with them until they get here. Thanks, Sheriff."

Walters hung up the phone and walked to Sarah as she was finishing a glass of water. Nick's arm was around her shoulders.

"The Sheriff is on his way," Walters said. "Are you okay, Sarah?"

She nodded. "I think so."

"When will your parents be home?"

"Around midnight, I think. They . . . they went to a dinner or something."

"Mr. Walters," Nick said, "why were you here tonight? You live outside of town, don't you?"

Walters sat down in a chair next to the sofa, the smell of chloroform still on his fingers. "Excuse me while I wash this smell off of my hands. The bathroom, Sarah?"

She pointed towards the hallway.

After Walters left, Nick looked at Sarah. "It was the black pickup, Sarah, just like you said. And he was wearing a red cap."

Sarah started to shake, so Nick held her tightly, wiping her eyes with a tissue. "I'm so sorry, Sarah. I put us in danger. I should have known better."

She wiped away a tear. "It was my decision, too, Nicky. We didn't know that he . . ."

Walters came back into the room and sat down in front of Sarah and Nick. "I went to the Frosty Freeze to find you, Nick, to see how your ribs were doing. I worked late at school, got bored, and knew that you two would be at the Frosty Freeze. Tim Preston told me that you were walking Sarah home, so I decided to see if I could catch you and give you a ride to her house."

"Your timing was unbelievable," Nick said. "If you hadn't come along, I . . . I don't know what would have happened."

"As soon as I turned onto Sarah's street I saw the truck parked at the end of the street, under a tree. Then I saw you two walking out of the woods and pulled over."

Nick looked at Sarah. "He was in the bushes right next to us."

Sarah stared at Nick, unable to speak.

"And we found two rags soaked in chloroform in the bushes next to the path, right where we stopped to talk to Mr. Walters . . . and a tire iron."

"He was that close to us?" Sarah's lips began to tremble and she began shaking. "Was he going to put those . . . those things over our mouth?"

"Apparently that was his plan," Walters said. "I think he was going to use the tire iron on Nick."

Sarah looked at Nick. "Nicky, I knew he was evil. I saw it in his eyes." She started crying softly.

They all jumped when they heard a loud knock on the door.

"Probably the sheriff. Sit still while I check it out." Walters walked to the front door. He peered through the peephole, breathed a sigh of relief and opened the door. "Evening, Sheriff. Come on in."

Sheriff Logan walked into the living room, taking off his wide-brimmed hat. "Evening, John." He looked at Nick and Sarah on the sofa. "Evening, Nick, Sarah."

Nick nodded. Sarah sat still, not moving, a frown on her face.

"Have a seat, Sheriff." Walters pointed to the chair next to the sofa. "Sarah's parents won't be home until around midnight."

Sheriff Logan sat down, put his hat on the coffee table, and leaned closer to Nick and Sarah. "What was that smell on the front porch? It smelled like—"

"Chloroform," Walters said. "We found them in the bushes next to the path coming out of the woods."

"No kidding? And the tire iron?"

Walters nodded.

"So tell me what happened." He was looking at Walters. "First of all, what brought you into the picture?"

"I was told that Nick and Sarah were walking home from the Frosty Freeze, so I wanted to see if I could catch them and drive them here. As I turned onto Sarah's street, I saw the black pickup sitting at the end of the street."

"How did you know it was black? It was dark out and there are no lights at the end of the street."

"Well, I just assumed, I guess."

Logan turned to Nick and Sarah. "Did you see the pickup prior to John driving up the street?"

Nick shook his head. "No, we were just coming out of the woods. The first thing we saw was Mr. Walters pulling up in front of us."

Logan's eyes grew wide. "You walked home through the Palmer Woods?"

Nick licked his dry lips. "Yes, sir, we did."

Logan looked at Walters. "Did you know this, Coach?"

"Not until I saw them coming out of the woods when I turned onto the street, after seeing the black pickup. I had no idea they were in the woods until then."

"What in God's name were you thinking, walking through those woods at night, with a killer out there?" Logan stared at Nick, then Sarah.

Sarah wiped her nose. "I talked Nicky into taking the shortcut through the woods. I do it all the time. It was my fault, not Nicky's."

Logan continued to stare at them.

"We think he was waiting for them in the bushes next to the entrance, where we found the chloroform rags and the tire iron," Walters said. "I don't know how he knew Nick and Sarah were in the woods, but he did."

Logan stood up and brushed his thinning gray hair. "If you hadn't come along, John . . ."

Walters nodded. "I know, Sheriff. It would have ended very badly."

Logan sat back down. "I want all three of you in my office in the morning at nine o'clock sharp." He rubbed his forehead. "And plan on being there most of the morning."

"We'll be there, Sheriff," Walters said, looking at Nick and Sarah.

"What happened to the man in the pickup?" Logan said.

"Well, Nick and I were going to sneak up on him in his pickup but then we saw him coasting down the street with his engine off."

"Did he see you?"

"Oh, yeah. We were yelling and flailing a couple of baseball bats at him. He probably pissed his pants trying to get out of there," Walters said.

Logan brushed his hair again. "I'll be damned. Did you at least get a good look at him?"

Walters shook his head. "No, too dark and he had his cap pulled too low over his face."

"I got part of his license plate number," Nick said.

Logan looked up in surprise.

"I saw part of it," Nick said. "I got closer than Coach did and saw the first three letters."

Logan smiled. "Finally, we may have a lead. What were the letters, Nick."

"MCF," Nick said. "And it's from Walnut County."

Logan's eyes opened wider. "You sure about that?"

"I saw it plain as day, Walnut, just above the letters."

Logan smiled and nodded. "Good work, son. Very good work. Now we're getting somewhere. No guess as to the three numbers on the plate?"

Nick shook his head. "Didn't have enough time, he was moving pretty fast."

Walters grinned. "Ah, to have young eyes."

Sheriff Logan stood up, closed his notebook and reached for his hat. "I think I've got enough here to get our investigation started. I'll take those chloroform rags and tire iron outside with me as evidence. Maybe we can get fingerprints off of them."

Walters stood up and shook the sheriff's hand. "Thanks for coming at such a late hour, Sheriff."

Logan nodded. "You staying with Nick and Sarah until her folks get home?"

"Yes, I'll be here."

"Okay, then. Be careful when you leave, and lock all the doors when I leave. He may still be out there, close by."

"Will do, Sheriff."

"Goodnight Nick, Sarah. Get some rest. And good work, Nick. You may have given us what we need to crack this case." Logan stopped as he reached the door. "Tomorrow at nine o'clock. We have a lot to talk about."

Logan walked out with Walters following him, closing the door behind him.

"Sheriff, this animal obviously knows where Sarah lives. He might be out in those woods across the street right now. Can you have someone check the street for a few days, just in case?"

"Sure, I'll have a deputy check on the area a few times a day on his normal patrol until we get this guy. Matter of fact, I'll have someone out here tonight to keep watch over the weekend. You never know what this kind of pervert might do."

"Goodnight, Sheriff."

Logan picked up the rags and tire iron and walked to his car. "Goodnight, John."

Walters walked back into the house, shut the door and locked the deadbolt. "Is your back door locked, Sarah?"

"We always keep it locked, ever since . . ."

"Okay, I'll go check it. Can you and Nick check all the windows, to make sure they're closed and locked?"

"Okay, Coach," Nick said.

After checking all the doors and windows, they came back and sat down in the living room, Walters in the chair and Nick and Sarah on the sofa.

"Well, it's almost eleven thirty, so your parents should be home soon, Sarah. It's been quite a night."

"Thank you for staying, Mr. Walters," Sarah said. "If you hadn't been here . . ."

Walters smiled. "I'm just glad I decided to check up on Nick, here." He looked at Nick. "By the way, how are those ribs, son? And don't sugarcoat it."

Nick laughed. "I haven't thought about them until just now. I ran down the street pretty fast after that pickup, so guess they're okay."

Walters laughed. "I think you ran faster than you did tonight on your touchdown run. At least you didn't have Grant chasing you."

Nick's smile faded. "Yeah, he was a bull, but now we have someone a whole lot more dangerous to worry about."

Walters shook his head. "That we do, Nick. That we do."

CHAPTER 35

Nick woke up at eight o'clock Saturday morning but couldn't get out of bed. His ribs hurt worse than when Grant clocked him the night before. He rolled over on his right side and slowly slid out of bed, the pain making him catch his breath. After a few seconds he stood up, wobbly at first. He shuffled to the bathroom, relieved himself then very slowly slid on his jeans and tee shirt. He opened his bedroom door and shuffled to the kitchen, where his mother was making pancakes.

"Morning, Mom," he said.

"Hey, Nicky, how you feeling?"

Nick grunted in pain. "Not good. I can hardly move."

Eloise walked to him and pushed the hair out of his eyes. "I can imagine, the hit that guy put on you last night."

Nick tried to chuckle, but it hurt too much. "He was a bull, Mom. No wonder he's all-state. I feel it in every bone in my body."

Eloise hugged him softly and patted him on the shoulder. "And you only played a few minutes, honey. Think how Mike Thomas feels this morning."

Nick tried to laugh, but held it in. "Can I have some coffee this morning, just this once?"

"Just this once, Nicky. I think you deserve it after last night."

Nick slowly sat down at the kitchen table and put his head in his hands. "I don't know if I can sweep the sidewalks downtown today, Mom."

"Oh, they can get by without you for one week," she said. "I'll call Mr. Krause and let him know. I'm sure he'll understand." She put his coffee in front of him.

Nick groaned as he tried to pick up his coffee cup. "Ahh. I can't even pick up my coffee cup. Everything hurts."

Eloise rubbed his back. "Give it time, Nicky, it'll get better." She sat down next to him. "The sheriff called a few minutes ago. He wanted to remind you and Sarah about the meeting this morning at nine."

Nick nodded. "Yeah, he told us last night. I hope he has some good news."

Eloise brushed his hair back. "Thank God for Mr. Walters."

"No kidding. Can you drive me to the Sheriff's office?"

"Can you make it the way you feel?"

Nick slowly took a long sip of coffee and nodded his head. "If you can drive me."

"Of course, honey. I have some shopping to do anyway. Why don't you go take a shower and clean up. We'll leave here at eight thirty, to give us plenty of time."

"Mom, can I call Sarah? I want to make sure she's okay."

"Sure, let me call Mabel so she can connect you." Eloise dialed zero, talked briefly with Mabel, the weekend switchboard operator, and handed the phone to Nick. "She's connecting you right now, Nicky."

Nick slowly lifted the phone to his ear and heard a man say, "Hello."

"Hi, Mr. Rogers? This is Nick Paxton."

"Hello Nick. How are you feeling this morning?"

"Pretty sore, sir. Is Sarah awake yet?"

"She's in the shower. The sheriff called and wants her to be in his office at nine this morning. Are you going to be able to make it?"

"Yes, sir, I'll be there."

"Okay, we'll see you then, Nick."

Nick handed the phone to his mother and took another sip of coffee. "I'm going to start getting ready, Mom. It'll take me quite a while."

"Okay, Nicky. Let me know if you need any help. We may want to see Doc Peters about your ribs while we're downtown."

Nick nodded and slowly stood up and shuffled to his room.

Nick walked into the Oak County Sheriff's office exactly at nine o'clock and saw Sarah and her father sitting in the waiting room. Sarah's eyes were puffy and red. Nick sat down next to her.

"Hi, are you doing okay?" Nick said, reaching for her hand.

Sarah squeezed his hand. "It was a long night, Nicky. I couldn't get to sleep until two or three in the morning."

"How are you feeling, Nick? Your ribs, I mean," Mr. Rogers said. "I heard you took a nasty hit last night."

Nick tried to smile. "Yeah, the guy clocked me pretty good. Ribs are real sore, but starting to loosen up some."

They saw a door to their right open as Sheriff Logan entered the waiting room. "Good morning," he said. "Sorry I'm a little late. Why don't you come on in to my office so we can talk in private. Larry, you can join us if you like," he said to Mr. Rogers.

Mr. Rogers looked at Sarah and Nick. "Do you mind?"

"No, not at all," Nick said.

Sarah shook her head. "I'd like you to be there, Daddy."

"Anyone heard from Coach Walters? I couldn't reach him by phone this morning," Logan said.

They all shook their heads.

"Okay, we can start without him. Hopefully he'll show up soon."

They all stood up and followed the sheriff into his office, taking chairs in front of his desk. Nick and Sarah held hands as they waited for Sheriff Logan to start. They heard a noise from the waiting room , then John Walters walked into the office.

"Sorry I'm late, everyone. A tractor was blocking my road this morning," Walters said.

"No problem, John. Have a seat." Logan pointed to the only available chair.

"Okay, let me bring you up to speed. We ran the letters 'MCF' through our database for Walnut County and came up with four possible matches. My deputy is checking them as we speak. However, one of the matches was on a vehicle owned by a deceased person. He was the first one that we checked. And here's the interesting part. The man's vehicle has been parked next to his house for several months since his death. He was a widower, so no one lives in the house. When we checked the car, both license plates were missing."

Nick glanced at Sarah. "You mean, they were stolen?"

"Appears that way. If that's the case, and it looks very likely, the man who was following you last night is untraceable, unless he's dumb enough to keep those plates on his truck."

"Which means he could live anywhere, not just Walnut County," Nick said.

"That's correct, Nick. He knows now that you and John saw him and his truck, but he doesn't know for sure if you got the license plate number. There's still a chance that he won't change plates, and if so, we have a shot at locating him at some point."

"Can you run a check on all black Ford pickups in the tri-county area?" Mr. Rogers said. "I know that's a long shot, but who knows?"

"That's more than a long shot, Larry. It's darn near impossible," Logan said. "So many farmers in the tri-county area have older pickups that are too old to trace. According to John here, this man's truck was at least five or six years old."

Sarah leaned forward. "So we're back to square one. We don't have a clue who this animal is?"

Logan shook his head. "Our only hope is that he gets cocky and keeps that license plate on his truck. Other than that, we would have to check every older black Ford pickup in the tri-county area and hope we get lucky. As your father said, it's a long shot."

"He may have another car or truck," Nick said. "He knows he's been spotted so he may stay low for a while, or use another vehicle."

"That's right, Nick. Our hope is that he stays out of Acorn because of what you just said. But if he has another vehicle, we'd have no way of identifying him."

"Will you give the description of the truck and license plate to the other counties in the area?" Mr. Rogers asked. "After all, Adams and Walnut counties have been his hunting ground, until now, at least." He looked at his daughter, putting his arm around her.

"Yes, we will. We don't have a decent profile on the kidnapper yet, just because he left no trail for us to follow in the three kidnappings. The two girls who were found in Adams County had no fingerprints on them, no hairs other than their own, and no footprints around the bodies. This man is meticulous and cleans up after himself extremely well. We know he's smart and that's why we believe he'll change the license plate, or use a different vehicle."

"So what do we do now?" Nick asked. "Do we hide in our homes?"

"That's a difficult question, Nick," Logan said. "I have a couple of deputies stationed close to your house, Larry, and we'll do patrols in the area on a regular basis. However, you live next to a large woods. It makes it much easier for someone to approach the house. He could park on the other side and walk through them to your house. Those woods compound the problem, I'm afraid."

Mr. Rogers still had his arm around Sarah. He looked at her and then turned to Logan. "Can we get full time protection from you?"

"Full time, meaning a deputy in your residence, or parked outside twenty-four seven?" Logan said. "No, we don't have the manpower for that. You could hire someone to do that, but that would be your cost, not Oak County's."

Nick saw the tears beginning to well up in Sarah's eyes. He squeezed her hand a little tighter.

"Or, we could move until this nightmare is over," Mr. Rogers said. "We won't allow Sarah to be used as bait, Sheriff."

"Whoa, wait a minute, Larry. We have no intention of using your daughter as 'bait,' as you put it. You're free to do whatever you need or want to do. We're here to serve and protect, and hopefully catch this animal before he strikes again. The Walnut Hills girl is still missing, and we're losing hope of finding her alive. If the man that was following Nick and Sarah last night is the same man who kidnapped the girls from Adams County and the one from Walnut County, it appears he is on the prowl again. That's does not bode well for the girl from Walnut Hills."

Logan stopped and let this sink in. "As of this moment, there is only one solid link between the kidnapper of the three girls and the man you saw last night."

"What's that?" Nick said.

"Chloroform. Traces of chloroform were found in the two murdered girls."

Sarah put her hands to her mouth and let a gasp escape.

"Is that enough to make him a prime suspect in the murders?" Larry Rogers said.

"Any link to those murders makes him a definite suspect."

"Sheriff, why do you think he wanted me too?" Nick asked.

"I thought about that, Nick, and all I can come up with is that you were in the way. It was obvious to him that he had to go through you to get to Sarah, so to him you were collateral damage."

"Meaning," Nick said, looking at Sarah, "he would have killed me to get to Sarah?"

"That's the only motive I can come up with, son."

"What about fingerprints on the tire iron?" Mr. Rogers said. "You must have found something there."

"Unfortunately, he must have been wearing gloves because the only fingerprints that came up were those of Nick. The tire iron had Nick's prints on them, evidently from when he picked it up last night. Every indication is that the kidnapper is smart, that he knows how to cover his tracks. But they all make mistakes. They always do."

"So getting back to the original question," Mr. Rogers said, "what do we do now?"

Sheriff Logan raised his hands in the air, palms up. "Secure your home as best you can, make sure Sarah is never alone, always with someone, preferably an adult, at all times, especially to and from school, and be vigilant. Never let your guard down and be cognizant of everyone and everything around you, day and night."

Mr. Rogers nodded. "Or we can move away until you catch this dirt bag."

Sheriff Logan nodded, shrugging his shoulders. "Or you can move away."

CHAPTER 36

Jimmy took the white breathing mask off and inspected his work. He'd been in the barn all morning repainting the black pickup, which was now green. He was expert at painting cars, having done it for a living in his younger days. He walked around the pickup, checking for any bleeding, any missed spots, and any indication that green was not the truck's original color. Once satisfied, he got his screwdriver and unscrewed the stolen license plates, front and back. He had several more available in a pile under the tool cabinet that he had stolen a few weeks before. He chose one from a county eighty miles away from Acorn. Once that was done, he went to the tack room and hung up the red cap. He put on a white cap with a John Deere logo on the front, one of his father's work caps. It was dirty, like a work cap should be. He then checked his supply of chloroform, hidden in the barn's hay loft under a tarp and some loose hay.

She had escaped him this time, the blonde cheerleader. He wouldn't make that mistake again. He could wait in the woods for hours, days if necessary, until she was alone in the house. Jimmy knew her parents left her alone a lot, so there would be an opportunity soon. He was also expert at picking locks, from his days as a burglar in his youth. His skill set was perfect for his avocation—collecting young girls. He couldn't remember how many there had been, maybe a dozen or more. He kept something from each one once he disposed of them. A ring from one, a sweater from another. He smiled his crooked smile when he thought of the Walnut Hills girl, so full of life, energy and spunk. She was his favorite so far. He had kept her cheerleader outfit as a memento, had it hanging in the cornfield cellar along with his other mementos. Now he wanted, needed, another cheerleader, the blonde from Acorn, and would kill anyone that got in the way. In the meantime, he would find a replacement, a stand-in until he could bring home his ultimate treasure.

He decided he would let the new paint job dry overnight, let things cool down some, and then drive into Acorn in his new green pickup, wearing his old white John Deer cap, to see if anyone recognized him. The man and boy last night hadn't gotten a good look at his face, so he felt confident, even bold. Afterwards he would hide his truck and go into the woods, close to the cheerleader's house, and wait. He had once waited two days for an opportunity, laying in the same spot, not moving, pissing into a bottle, his eyes always on the target. That's how he got the cheerleader from Walnut County, waiting in the woods close to the high school, knowing she walked through them on her way home. Jimmy's eye began twitching at the thought of the blonde cheerleader.

CHAPTER 37

The Paxtons sat at the kitchen table having their after-church lunch of fried chicken, corn and mashed potatoes and brown gravy. It was Clint's favorite, so it was a Sunday afternoon staple.

While Clint and the two younger Paxton boys gobbled up their chicken and fixings, Nick sat silently, moving the corn around on his plate.

"Nicky, not again," Eloise said, looking at her son. "You hardly touched your breakfast and now you haven't taken one bite of your lunch. You need to eat, honey."

Nick rested his head in his left hand, looking at his mother. "Not hungry, Mom."

Clint stopped eating and looked at Nick. "What's eating at you, son? You've been a statue ever since I got home from work last night. Want to talk about it?"

Nick slowly shook his head.

"If you don't start eating, Nicky, I'm going to start feeding you like when you were Ethan's age. Eat, now."

Nick looked at his little brother, Ethan, whose face was just inches from his own plate, almost shoveling the corn and mashed potatoes into his little mouth. He looked at Bo, who was doing the same thing while swaying to some song in his head. Nick got a fork-full of mashed potatoes and put it in his mouth, looking over at his mother.

"Okay, that's a start, keep it going," Eloise said, smiling.

Clint, taking a break from filling his belly, put his fork down and glared at Nick. "Your mom told me about what happened on Friday night, Nick.

I'm sorry I had to leave so early for work yesterday because I wanted to talk to you about it. But I'm here now, son."

Nick raised his head up, wincing from the pain in his ribs. "Maybe after lunch, Dad, okay?"

"Okay, son. What did the doctor say about your ribs? Are they cracked, broken, what?"

"Just bruised. He said bruised ribs can hurt worse than broken ribs sometimes."

Clint nodded as he grabbed his pipe out of his shirt pocket and began stuffing it with tobacco. "I remember once, when I played football back in the stone age, I bruised my ribs. I couldn't move, it hurt so bad. You think you'll be able to practice this week?"

"I don't know, Dad, and don't care."

Clint took out his lighter and lit his pipe, puffing on it until he got a bright orange glow. "What do you mean you don't care?"

"I don't care, all right?" Nick said loudly, his face turning red. "I don't care anymore!"

Clint puffed on his pipe, looking at Eloise and then at his two younger boys. "Let's go, son. If you're not going to eat your lunch, you and I are going into the living room to have a talk. Now."

Eloise reached over and patted Nick's arm. "I'll heat up some chicken for you when you get hungry, honey."

Clint slid his chair back and stood up. "Let's go, Nick."

Nick got up slowly, holding his side. "Just bitchin'."

Clint stopped and glared at him. "What did you just say?"

"Just bitchin'. It's just a saying going around school."

"Well, I won't allow it in this house, whatever the hell it means, got it?"

Nick slowly nodded, following his dad into the living room.

"Sit down on the couch," Clint said, as he blew out a large cloud of pipe smoke. "Now tell me what's going on."

Nick let out a big sigh, then started in, telling his father all about what happened Friday night and about the meeting with the Sheriff and Sarah and her dad on Saturday morning. After he was done talking, he had tears welling up in his eyes.

Clint leaned back, took a puff on his pipe then leaned forward, looking into Nick's eyes. "I'm sorry you had to go through that, son, I really am. I don't know how you feel because I've never had to go through anything like that before. It must have been, well, frightening, to know someone was following you."

"Dad, he had rags soaked in chloroform that he was going to use on Sarah, and a tire iron for me. I think I could've fought him off, but he was waiting for us in the bushes."

"I know, son, but your guardian angel was with both of you Friday night. He's a little big to be an angel, but John Walters qualifies, I think."

Nick wiped his nose with his sleeve and sniffled. "If he hadn't come along when he did . . ."

Clint took a long puff on his pipe and blew out the smoke. "Have you talked with Mr. Walters since it all happened?"

"Only when he drove me home on Friday night, after Sarah's parents got home. He's my coach and my teacher, but I think of him as my friend, too."

"I know for a fact he thinks very highly of you, Nick. He talked to me one night a couple of weeks ago after one of your games. I think it was the one in Lynn. Your mom and I were waiting for you to shower once we got back to Acorn. He told me how smart you are in class, how everyone looks up to you and likes you. Nothing about football, but about you as a person. I thought that was pretty special."

Nick smiled. "Thanks for telling me that, Dad. He's a great man, a really good teacher."

"So are you worried that the Rogers family will move away, is that what this is about?"

Nick shifted on the couch, wincing again from the pain in his ribs. "Sort of, I guess. I really love her, Dad, and I don't know what I'd do if she moved away." He wiped his nose again. "But I don't want her to be put in danger and if she stays in Acorn, who knows what that crazy animal might do."

"That's a tough spot to be in, I won't lie," Clint said. "Larry Rogers has a very difficult decision to make, but his first priority is the safety of his daughter. Do they have any other children?"

"Just her brother, who's in college up in Sioux City. That's where they'll probably move to, if they . . ."

Clint nodded. "Well, you know Sioux City isn't on the other side of the world, it's only about two hundred miles away. We could drive up every now and then on a weekend to visit. I have a sister in Sioux Falls, South Dakota, not far from Sioux City."

Nick smiled. "That'd be cool, Dad. I didn't think about that."

"But let's tackle that when the time comes. Maybe they'll catch this guy before he has a chance to do anything. Then life can get back to normal around here."

"Maybe, but Sheriff Logan doesn't seem too optimistic. He says the guy is probably smart enough to change his license plate, maybe even dump his pickup and use another car. We don't know anything about him, just that he's a whacked out pervert who preys on young girls."

Clint blew out more smoke and wiped his mouth. "What about what you said at the table, about not caring about football?"

Nick shifted again, holding his ribs. "I don't know, I'm just frustrated, Dad. With my bad ribs, with Sarah's situation, with what's going on in Cuba, with everything. Football doesn't seem important right now."

"I can see your point, son. It does seem unimportant next to those things. But you have a gift, Nick. You have the gift of speed, of natural talent, that most people never get close to. People in this town look at you as a local hero. Let's face it, there's not much else in this two-bit farm town for people to get excited about. But on Friday nights, they get to watch a very talented football team, and cheer for their local heroes. If you didn't play anymore, you'd be hurting not just yourself but this entire town."

Nick stared at his father, his words beginning to sink in. "I guess you're right, Dad. Coach Walters said the same thing, about my speed and talent. He said it doesn't come around that often and that I should take advantage of it while I can."

"He's a smart man, Nick. When you get older, like me, you'll think back to these days on the football field as some of the best days of your life. Don't give it up, son."

Nick stood up slowly, wincing, and walked to his father. They hugged for several seconds until Nick's ribs began to ache. "Thanks, Dad, for everything."

"You're welcome son. You know, my dad used to have a saying. 'It's always darkest before the dawn'. These are dark days, with a killer loose in our area and our country on the brink of nuclear war. But, God willing, these things will pass and we can all get back to our normal lives. I just hope our President has the courage to do the right thing when the time comes."

"Mr. Walters had a discussion in our World History class about the Cuban crisis. He's so smart. He told us to learn everything we can about what's going on so when the real crisis happens, we'll be informed. Do you think it could lead to a nuclear war, Dad?"

Clint puffed on his pipe, looked at the ceiling, and blew out another cloud of smoke. "It's probably the closest we've ever been to one, son. It all depends on the leadership of not just the United States, but of the USSR. All it takes is for one of them to pull the trigger."

"That's what Mr. Walters said, too," Nick said. "I hope they realize what would happen if they do pull the trigger."

"God help us if they don't," Clint said, putting his hand on his son's shoulder.

CHAPTER 38

It was almost dusk when the green pickup pulled onto Main Street in Acorn and slowly drove through downtown. Jimmy had his white cap pulled low on his head, looking at each person he passed, searching for any sign of recognition. No one paid him any attention. Sunday evening on Main Street was pretty dead, with most of the stores closed for the day.

He turned right on Chatauqua Park Drive and drove past the Sheriff's office, even stopping on the side of the street as a deputy came out of the building. The deputy glanced at the green pickup and continued walking, not giving it a second thought. Jimmy smiled as he passed a large park where some children were playing on the swings and big metal slide. He continued on around the park, ending up at the entrance to Highway Six. At the stop sign, he could see the Frosty Freeze, which was nearly deserted on a Sunday night.

He made a left turn onto the highway and drove to Oak Street, which would take him to the street where the Rogers family lived. He thought about driving by their house, but it was a dead end and would probably look suspicious. Instead, he took a side street that skirted the wooded area and drove to the other side of the woods. He found an isolated spot under a large oak, off the street, and parked.

Jimmy got out of the pickup, grabbed his large duffel bag from the bed of the truck, and found the entrance to the walking trail that would take him deep into the woods. He followed the trail in the fading light until he was just a few feet from the spot where he had waited for the cheerleader just two nights earlier. He looked through the bushes for the rags and tire iron but found nothing. His heart began to race. Someone must have found them. *Dammit!* At least he'd been smart enough to wear gloves that night. No fingerprints.

He saw lights coming on in the houses beyond, so began walking into the woods, low enough to not be seen, and found a secluded spot in some bushes with a perfect view of the gray and white house, just fifty feet away. He spread his tarp out under the bushes, grabbed his binoculars, and sat down, facing the house.

Jimmy raised the binoculars to his eyes and focused them on the front window, watching for any movement. He scanned the second story, looking for lights on in a bedroom, but it was dark. Then he saw a light on the ground floor and focused his attention on that. Nothing. He checked behind and around him to make sure he couldn't be seen, even in the daylight, and was satisfied that he was nearly invisible in the thick brush. He turned back to the house and watched . . . and waited.

He crouched lower as he saw headlights coming up the street. The car was going very slowly, as though the driver was looking for something or someone. As it got closer, he saw that it was a brown Oak County Sheriff's cruiser. The driver shined a spotlight into the woods, just to the left of him, and he bent down until it passed. The cruiser stopped in front of the Rogers house and parked for ten minutes, every now and then turning the spotlight onto the woods.

Jimmy sat motionless, not making a sound, until the cruiser started up again and made a U-turn and drove back down the street. Jimmy watched it turn the corner at the bottom of the street.

When he picked up his binoculars and looked at the house, Jimmy saw someone at the upstairs window, peering out, looking in his direction. The silhouette looked like the cheerleader. His eye began twitching as he kept the binoculars trained on the shadow in the window. She finally closed the curtains and turned off the light.

Out of the corner of his eye, he saw the sheriff's cruiser coming up the street again, the spotlight shining on the woods. *Damn!* This wasn't going to work. Obviously the local cops were aware of what happened on Friday night and were patrolling the area regularly.

He waited until the cruiser made a U-turn and began driving back down the street before gathering up his tarp and duffel bag, slowly walking to the path and returning to his truck. Throwing everything in the bed of the pickup, he got in and started it up. His eye twitched, his heart beat fast. He would have to find a replacement for the time being, until things quieted down in Acorn.

Jimmy backed out of his secluded parking place and returned down Oak Street to the highway, headed for another town to search for his next treasure. But he would be back to get the blonde cheerleader and she would be his ultimate, the one that he would keep forever.

CHAPTER 39

After Nick dropped off Ethan at his pre-school classroom, he walked quickly to the stairs, watching for Sarah. The large white clock in the hallway showed it was seven fifty-five, so he had five minutes before class. He climbed the stairs to the second floor, holding his ribs as he took each step. A few students passed him going down the stairs, but said nothing. When he finally reached the second floor landing he saw Tim Preston standing next to the World History classroom, talking with three other boys.

"Hey, Tim," Nick said.

"Nicky." Tim walked over to him. "Still holding those ribs, huh? They still hurt?"

"Oh, yeah. No practice for me for a day or two. Doc Peters said they weren't broken, just bruised, but said it would take a week or more to start feeling better. Not sure about Friday's game."

"That's tough. We play Madison on Friday, and it should be a cakewalk. I don't think they've won a game all year. Hey, did Mr. Walters find you and Sarah on Friday night? He came to Frosty Freeze looking for you."

Nick quickly told Tim about what happened on Friday night and finished right before the bell rang.

"Geez, Nick. Is Sarah okay?"

Nick looked around but didn't see Sarah anywhere. "I hope so. I called her last night and she was pretty depressed. We better get inside before Mr. Walters comes looking for us."

The two boys walked into the classroom, looked at Mr. Walters' empty desk, and walked to their desks. He glanced at Sarah's empty desk and got a queasy feeling in the pit of his stomach until he heard the door open and watched her walk in. She quickly went to her desk and sat down, glancing at Nick, but not smiling.

There was quiet chatter in the classroom as the students fidgeted, wondering where Mr. Walters was. Nick slid out of his desk and knelt down next to Sarah.

"Are you okay, Sarah?" he said, looking at her puffy eyes.

"No, I'm not okay," she answered.

At that moment, Mr. Walters walked in and strode to his desk, put his briefcase down and faced the classroom. He had a serious look on his face, not normal for a Monday morning.

"Good morning, everyone," he said, looking directly at Nick, then at Sarah. "Sorry I'm late, but we had a last-minute meeting in the teachers' lounge." He pulled out a piece of paper and showed it to the class. "I got a memo from Principal Hayes, with some very serious news about Cuba."

Nick walked back to his desk and looked at Sarah, who intently watched Mr. Walters.

"The State Department issued a memorandum this morning, claiming a U-2 spy plane was dispatched yesterday, October 14, to fly over Cuba at low altitude to search for Soviet missile sites and/or stockpiles of medium and intermediate range missiles. The pilot took low-level pictures and flew back to Andrews Air Force Base, outside of Washington D.C. The pictures evidently are proof positive that the Soviet Union has established and is constructing ballistic nuclear missile launch sites in Cuba. So it is clear now that the Soviets have and are introducing offensive nuclear weapons there."

Walters sat on the edge of his desk and looked out over the classroom. "Our worst fears are being realized about the Soviet Union and Cuba," Walters said. "Now it's up to the President and his civilian and military advisors to decide what to do about it. Any questions?"

Half the class raised their hands at once. Walters pointed to a boy in the front row. "Bruce?"

"We have to go in and bomb them, right? We can't let them do this without doing something."

Walters pointed to the girl next to Bruce. "Linda."

"If we bomb Cuba, won't the Soviet Union retaliate? That's what you said last week."

Walters nodded and pointed to Tim Preston. "Tim, you want to answer these questions?"

"If we bomb Cuba without some kind of diplomatic negotiation, it will force the Soviets to retaliate, possibly with long-range nuclear weapons. My cousin is stationed at Offutt Air Force Base in Omaha, and is with the Strategic Air Command, and they know instantly when the USSR has launched long-range missiles, so we would have to counterattack with our own launch, and . . . World War Three."

Walters was grim-faced as he stood up. "Tim hit the nail on the head. Attack, counterattack, and the world as we know it is over. It's time for cooler heads to prevail in Washington and in Moscow, and let's pray that they do. We'll follow the events every day at the beginning of class, but I encourage you to watch television, read the newspaper, and talk to your parents. Like it or not, we are on the brink of . . . well, something very dire." Walters listened to the deafening silence and saw the fear in the eyes of his students.

"I have another memo from Principal Hayes. This one is very important so everyone listen up. 'On this past Friday night, there was an incident in Acorn of a possible kidnapping of two of our students. The kidnapping was thwarted by one of our teachers, John Walters, who happened upon the scene just as the kidnapping was about to happen. Thankfully, no one was hurt. However, it appears that the alleged kidnapper could be the same man that abducted the two girls from Adams County and possibly the girl from Walnut County. We all need to remain vigilant and do not, I repeat, do not walk anywhere in Acorn by yourself. Be on the watch for a black Ford pickup. If you see it or anyone that looks suspicious please call the Oak County Sheriff's hotline posted on the bulletin boards around school. Be cautious, be careful and be safe. Principal Hayes.'"

Walters looked around the room, listening to the gasps and the whispering, seeing the fear in every student's eyes. "The kidnapper was following two students on Friday night in a black pickup truck." Walters looked at Nick and Sarah. "Nick Paxton and Sarah Rogers were walking together around ten thirty in the evening and were close to her home. I came along just in time to scare the kidnapper off."

Everyone stared at Nick and Sarah, the whispers getting louder. "Okay, okay, settle down. I didn't mention Nick and Sarah's names to embarrass them, only to let the rest of you know that we have a very bad man roaming around our area, seemingly intent on another abduction. Hopefully he was scared off on Friday night, but we can't be sure. As Principal Hayes' memo stated, be cautious, be careful and be on guard. Do not walk anywhere alone, even in your own neighborhood. Stay away from dark, wooded areas where someone could be lying in wait."

He looked at Nick and Sarah again. "Lock your doors and windows when you're home and know who it is before opening your door. This man will be captured, sooner or later, but we don't want any victims in Acorn. The sheriff's office has cruisers patrolling the area around school regularly, as well as two deputies, one at the front entrance and one at the back entrance to the gym, standing guard during school hours. But it's still up to you to be vigilant and watchful. Questions?"

Walters answered questions for the next ten minutes until he held his hand up. "Okay, it's time to get some learning in. Let's finish up with the Roman Empire. Turn to page one fifty-seven in your text."

CHAPTER 40

Nick and Sarah were surrounded after class by other students asking questions. Nick wanted to talk to Sarah but couldn't get to her before the bell rang for the next class. He put up with the stares and whispers in every class until lunchtime, then he sped out of the classroom with Tim Preston running interference for him. He searched the hallway for Sarah and finally spotted her, surrounded by six or seven other girls. He walked up to her, grabbed her hand and led her down the hallway to the lunchroom, with Tim behind them fending off curious students. They found a table in the corner and sat down. Sarah had been crying, her eyes red and puffy.

"What a nightmare," Nick said, rubbing her hand. "Are you okay, Sarah?"

She was visibly shaken, her lips trembling. "I want to go home, I can't stand it here."

Nick looked at Tim. "I don't know if they'll let you go without your parents picking you up. Is your mom home?"

She shook her head. "No, she's with my dad in Council Bluffs. They're talking to a private investigator over there. They'll pick me up after school, but no one's home right now."

Nick slid his chair over and hugged her, brushing hair out of her eyes. "Maybe we can talk to Principal Hayes about missing our afternoon classes and then go somewhere until school is out. Do you want to do that?"

She nodded, still shaking.

"Tim, could you go to the Principal's office and ask him if we can talk to him?" Nick said.

"Sure, be right back," Tim said, and he walked quickly out of the lunch-room.

Nick looked around the cafeteria and saw everyone staring at them, still whispering and pointing. But they stayed away from their table, at least giving them some privacy.

"Nicky, what's happening? Why did this happen to us? I can't stand the stares, the whispering, and the pointing. Can't we get out of here?"

"We will, Sarah. Tim's talking to the Principal now."

Nick felt a tap on his shoulder. He looked up at Mr. Walters.

"Mind if I sit down?"

Nick shook his head. "No, Coach."

Walters sat down with his back to the rest of the cafeteria. "I wanted to apologize for naming you guys this morning in class. I didn't think it would turn into this." He looked around the cafeteria. "This circus. I thought by letting the others know that two of their classmates were almost abducted might make them act more cautiously, take it seriously. My mistake, I screwed up by giving them your names. I'm really sorry."

Sarah, her lips still trembling, blinked back a tear. "It's not your fault, Mr. Walters. Everyone would have found out anyway. But my nerves are shattered, I can't think, I just want to go home."

"I know, I caught Tim in the hallway and he told me. We can't let you go home if your parents aren't there, though. When do you expect them home?"

"They said they would pick me up from school at three."

"Okay," Walters said, "there's an empty classroom on the first floor that isn't being used. We can put you in there until three, you and Nick. You'll be alone and no one will bother you. Is that good?"

Sarah nodded.

"Thanks, Coach," Nick said. "Can you stay with us?" He looked at Sarah and she nodded. "We feel like this happened to all of us and being able to talk about it might help us understand everything."

Walters sat silent for several seconds. "Sure, let me talk to Principal Hayes about getting a substitute for my last two classes. You going to football practice, Nick?"

"I don't want to leave Sarah until her parents get here, plus my ribs are still really sore. Can I skip this one practice?"

"Yeah, I'll explain it to Coach Davis. I can stay here with you until two, but then I have to get ready for practice. That okay?"

Nick and Sarah nodded. "Thanks, Coach," Nick said.

They spent the next hour and a half in the empty classroom, talking about what happened Friday night, about the meeting with the Sheriff on Saturday, and about Sarah's parents talking with a private investigator. Mr. Walters mostly listened, letting them get things off their chests.

"Sometimes," Walters said, "it's hard to understand why things happen to us, why we were selected, why we have to go through this pain and suffering. There's no easy answer, it just is. You two are strong and the other students look up to you. If you show weakness and fear, they feed off of that. If you show strength and resolve, they see that and feel better about themselves."

"But it's hard being strong when everyone is staring and whispering and saying who knows what," Sarah said.

"I know, Sarah. It's human nature for people to be curious, to judge others. Just remember, you guys did nothing wrong the other night. You were the victims, not the perpetrator. And you both were strong, especially for each other. Don't forget that. Sure, I happened along at the right time, but you beat him, the kidnapper. He ran away, beaten. That probably hasn't happened to him before."

"I'm so scared that he's still out there, watching me, waiting for, for . . ." Sarah said.

"He could be, but chances are he's smart enough to know that Acorn is dead to him for a while. Too much publicity and people are on guard. I don't know if you've noticed, but there are sheriff's cruisers patrolling all over Acorn, especially around your home, Sarah, and around school. He won't take any chances as long as that keeps up. And hopefully, he'll make another mistake and get caught."

Sarah wiped her eyes. "Thank you, Mr. Walters. You always have a way of calming everyone down, of explaining things so well."

Nick laughed. "My dad called you our guardian angel."

Walters smiled. "That's nice to hear, Nick. Tell your dad thanks." He looked at his watch. "I have to go to practice. You two stay here until the three o'clock bell rings. Have some alone time. I think you deserve it. And if you want to talk some more tomorrow, just let me know."

"Thanks, Coach. I hope Coach Davis won't be too mad that I'm missing practice."

"Don't worry about it, I'll explain the situation to him. You rest those ribs and we'll hopefully see you tomorrow at practice."

"Thank you," Sarah said, leaning over and kissing Walters on the cheek. "I feel much better now."

"Bye, guys. See you tomorrow."

Nick and Sarah watched him walk out of the empty classroom.

"So you're not going to move after all?" Nick said, holding her hand.

Sarah smiled. "No, my dad said he didn't want the animal to dictate where we live. That's why he's hiring a private investigator."

Nick grinned broadly. "That's the best news I've heard all day."

The bell rang and they hugged one more time before standing up and walking out of the empty classroom, ready to face the stares once again.

CHAPTER 41

After dinner, the Paxton family gathered around the television set to watch the evening news. Nick had told his parents about what Mr. Walters had said about Cuba, so they wanted to hear what, if anything, the President had to say.

"I doubt if he will have much to say, Nick," Clint said in between puffs on his pipe. "It just confirms what they already knew."

"But he needs to tell the world, especially the American people, about what the Soviets are doing," Nick countered. "We have a right to know."

"Maybe, but U-2 flights are surveillance, meaning they're spy planes. Usually the military doesn't want anyone to know that they're up there. It's like telling the Soviet Union our secrets."

Nick shook his head. "Not in this case, Dad. We have to let Khrushchev know that we know what they're doing. Mr. Walters said it's the first stage of negotiation, letting your enemy know that you know, making it public knowledge."

They watched the news on their black and white TV, but other than a cursory comment about Cuba, no mention was made of the U-2 flight or the pictures.

Clint blew out a puff of smoke. "Looks to me like Kennedy doesn't want Khrushchev to know we're spying on him."

Nick was about to go into his room to study when the news announcer switched to local news. He sat back down, wondering if they would say anything about Friday night.

"In local news, it appears the Southwest Iowa kidnapper has reappeared." Nick glanced at his father, his eyes growing wide. "After several weeks of inactivity, and nearly two weeks after two girls were found dead in Adams County, another missing teenage girl has been reported, this time in Walker County. Walker County Sheriff Ervin Larson issued a statement at four o'clock today, advising that the missing girl, a fifteen year old sophomore at Walker High School, left for school this morning and never made it. The disappearance is similar to those of the two Adams County abductions and the one in Walnut County just over three weeks ago. The Walnut County girl has still not been found."

Nick stared at the TV set, his mouth hanging open. His mother sat next to him and silently rubbed his back.

"It is important to note that both the Walnut County and Walker County girls are cheerleaders for their local high schools. Now, turning to weather—"

Clint turned the television off and stared at Nick. The ringing of the telephone made them all jump.

"I'll get it," Eloise said, quickly walking into the kitchen.

"Sarah. I have to call Sarah." Nick jumped up from the sofa.

"Nicky, it's Sarah," Eloise yelled from the kitchen.

Nick ran to the phone and grabbed it from his mother. "Sarah, did you see the news?"

"Yes, that's why I called. Is it the same man, Nicky?"

"It has to be, Sarah. Walker County is not that far away, maybe seventy miles or so. He probably got scared off from Acorn after Friday night and moved elsewhere."

"Nicky, that could have been me."

"I know, sweetie, but like Mr. Walters said today, we beat him, so he left us alone."

"But for how long? Will he just keep kidnapping girls until he gets caught?"

Nick didn't know what to say. "Yeah, I guess so. He's sick, Sarah, and doing this feeds his sickness. He'll make another mistake and get caught, don't worry."

Nick heard two clicks in the receiver, meaning someone was trying to call him. "Sarah, I'll call you back. Someone's trying to call us. I love you."

"I love you, Nick. Bye."

Nick pressed down once on the phone and said, "Hello?"

"Hello, Nick?"

"Yes, this is Nick Paxton. Who's this?"

"My name is Robert Douglas of WOMA-TV in Omaha. I'm reporting on the Southwest Iowa kidnappings. Can I speak to you for a few minutes?"

Nick held his hand on the phone and mouthed, "A television reporter" to his parents, who were standing next to him. Clint grabbed the phone.

"This is Clint Paxton, Nick's father. What do you want?"

"Mr. Paxton, my name is Robert Douglas of WOMA-TV in Omaha. I'm a reporter working on the Southwest Iowa kidnappings and—"

"What's that got to do with my son?" Clint said.

"We heard about the incident in Acorn last Friday night and are following up on it, in light of the news today."

"Again, what has this got to do with my son?"

"Well, sir, your son and his girlfriend were alleged targets of a possible kidnapper."

"Nothing was proven or substantiated about what happened. He has nothing to say. Goodbye," Clint hung up the phone.

"Why did he want to talk to me?" Nick said.

"He wanted to ask you about Friday night. I told him no."

Eloise held her son around the shoulders. "Your Dad is just trying to protect you, Nicky."

Nick nodded. "Yeah, I understand." Nick suddenly jerked his head up. "Sarah! He'll try to talk to her, too!"

Nick picked up the phone and dialed zero. The switchboard operator came on.

"How may I help you?"

"The Rogers residence, please," Nick said.

"Just a moment while I try that line."

Nick waited several seconds. "I'm sorry, but that line is busy. Do you want to try again later?"

"Can you break into the call? This is an emergency, Mabel."

"Is this Nicky Paxton? Just a moment, Nicky, while I try to break in."

Nick shuffled from one foot to another, glancing at his parents, who had worried looks on their faces.

"Hello, Nicky? The line is open now."

"Hello."

Nick recognized Sarah's voice. "Sarah, it's Nick. Did a reporter from Omaha try to call you?"

"Yes, I just hung up on him. Did he call you, too?"

"Yeah. They're trying to tie in what happened Friday night with the kidnappings and the missing girl from Walker."

"I know. My Dad told the reporter to go to hell and hung up."

"This is becoming too much, Sarah. I don't want to be on TV, and I don't want the kidnapper to know our names, especially yours."

"That's what my Dad said, too. It would make us an even bigger target for the sicko."

"I'm going to call Mr. Walters. They may have tried to contact him, too."

"Okay. Should we call the Sheriff?" Sarah said, sounding nervous.

"Not yet, let's wait to see what Mr. Walters says. I'll call you back, Sarah."

"Okay. Bye."

Nick dialed zero again and waited for Mabel to answer.

"How may I help you?" the sing song voice said.

"Mabel, it's Nick Paxton again. Can you connect me with John Walters, please?"

"Why certainly, Nicky. You're a busy little beaver tonight, aren't you?"

Nick ignored her, waiting for the dial tone. He heard someone pick up the phone.

"John Walters."

"Mr. Walters, it's Nick Paxton."

"Hi, Nick. Did the reporter call you, too?"

Nick let out a sigh. "Yes, and he called Sarah, too."

"Did you or Sarah talk to him?"

"No, we hung up on him."

"Good. That was good thinking, son. We don't want your names and faces broadcast all over southwest Iowa, especially with the kidnapper still out there."

"Mr. Walters, how did they get our names?"

"Probably from the Sheriff's office. They keep official records and that's where the news agencies get most of their information. I'll call Sheriff Logan tonight and let him know we don't want your names in the news."

"Thanks, Mr. Walters. Did you hear about the girl in Walker County?"

"Yes, I saw it on the news. It appears as though our Friday night friend may have found a new target, if it turns out to be a kidnapping. Walker County isn't too far away. He may have been frightened off from Acorn, exactly what we were hoping for."

"Is Sarah out of danger, you think?"

"No, unfortunately I don't think so. This guy doesn't like to lose, and Sarah beat him—not once, but twice. That will just feed his hunger. I think the girl in Walker was just a temporary substitute until . . . until things quiet down in Acorn."

Nick felt sick to his stomach. "Can you ask the Sheriff to continue the patrols on Sarah's street?"

"I will, Nick. Get some rest and I'll see you tomorrow. Oh, how are your ribs? Coach Davis wants you at practice tomorrow, even if you can't play."

"They're getting better. I'll be at practice tomorrow. Don't know about any contact, though."

"We'll limit your contact until they're healed up. We just want you with the team whether you play Friday night or not. See you tomorrow, Nick."

"Okay, thanks Mr. Walters. See you tomorrow."

Nick hung up the phone and sat down at the kitchen table, putting his head in his hands. *When is this all going to end?*

CHAPTER 42

Nick avoided everyone at school on Tuesday except for Sarah and Tim. He saw the stares and finger-pointing throughout the day, but no one came up to him or Sarah. During lunch, they sat in the corner with Tim, away from the main body of students.

"What is everyone saying, Timmy?" Nick said.

"You know, just gossip, stuff they heard from someone who heard something from someone else. They don't mean any harm to you and Sarah, they're just curious."

"A reporter from a television station in Omaha called Nicky and me last night," Sarah said. "We hung up on him, but they may still use our names if they run the story about what happened Friday night. That would really get everyone talking."

"Mr. Walters was going to talk to Sheriff Larson about it, to try to keep our names out of any story. I didn't have a chance to ask him if he did that," Nick said.

"My Mom was watching the news this morning before I left for school," Tim said, "and they were talking about the Walker County girl. She's still missing, no trace of her anywhere. How does the guy abduct someone in broad daylight without anyone seeing anything?"

"I think he probably stalks them, watches their patterns to see when they will be alone or isolated," Nick said. He looked at Sarah. "Sarah lives across from the woods, which makes for a perfect place to kidnap someone. I think that's what he was trying to do Friday night, get us in the woods."

"That's scary. How many times did we play in those woods when we were kids? It makes the hair on my neck stand up." Tim shivered.

Nick shrugged his shoulders. "All I can say is, thank God for Coach Walters."

Sarah continued to stare at Nick, saying nothing.

Tim looked at Sarah and then at Nick. "Well, maybe he won't come back to Acorn. Too many people are on the lookout for him."

"Yeah, maybe." Nick watched the crowd of students in the cafeteria, most of whom were looking at them in the corner, whispering and pointing. Nick saw Allen Neal walk towards them, a worried look on his face. He stood next to Tim, looking at Nick.

"You guys were on the noon news," Allen said. "Some reporter talking about what happened last Friday night, tying it into the disappearance of the Walker County girl."

"He used our names?" Nick said, grabbing Sarah's hand.

"Yeah, and Coach Walters's. The reporter said that Coach foiled the kidnapping attempt. He said something about some evidence left at the scene by the kidnapping suspect."

Sarah was staring down at the table, looking like she was about to lose it. Nick squeezed her hand.

"Well, I guess the Sheriff couldn't talk the reporter out of using our names," Nick said. "Damn it."

"Nick, we're all behind you and Sarah," Allen said, looking around the cafeteria. "It could have happened to any one of us. We want to help you guys in any way we can."

Nick nodded. "Thanks, Allen. Tell them that right now we just want to be left alone. Okay?"

"Sure, I'll tell them. You going to be at practice today? We missed you yesterday."

"Yeah, I'll be there. My ribs are still pretty sore but I can do everything except heavy contact, according to Coach Walters."

Allen nodded, slapped Tim on the shoulders, and walked back to the group of students. He said something to them and they immediately dispersed, going back to their tables to eat lunch. Allen gave Nick and Sarah a thumbs-up and smiled.

"He's a good guy," Tim said. "Glad he's our quarterback and captain."

Nick wiped a tear from Sarah's eyes. "It'll be okay, Sarah. We'll get through this."

She put his hand on her cheek and tried to smile. "As long as we do it together."

Nick ran wind sprints, did calisthenics and ran non-contact plays with the team. Coach Davis ordered the defense not to hit him or block him. Nick felt embarrassed to be treated with such kid gloves, but bruised ribs took a long time to heal and any contact could set his recovery back weeks. But it felt good to be with the team, to hear the shouts and laugh at the jokes. It took his mind off what happened Friday night, at least for a couple of hours.

At the end of practice, Coach Davis blew his whistle and yelled, "On me," waving everyone to circle around him. "Take a knee."

Everyone took their helmets off and bent down on one knee, waiting for the coach to speak.

"Good practice and good to have Paxton back with us. We play an away game on Friday, over at Oak Bluff. They're winless this year, but they won't be a cakewalk by any means. They have a good defense against the run, but are weak on pass defense, so we're going to work on our passing game this week. We're not planning on Paxton playing on Friday because of his ribs, so Jansen and our ends will be the prime targets.

Let's stay focused, learn our plays, and don't get cocky. We need to win the rest of our games to have a chance at the conference championship, so let's take them one at a time. Okay, two laps around the field then hit the showers."

Nick and Tim began jogging around the field together, nothing being said. Once their two laps were completed, they stopped at the water jug and chugged down a bottle each, and then started walking towards the locker room.

"So you don't plan on playing Friday?" Tim said. "I didn't realize your ribs were that bad."

"They're getting better, but one good hit and I lose two or three more weeks. Coach Walters thought it best to give it another week and then tape them up for the Woodland game a week from Friday."

"Wish I could get a shot at right halfback, since you're going to be out this week. Always wanted to play the glory position, like you," Tim said, laughing.

"Why don't you talk to Coach about it, see what he says? This would be the week to try something out, against a weaker team. Want me to talk to him?"

"No, maybe I'll give it a shot with him. It would be fun to see how the other half lives."

CHAPTER 43

As Nick began walking up the stairs to his first class he heard a voice behind him. He turned and saw Principal Hayes and Mr. Walters. He walked back down the steps and faced them.

"Good morning, Nick," Principal Hayes said. "I need you and Mr. Walters to join me in my office. Sarah Rogers is already waiting for us."

Nick glanced up at Mr. Walters, who had a grim look on his face and was looking straight ahead as they followed the Principal to his office. Nick had a bad feeling about whatever was about to happen. They entered Principal Hayes' office and saw Sarah sitting in front of the desk by herself. She looked up at Nick and smiled weakly. Nick sat next to her, with Mr. Walters taking the chair next to the Principal's desk.

"What's going on?" Nick whispered to Sarah.

Sarah shook her head slowly, shrugging her shoulders.

Hayes closed the door and walked around and sat at his desk. They heard the bell ring for the first class of the day.

"Don't worry, John, I have someone in your classroom until you get there. This won't take very long," Hayes looked at Nick and Sarah. "You two have become celebrities here at Acorn High the last few days, and it's about to get worse."

Nick looked at Sarah and Mr. Walters, his eyes growing wider. "What do you mean?"

"A news crew from WOMA-TV in Omaha will be here at noon to interview the three of you about what happened last Friday night," Hayes said. "They called and asked my permission, which I initially refused. But then I got a call from the Sheriff and he convinced me to allow it. They'll be setting up in the cafeteria."

Mr. Walters had remained quiet and solemn-faced up to now. "Principal Hayes, all three of us refused to talk to the reporter when he called us on Monday night. Don't we have a right to refuse to talk to them?"

"Yes, you do, John, but the Sheriff convinced me that talking about your confrontation will be good for the community and the school. It will bring awareness to the citizens of Acorn and to the students here at school."

"And publicity, which we don't need. It's disruptive and potentially dangerous."

"Dangerous in what way, John?"

"A psychopath is out there somewhere kidnapping young girls and killing them. He's sick and demented. If he can put a name to our faces, that puts Sarah and Nick in real danger. They become even bigger targets for this psycho."

"Well, John, that may be true, but it appears they're already targets of this 'psycho,' as you put it. If it weren't for you, they might have become victims on Friday night. You three are the only people that have seen him up close, seen his truck and looked into his eyes. Your description of this man could potentially save someone's life, maybe even here in Acorn."

"We can give a description of him without being paraded on TV," Walters said. "As a matter of fact, we gave a description to the Sheriff last week. Why don't they interview him instead?"

Nick and Sarah held hands, silently watching the two men.

"The Sheriff will also be in the interview at noon," Hayes said. "The public has a right to know what happened, and hearing it from eye witnesses carries much more weight and credence. It's the news process, John. The more the killer hears that Acorn is aware of him and what he looks like, the less chance of him coming back here. We have to think about the safety of this town and our children."

Walters leaned forward, staring at the Principal. "What if it enrages him, stirs something up inside of him that he can't control, like revenge, retribution, anger? What about the safety of these two kids?" Walters pointed at Nick and Sarah. "I believe that the risk is not worth the public's need for information, and I oppose it."

Hayes nodded. "Well noted, John, but the interview will proceed on schedule. Please be in the cafeteria at noon. Thank you, you can go to your classes now."

Walters remained seated, glaring at the Principal. Nick and Sarah slowly stood up, watching Mr. Walters. He slowly stood up and put his hands on the Principal's desk. "I'm holding you personally responsible if anything happens to these two kids."

Hayes stared back at Walters, not responding.

Walters followed Nick and Sarah out of the waiting room and into the deserted hallway. He stopped them a few feet from the Principal's office.

"Your names are already out there, so we can't do anything about that," Walters said. "But you don't have to go on TV unless you want to. Principal Hayes can't force you to do this interview. I can do it alone and speak for all three of us. That way the kidnapper will only see my face, hear my voice."

Nick looked at Sarah. "What do you think, Sarah?"

"He already knows what I look like. He stared into my eyes for a long time on the day of the Fall Festival. I know his face better than anyone."

"What do you want to do?" Walters looked at them.

"I want to do the interview," Sarah answered. "I want to stare into the camera and tell everyone about him, the evil and dark eyes, the dark hair, everything. If it can save one girl's life, then it'll be worth it." Sarah folded her arms in front of her.

Walters put his hands on her shoulders. "What about saving your life, Sarah? We don't know what this man is capable of, or what drives him. Lust, yes, but maybe he likes to be in control. If he sees you on TV, talking about him, it may unleash something in him that's uncontrollable. Do you want to take that risk?"

Sarah wiped away a tear. "Yes, I don't want to hide from him anymore. I have Nicky beside me, my parents . . . and you, Mr. Walters. We're all in this together."

Walters stared at her for several seconds and then looked at Nick. "How do you feel, Nick?"

"I'm with Sarah, Mr. Walters. It's time to tell everyone as much as we can about this weirdo and maybe, by doing that, we can save someone's life."

Walters smiled. "Okay, let's go on the offensive and bury this madman."

Nick and Sarah walked into the cafeteria and noticed the lights and cameras set up in the corner where they usually sat. They saw Sheriff Logan talking with Mr. Walters and another man.

"You ready?" Nick smiled as he held Sarah's hand.

"Yes, as long as I'm with you."

They walked up to the three men. "Where do you want us?" Nick asked.

The man talking to Walters and the Sheriff turned and smiled a big, toothy smile. His hair was perfect, his complexion perfect, and his expensive-looking suit fit him well.

"Nick and Sarah, I presume?" he said. "I'm Robert Douglas of WOMA-TV. We spoke on the phone the other night."

Nick shook his hand but Sarah held back. "Yeah, I remember."

Mr. Walters stood next to Nick and Sarah. "They're going to interview the Sheriff first," he said, "then me, then the two of you together. You guys okay?"

They both nodded, blinking at the bright lights behind the camera.

"Don't look directly into the lights," the reporter said. "Look at me the entire time. You'll do fine."

Douglas and Sheriff Logan stood in front of the camera as Walters, Nick and Sarah stood to the side, watching. The Sheriff answered the reporter's questions, looking relaxed and confident. Next, Mr. Walters stood next to the reporter and responded to his questions with one- or two-word answers.

"And finally, John, what were you doing on that dark, isolated street so late at night. Why were you there?"

Walters glanced at Nick and Sarah. "I wanted to talk to Nick about his football injury and was told they were walking to Sarah's house, so I decided to find them to give them a ride."

"And what did you see when you turned onto her street?"

"I saw a black Ford pickup, an older model, at the end of the street."

"And that sent up a red flag in your mind?"

"Yes, and then as I was driving past the entrance to Palmer Woods I saw Nick and Sarah."

"Were they in the woods?"

"Yes, just emerging from the woods."

"And then what happened?"

"I told them about the black pickup and we drove quickly to Sarah's house and ran inside."

"And did you stay in the house?"

Walters hesitated. "No, Nick and I grabbed a couple of baseball bats and went outside to confront the man in the pickup."

"And what happened?"

"We saw him coasting down the street with his headlights off, so we began running after him."

The reporter looked into the camera and back at Walters." And then what?"

"The driver started up the engine and took off before we could catch him."

The reporter looked into the camera. "A possible kidnapping thwarted by the fortunate appearance of teacher and coach, John Walters." He turned back to Walters. "Thank you, John."

The reporter then motioned for Nick and Sarah to stand next to him.

"Can you tell us your names?" the reporter said.

"Nick Paxton and this is Sarah Rogers."

"And Nick and Sarah, are you boyfriend and girlfriend?"

Nick looked at the reporter and frowned. "Yes."

"Why were you walking alone last Friday evening at ten o'clock, knowing that there was a kidnapper, a killer, in the area?"

Nick fidgeted, the question catching him by surprise. "Well, I, uh . . ."

"Because I wanted to be alone with him," Sarah said, confidently.

"You weren't able to be alone with Nick somewhere safe?"

"No, there were always people around. I asked him to walk me home."

"And why did you decide to walk through the Palmer Woods instead of staying on the lighted streets?"

"It was a shortcut to my house, one that I've taken many times," Sarah said.

"But never with a kidnapper and killer in the area. Did this worry you?"

Nick shuffled his feet. "I saw a black pickup pass by the Frosty Freeze where we were earlier, so yes, it worried me. But unless he was following us he wouldn't have known that we took the woods shortcut."

"And why was seeing a black pickup a concern to you, Nick?"

Nick looked at Sarah, who squeezed his hand.

"I saw the man in the black pickup a few weeks earlier," Sarah said, "on the day of Acorn's Fall Festival."

The reporter raised his eyebrows. "You did? The same one from Friday night?"

"Yes, we think it was the same man."

"Can you tell us what happened that day? Why would you remember something from over a month ago?"

Sarah cleared her throat. "I was supposed to be in the parade but I was running late, so I rushed out of my house and began running down the street. I noticed a black pickup that began following me, so I ran into the street to get to the woods next to our street, to take a shortcut to downtown."

The reporter was obviously excited about this new piece of information. "And what happened then?"

"The man in the black pickup slammed on his brakes right in front of me. We stared at each other for several seconds."

The reporter looked at the camera and then back at Sarah. "And what did you see?"

Sarah looked directly into the camera. "I saw evil eyes, and a face that could have been the face of the devil himself."

The reporter was silent for several seconds. "And you believe that this man is the same one that was on your street Friday night?"

"I know it was him."

"And you believe that he is the kidnapper of the four missing girls, the killer of two of them?"

"Absolutely, without a doubt."

The reporter was beside himself with excitement. "And would you recognize the man you saw if you saw him again?"

"Yes."

"Thank you, Sarah and Nick," the reporter said. Turning to the camera he recounted what Sarah had just said. "And she said that his face was the face of the devil himself," he said slowly and with emphasis. "Back to you, Mary."

The lights clicked off and the interview was over. Nick and Sarah stood still, waiting for someone to tell them what to do.

"That was perfect, Sarah. Perfect. You too, Nick. Thank you," the reporter said as he walked away, smiling broadly.

Walters walked up to Nick and Sarah. "That was some description, Sarah. If that doesn't scare everyone to lock their doors, nothing will."

Nick frowned. "If he sees this," Nick said, looking at Sarah, "he'll know that you can identify him. The only person still alive that can identify him. That makes you a big target, Sarah. Why did you have to call him the devil?"

Sarah had fire in her eyes. "Because he is, and I looked straight into his black soul that day, Nick. You weren't there, you haven't seen him up close. And the only ones that do end up dead."

Walters listened to the exchange quietly. "Sarah, that was a brave thing to do, or a very stupid one. Time will tell, I guess. But one thing is certain. We haven't seen the last of this guy."

CHAPTER 44

Jimmy was eating his dinner at a roadside diner close to his father's farm. He'd been a regular there since he arrived and everyone knew him as the son of a local farmer, so they never gave him a second look. He blended into the scenery, part of the Iowa landscape of corn, oats, and the farmers that tilled the soil.

He usually didn't pay any attention to the small television behind the counter but something caught his eye. The six o'clock news was on and the talking heads were discussing the crisis in Cuba, wringing their hands, saying the world is on the brink.

Bullshit, he thought.

But what came next caught his attention. A local reporter named Douglas was standing next to the Oak County Sheriff, talking about an incident in Acorn on the previous Friday night. Jimmy dropped his fork on his plate and stared at the black and white TV. He stood up and moved closer so he could see the images. After the Sheriff, the reporter interviewed the big man who had foiled his plan on Friday night. He talked about how he had seen a black pickup on the girl's street and intercepted the young couple as they emerged from the woods.

Jimmy's left eye began twitching when he saw the next two people, the cheerleader and her football-player boyfriend. She was looking straight into the camera, as if she was staring at him, just the two of them. He wanted to reach up and touch the screen, to connect with her, but glanced around the small diner first. Several people were watching the TV and glancing at him standing in front of it. He moved back, staring at the girl on TV, his left eye twitching, a crooked smile creasing his face. Then he heard her voice.

"I saw evil eyes, and a face that could have been the face of the devil himself."

She was looking directly at him, staring at him, just like she did on that first day. They had a connection, a bond that was being proven to the world. He took several steps back from the TV, keeping his eyes on hers. His heart ached, he wanted her so bad.

The reporter repeated their names. Nick Paxton and Sarah Rogers.

Sarah, Sarah. He'd never known the names of his victims before he abducted them, but now he knew everything about his next and last conquest, his final treasure. He would keep her forever as his own.

Jimmy froze when the reporter mentioned the name of the tall dark-haired man. He sat down and stared at the television set, his mind racing. He put three dollars on the table, grabbed his white cap and walked out of the diner. No one noticed.

CHAPTER 45

It was nearly seven o'clock as Nick sat in the locker room, fully dressed in his home uniform, jersey number twenty-five. He knew there wasn't much of a chance that he would get to play, his ribs still sore and bruised, but Coach Walters wanted him to suit up anyway.

"You're part of this team and we want you on the sideline, Nick," Walters had said.

Tim sat next to him, his nerves getting the best of him.

"Timmy, you okay?" Nick said.

Tim looked up, sweat gleaming on his forehead. "I should've left it alone, Nick. I wanted to see what it would be like to be a star like you. Now I have to prove it and I'm scared, man."

Nick slapped his friend on the shoulder pads. "Hey, you'll do fine. Just follow your blockers and look for an opening. That's what it's all about."

Tim stared at him. "But I'm not anywhere near as fast as you, Nick. I'm gonna get creamed out there."

Nick chuckled. "Hey, you wanted to see how the other half lives. Now you'll find out. Just keep your hands on the football. One thing Walters hates is fumbling."

Coach Davis walked into the locker room. "Listen up," he said loudly, as the players gathered around him. "We had a good week of practice, we have a good game plan. If we play our game, we'll win tonight, but we have to fight hard to the last whistle. It's going to be cold out there, so keep loose. All right, gather up."

Everyone gathered into a circle, putting their hands together in the middle.

"Who are we?" Coach Walters yelled.

"Mighty Oaks!"

"Louder, I can't hear you!"

"Mighty Oaks! Mighty Oaks, Mighty Oaks!"

"All right! Let's hit the field!"

The game went according to the coach's plan, with the Mighty Oaks using their pass attack to perfection. Allen Neal threw for three touchdowns and had a big night. Tim got to run the ball twice, both times being stopped with a short gain, and caught two passes out of the backfield, one for a fifteen yard gain. He played his normal strong game on defense, intercepting a pass in the fourth quarter to put the game away. Nick sat on the bench, as expected. The Mighty Oaks beat Oak Bluff easily, twenty-seven to six.

Frosty Freeze was nearly deserted after the game. The bitter cold, the easy game, and the events of the past week put a damper on any celebrating. Nick and Sarah, along with Tim and Susie Daniels, went with their parents to a diner called the Shady Oak, on Highway Six on the north edge of town. The parents, along with Nick's two little brothers, got a separate table in the diner, leaving the teenagers alone at their own table in the corner. The conversation was subdued.

"This kinda sucks," Tim said, looking over his shoulder at his parents talking to Nick and Sarah's parents.

Nick chuckled. "Better than just going home, Timmy. Besides, they have the best fries and cherry coke here. My Dad takes us here on Sunday after church sometimes."

Sarah, still in her cheerleader outfit, was staring at her French fries, not smiling or looking up.

"What's wrong, Sarah," Susie Daniels said. "Aren't you feeling well?"

Sarah looked up and smiled weakly. "No, just tired from this past week. I think everything just wore me out."

Nick tried to lighten the mood. "Plus, your boyfriend didn't get to play tonight. He had to watch the second-stringer play his position," he said, nudging Tim.

"You can have your position back," Tim said, "I don't want to play offense anymore, too much pressure and too much to learn."

Nick laughed. "You did okay, Timmy, but I have to admit, you're a whole lot better on defense."

The jukebox in the small diner had a Beach Boys song playing. Nick shook his head as he watched Bo doing his swivel-hip dance in front of the parents.

Susie put her arm on Sarah's shoulder. "You've had a rough week, Sarah. Want to talk about it?"

The front door to the diner opened and a man in a white cap and farmer's overalls walked in. He wore glasses and had the cap pulled low over his face as he looked around the diner. He quickly looked at the table of teenagers as he strode to the bar in the back. Sarah followed him with her eyes until he disappeared into the bar.

"Sarah, do you want to talk about it?" Susie repeated.

"What? Oh, no, not really. I'm just so tired of the finger pointing and the stares. I'm starting to think that moving away might not be such a bad idea." She looked at Nick when she said this, but avoided eye contact.

Nick looked at the bar in the back of the diner. Something about the man that just walked in unsettled him. He turned around when he heard Sarah's comment.

"Are you serious?" Nick said. "I thought you and your parents put that idea to bed."

Sarah grabbed his arm and put her head on his shoulder. "I won't leave you, Nicky. Not now, not ever. I'm just really tired of everyone staring at us. Aren't you?"

Nick nodded. "Yeah, it gets old, but we put ourselves in that position, Sarah. The TV interview on Wednesday was probably not such a good idea."

Tim leaned in, looking at Nick, then Sarah. "I thought you guys did a great job. Sarah, you were brave and confident in front of the camera. Even Mr. Walters said so."

Nick turned and looked at the bar in the back again. "Did you guys see the man that just walked in?"

"Yeah, just some farmer getting a drink. What's the big deal, Nick?" Tim said.

Nick shook his head. "I don't know, something about him, something that I've seen before, but I can't remember where or when."

Sarah took her head off Nick's shoulder and stared at him. "He had his cap pulled low over his face. Why would he do that unless he had something to hide?"

They stared at each other until the light bulb came on in their heads at the same time. Their eyes grew big as they realized where they had seen him before.

"Change the white cap to a red cap," Nick said.

"And remove the glasses," Sarah added.

Nick slid his chair back and stood up. "I'm going in there."

"Nicky, no—please," Sarah pleaded.

"I have to know, Sarah. *We* have to know."

Nick took a step towards the bar, but Tim held him back. "You're not going in there alone, Nicky. I'm coming with you."

The two teenagers slowly walked to the bar, hearing the country western music and smelling the smoke and liquor. They stood in the opening, peering into the dark room. Three men were sitting at the bar, but they had their caps off. Nick walked slowly up to the bar, Tim right behind him. He put his elbows on the bar and peered down, looking at the three men. One was wearing farmer's overalls and wore glasses, the other two were in jeans and flannel shirts. Nick concentrated on the one in farmer's overalls. He squinted his eyes, trying to adjust to the dim light. The man in the overalls turned to look at him.

"You lookin' for somebody, kid?" the man said.

"Uh, no."

Nick heard the back door of the bar open and turned around quickly and saw a man in a white cap disappear through the door.

"Tim, he went out the back door," Nick said. "Let's go!"

The two boys ran to the door and opened it, peering into the darkness. The silhouette of a man disappeared around the corner. They ran to the corner of the building and Nick carefully craned his head to look. The lights in the front of the diner illuminated the man in the white cap walking towards the parking lot.

"Follow me," Nick said, inching his way up the side of the building, keeping his eyes on the man in the white cap. "If he's driving a black pickup . . ."

He watched the man get into a dark-colored pickup. Nick quickly walked into the light to get a better look. The driver started it up and began to pull out of the lot, past the two boys. When the pickup passed under the lights, Nick saw that it was green. He squinted at the license plate as it passed by them, then relaxed his shoulders and shook his head.

"It's not him," he said. "It's green, not black, and the license plate was from a different county."

Nick stared at the man in the pickup as he pulled out onto the highway and froze when he turned around to look at him.

"What's wrong?" Tim said.

"That's him."

"Who?"

"The man from the hardware store . . . the man in the black pickup."

"It's green and you said yourself—"

"It's him."

CHAPTER 46

A light snow was falling as Jimmy put on a heavy parka and pulled the hood over his red cap, looking out his back door at the fading light. He picked up his green duffel bag, partially filled with food and water and necessities, and opened the door into the cold night air. He felt the snow on his face as he looked up into the twilight sky. He trudged to the edge of the cornfield, dropped the duffel bag and looked around. Even though he lived far away from the closest neighbor, he never knew when someone might drop by. Feeling secure, he picked up the bag, threw it over his shoulder, and began walking into the dying, brown cornstalks. He walked through the field to the open area, being careful not to break any cornstalks and leave a path that others could follow.

Once he reached the open area, he removed the dead cornstalks from the top of the shelter door, feeling his pulse race as he thought about what was inside. He opened the heavy door, the loud creaking sound lost in the cold night air, and carried his duffel bag down the dark stairs until he came to the locked door. He opened the peephole and peered inside, seeing the orange light of the space heater, but not much else. His pulse quickened as he unlocked the padlock and slowly opened the heavy metal door. He heard scuffling as his flashlight illuminated the dark room. He panned the flashlight on the back wall and saw her, huddled against the wall, a green wool blanket around her shoulders. He lit the kerosene lamp and slowly walked towards her, dragging the duffel bag behind him. She cowered in the corner, covering her eyes with the blanket.

"How's my little treasure tonight," Jimmy said. "Is the space heater keeping you warm enough? It's getting cold outside, so I have to keep my little treasure warm and healthy. Are you healthy?"

The cowering girl didn't respond, keeping her head covered with the blanket.

"I'll check you out, make sure you're healthy, don't you worry." He pulled the duffel bag close and unzipped it. "I brought you some food, water and, uh, some female essentials. You want to clean up for me, right?"

The girl peeked out from the blanket at the duffel bag. She nodded her head.

Jimmy knelt down and held a banana out. "Here, take it."

The girl grabbed the banana and ripped the peel off, shoving the fruit into her mouth as she looked at him. She snatched another one when it was offered and held it close to her, then took the water jug and drank as much as she could.

"Well, you sure have your appetite. Now, let's see if you're healthy." He stood over her and grabbed the blanket, ripping it away from her, holding the lamp up so he could see her better.

"You've lost some weight," he said, dropping to his knees.

The Paxton's had an early dinner and then gathered in the living room to watch the evening news. Bo and Ethan were lying on the floor, playing with their toys, uninterested in anything on the television until the news was over. Eloise and Nick occupied the sofa, one at each end, Eloise doing her usual knitting. Clint sat in his chair, puffing on his pipe, trying to get it lit.

"There's supposed to be some big announcement about the President tonight," Eloise said, looking up from her knitting.

Nick stared at the TV, watching a commercial about Kent cigarettes. He had not been following the Cuba crisis the last few days because of everything else that was happening. His mind was on Sarah and the man in the green pickup. He couldn't get the vision of the man turning around to look at him out of his head. It was exactly the same as the Saturday afternoon on Main Street, after he followed the man in the hardware store out to his pickup. It looked like the same man, but now his pickup was green.

"It's on," Eloise said, dropping her knitting into her lap.

"Good evening." Walter Cronkite said, "It's Sunday, October 21ˢᵗ, 1962. We start tonight's telecast with an important announcement from the White House. President Kennedy will be addressing the nation tomorrow night at six o'clock Eastern Standard Time regarding the escalating tension in Cuba. The missile crisis has reached a critical stage and the President will be outlining his response to Soviet Premier Khrushchev to the American people. The world is on the brink of an unimaginable catastrophe, one that we all hope can be averted."

Nick leaned forward as he listened to Cronkite explain recent events and the building tension between the U.S. and the U.S.S.R. *If Walter Cronkite said it, it must be true. The world is on the brink.*

After the newscast, Clint stood up and turned the television set off. Puffing on his pipe, he looked at his two youngest sons playing on the floor, knowing they were oblivious to the danger that was facing their world. A tear formed in his eye as he bent down and rubbed their heads. They glanced at him, smiled, and went back to playing. He stood up and walked to the sofa and sat next to Nick. Nothing was said as he put his arm around his oldest son. Eloise hugged him from the other side, softly crying.

CHAPTER 47

On Monday morning, October twenty-second, Mr. Walters opened the door and walked to his desk. He sat on the outer edge and looked out at his twenty-five students. He locked onto Nick's eyes and lingered, nodding slightly.

"Morning, everyone," he said. "I have a memo from Principal Hayes, but I'm not going to read it. I can see in your eyes that you know what it's about." He placed the memo on his desk. "We're living in a time of great anxiety, as you all know now. Tonight, President Kennedy will address the country about how he plans to deal with the Soviet buildup of missiles in Cuba. He has no simple or easy choices. Every option has the potential for thermonuclear war, which means we are on the brink of global annihilation." Walters walked around his desk and sat down. Every student's eyes were focused on him.

"I strongly encourage you and your families to watch and listen to the President's speech tonight. Tomorrow we'll discuss it and everyone will have an opportunity to ask a question, make a comment or just listen. It will be your time to express your feelings." He forced a smile. "But today we'll discuss the final days of the Roman Empire. Turn to page one seventy-one in your text."

Nick, Sarah, Tim, and Susie sat stone-faced at their corner table in the cafeteria. The mood of everyone in the lunch hall was subdued, the thought of that evening's Presidential address weighing on their minds.

Sarah was the first to speak. "This could be our last few days together," she said, holding Nick's hand and staring into his eyes. "How can this be happening?"

Nick squeezed her hand. "I have confidence in Kennedy. He'll figure it out and get us out of this mess."

"I do too, Nick, but what about Khrushchev? All it takes is for one of them to pull the trigger," Tim said. "This thing is escalating to a point where it may be too late to stop it."

Susie sat solemn-faced, blinking back tears. "How did the world get this way?"

Nick shook his head. "It just did and nobody cared, until now. Now that we're on the brink, it may be too late, like Tim said."

Coach Davis canceled practice on Monday so that all the players could go home and be with their families. Eloise picked up the three Paxton boys at three o'clock, but they didn't go straight home.

"Where you going, Mom?" Nick said. "This is the opposite direction from home."

"I know, Nick. I thought we'd stop at Frosty Freeze and get some ice cream cones first."

Bo and Ethan let out a happy yelp, but Nick just stared at his mother. "Why, Mom?"

"Because I want you boys to have some normalcy in your lives right now."

"That sounds great, Mom," he said, as he reached over and grabbed her hand. "Thanks."

At five o'clock Central Standard Time, the Paxton family was gathered in their living room. Clint was lighting his pipe in his easy chair; Eloise was pretending to knit something on the sofa, with Nick next to her. Bo and Ethan were lying on the floor, their heads propped up in both hands, looking at the television set. Nick had the feeling that every family in the United States was doing the exact same thing.

Walter Cronkite spoke solemnly about the upcoming Presidential speech and the grave situation America was in. Finally, President Kennedy was on the black and white screen, sitting at his desk in the Oval Office, looking grim, drawn and tired.

For the next seventeen minutes, President Kennedy spoke about the gravity of what the United States and the USSR—in fact, the whole world—faced. Moscow had created a 'nuclear strike capability' in Cuba, with missiles that could hit Washington, D.C., or any other city in the southeastern United States. Intermediate-range ballistic missiles could strike most of the major cities in the Western Hemisphere. Kennedy condemned the USSR for lying, speaking of the breach of faith of many Soviet promises to supply Cuba with only defensive weapons. The United States would not tolerate this threat to its security and would therefore quarantine Cuba to block all offensive weapons from reaching the island. Any Soviet failure to comply would justify additional U.S. action, including retaliatory attacks against the Soviet Union. He also promised to counter any threat to America's allies, including Berlin.

When President Kennedy's speech was over, a grim-faced Walter Cronkite repeated the main points to the American people and called the quarantine a "blockade of Soviet ships." He signed off by requesting prayers from every single American.

After Clint turned the TV off, he returned to his easy chair and resumed puffing on his pipe. Eloise continued to stare at the blank television set, her hands in her lap. Nick sat silent, looking down at his two brothers, who were lying with their heads resting on their hands, staring at their father and mother.

Finally, Clint took the pipe out of his mouth. "Well, there it is," he said. "A naval blockade or quarantine, whatever they want to call it. Regardless, it's a military action, an act of war."

Nick stared at his father, a shiver running up his spine at the mention of war. "It's not really war, Dad, is it? I mean, we're just making sure the Soviets don't send any more missiles to Cuba."

"That's right, Nick, but what if the Soviets don't stop and continue to sail to Cuba. What then?"

Nick thought a moment. "I guess we have to stop them."

Clint nodded. "And how do we do that? By shooting at them, ramming them, having submarines launch torpedoes at the ships? That sounds like war to me, son."

Nick leaned forward on the sofa. "So our fate is up to what the Soviets do?"

Clint nodded. "That's right, Nicky. It's in their hands now."

CHAPTER 48

As Nick dropped Ethan off at his pre-school room he overheard the teacher tell another parent that the school would be conducting drills for the next few days, having the children get under their desks or tables whenever they heard a bell ring twice. He watched Ethan run to the toy box as soon as he checked in with his teacher. *He's the only one that isn't afraid,* Nick thought. *He's too young to know any better.*

Nick was halfway up the stairs when he felt someone touch his arm from behind. He turned and saw Sarah one step below him. She was dressed in a plain beige pleated dress and a light green pullover sweater, her hair in a ponytail, a sad look on her face.

"Hi," Nick said, taking her hand. "You okay?"

Sarah walked next to him as they climbed the remaining stairs. "It's all so frightening, Nicky."

Nick pulled her away from the main hallway, into an empty corner near some lockers. "I know, sweetie. But we have each other."

She rose on her tiptoes and kissed him long and hard, her hand on the back of his neck.

"Good morning," they heard someone say behind them. Mr. Walters was standing in the hallway, smiling. "You two ready for class?"

Nick smiled sheepishly and followed Walters into the classroom, letting go of Sarah's hand when they got to her desk. He sat down at his desk and waited for Mr. Walters to begin.

Every student was sitting up straight, eyes on Mr. Walters. He took some books out of his briefcase and laid them on his desk, seemingly unaware of the attention he was getting. When he looked up, he smiled at his students.

"Good morning, everyone," he said. "I wish I had this kind of attention every morning."

There were a few laughs, but mostly silence.

"Who has a question?" Walters said.

Nearly every hand in the room went up.

"That's what I thought. Let's start in the back and work our way forward. Debbie?"

A short blonde-haired girl stood up. "Why did President Kennedy call it a quarantine instead of a blockade?"

Walters nodded and looked around the room. "Who wants to answer that?"

Nick raised his hand.

"Nick, what's the difference between a quarantine and a blockade?" Walter said.

Nick slowly stood up. "A quarantine is less threatening, less militaristic," he said. "A blockade is usually used in a war or confrontation. I think President Kennedy was trying to keep his response to the Soviets as non-confrontational as possible."

Tim raised his hand.

"Tim?" Walters said.

"But doesn't that make us look weak, less committed?" Tim said.

"Nick, what's your response to Tim's question?"

Nick cleared his throat as he looked at his best friend. "Yes, it does make us look weak. But I think the President is reaching out to Khrushchev, giving him a chance to back down without too much strong talk."

Walters smiled. "Good answer, but there are those in power, here in the United States, that think it's too weak for a world power. Even using the word blockade they think is a too-weak response."

Sarah raised her hand.

"Sarah?"

"What other option did the President have?" Sarah said.

Walters waited for a hand to go up, but saw none. "I'll bet the Joint Chiefs of Staff, our top military leaders, wanted a full-out air strike of Cuba to eliminate the missile sites. They all think that a blockade is a sign of weakness."

"But wouldn't that create the one thing no one wants?" Sarah said. "Russia would have to retaliate, and then we would retaliate."

Walters nodded vigorously. "Exactly right, Sarah. This is what we've been talking about for weeks now. How does the U.S. and USSR get out of this crisis without having to retaliate, which would result in thermonuclear war?"

Walters and his class bounced questions back and forth to each other for the next thirty minutes, until they heard the bell ring twice in the middle of the period. Everyone looked at each other.

"It's only eight thirty," someone said.

"Everyone, under your desks," Walters said. "And keep your heads down."

Every student ducked under his or her desk, the tension in the room palpable. Nick glanced at Sarah, who was looking back at him.

After ten seconds, the bell rang twice again. "Okay, everyone back in your seats," Walters said.

There was lots of grumbling and whispering as the students stood up and sat back down at their desks.

"Sorry for not telling you about the drill," Walters said. "I have the memo on my desk, I just forgot to read it to you. The school will be conducting drills like this randomly every day until this crisis is over. When you hear the bell ring twice, duck and cover. Everyone okay?"

Everyone started talking at the same time until Walters held up his hand for silence.

"Mr. Walters, what good would this do if there was a nuclear war?" one girl in the back said.

Walters shrugged his shoulders. "I don't know, maybe save you from something falling from the ceiling. It's just a precaution."

Tim raised his hand. "Or maybe keep us from panicking?"

Walters smiled. "Or that."

The bell rang again and several students ducked under their desk.

"That's the normal bell," Walters said. "See everyone tomorrow."

"We hope," someone said.

CHAPTER 49

It was cold and snow fell at football practice that afternoon. The team moved listlessly from one drill to another until Coach Davis blew his whistle. "On me!"

The players jogged over to their coach and took a knee, some shivering from the cold, others wiping sweat and snow water from their faces.

Coach Davis and Coach Walters stood in front of the team, hands on their hips.

"It's been a tough couple of days, and this weather isn't helping," Coach Davis said. "Coach Walters and I understand what you're going through, mentally and physically. The world is in a big mess, just like our football field this afternoon. It's cold, wet, and miserable—we get it." Davis held up his clipboard. "But we've got a game against one of the best teams in the conference in three days, and . . ."

Davis stopped when he saw two players whispering to each other in the back of the group. "Smith, Jenkins—you have something you want to say to the rest of us?"

Scott Jenkins, a first-team guard, stood up. "Coach, we don't know if we'll be around in three days, what with—"

"What with the Cuban crisis, and missiles, and all that other crap going on?" Davis said, finishing Jenkins' sentence. "You're right, we don't know. But, by God, this football team will be ready to play Woodland on Friday night. The only way to fight the anxiety that all of us are feeling is to live our lives just like before. Sure, you're afraid, I'm afraid, even Coach Walters here is afraid." He looked at Walters and smiled. "But that doesn't mean that life doesn't go on. We need to focus for two hours a day on beating Woodland. For those two hours we won't be afraid, we'll be the Mighty Oaks." Davis wiped his face with a towel. "This weather isn't going to get any better. The world situation may not get any better. But as God is my witness, this football team is going to get better in the next three days!"

Allen Neal stood up, raising his helmet into the air. "Let's go, Mighty Oaks!"

Davis blew his whistle. "All right! Offense with Coach Walters, defense with me."

Nick put on his helmet and jogged to Coach Walters, with the rest of the first and second string offensive players circling around him.

Walters walked over to Nick and put his hand on his shoulder pads. "How are the ribs, Nick?"

Nick smiled up at him. "I'm ready to go, Coach."

Walters slapped him on the helmet. "That's what I wanted to hear." He turned to the group. "Woodland has a damn good defense, especially up the middle. But they're weak around the ends. We're going to practice running Thomas up the gut, to soften them up, and then run Paxton and Jensen around the ends." He clapped his hands. "Let's go!"

Walters grabbed Nick as the rest of the team ran onto the field. "You sure those ribs are okay, Nick? I don't want to take any chances. Give me a straight answer, son."

"They're still a little sore, Coach, but I taped them up before practice. I need some contact to make sure."

"Okay, let's get into the huddle, but you let me know how you feel later."

"Coach, can I talk to you after practice for a few minutes? Something personal, about Sarah and . . . and . . ."

"Sure, Nick. Come to my office after you shower. Go get in the huddle."

After showering and dressing, Nick walked to Coach Walters' office and knocked on the door. Walters waved him in.

"Sit down, Nick. How did the ribs hold up?"

"I gotta admit, Coach, they're sore as hell," Nick said, "but I took some good hits today and they held up pretty good. I'll be ready by Friday night."

Walters nodded. "Good, we'll need your speed against Woodland. What's on your mind, son?"

Nick leaned closer. "I think I saw our guy last Friday night."

Walters sat up straight. "Where?"

"At the Shady Oaks diner, out on Highway Six. Me, Tim, Sarah, and Susie Daniels were sitting at a table, having a late dinner after the game."

"You were there alone, the four of you?"

"No, our parents were at a table on the other side of the diner. Anyway, a man walked in while we were there. Looked like a farmer, in overalls and stuff, and he had his cap pulled real low over his face, like he was hiding something, but he had dark hair."

"A red cap?"

"No, it was white. And he had glasses on."

"So, what made this guy so special?"

Nick leaned closer. "He glanced at Sarah and me. There was something about him, something familiar about his walk and the way he looked at us. He walked into the bar in the back of the restaurant. Tim and I followed him."

"You did what? Are you crazy, Nick?"

Nick fidgeted in his chair. "I just had to get a better look at him. Anyway, I thought he was sitting at the bar, so we went to the bar and looked at the three men sitting there, but he wasn't one of them. Then we heard the back door to the bar open and I turned and saw the man with the white cap walk out, real quick and all."

"And let me guess, you followed him."

Nick nodded. "We followed him out to the parking lot and saw him get into a Ford pickup, an older Ford pickup."

Walters' eyes widened. "Black?"

Nick sat back in his chair. "No, it was green."

Walters' shoulders sagged. "Green? So it wasn't him?"

"I didn't think so, and I got a look at his license plate when he drove away, and it wasn't the same as the one we saw."

"So, again, what made this guy so special?"

Nicked cleared his throat. "The way he looked back at me."

Walters leaned forward. "He looked back at you? That's what made him special?"

"Coach, it's the same guy I saw at the hardware store downtown a couple of weeks ago, I'm sure of it. He turned and looked at me like he knew me."

"And you think that's the guy we saw at Sarah's house?"

"He was driving a black pickup then, but it was the same guy. I'll never forget his eyes."

Walters leaned back in his chair and was silent for several seconds. "So two weeks ago he was driving a black Ford pickup—"

"And was looking at shovels," Nick said.

"And a week ago Friday, the guy that we saw at Sarah's house was driving a black Ford pickup."

"That's right, Coach. He could have painted his truck green and changed the license plate, and the color of his cap. All those things are what we recognized, and he knew that."

Walters nodded. "It's possible, but all circumstantial. The sheriff would laugh us out of his office with this story."

Nick's shoulders slumped. "I know."

Walters looked at Nick. "But if it's true, we now know to look for a green pickup instead of a black one. Did you get the license plate number, something we can give to the sheriff?"

Nick hung his head. "No, it was too dark, but I did see the name of the county."

"What county is that?"

"Walker County."

Walters stared at him. "Walker County, that's seventy miles away—"

"The last girl kidnapped was from Walker County."

"And she was kidnapped a couple of days after we saw him," Walters said. "Enough time to paint his truck and pick up the new license plates while he was in Walker County. It all makes sense, sort of."

"Coach, I know it's him. Just the way he pulled the cap low over his eyes, the way he looked at Sarah and me, the way he left the bar when Tim and I went in, and the way he looked back at me when he drove off, like he recognized me. He was testing us, Coach, to see if we recognized him."

Walters nodded. "He's getting bolder, taking chances." He looked up at Nick. "And that also means he's still after—"

"Sarah."

CHAPTER 50

Nick glanced at Mr. Walters, who was sitting at his desk, when he walked into the classroom at eight o'clock. Walters glanced up, a grim look on his face, as Nick sat down at his desk just as the bell rang.

The classroom was dead silent, everyone waiting for Mr. Walters. There were rumors of something big regarding the Cuban situation. Mr. Walters finally stood up, walking around his desk to face his students. He was holding a piece of paper.

"President Kennedy received a reply from Nikita Khrushchev early this morning. The Soviets are taking the position that the U.S. blockade is "an act of aggression" and that their ships bound for Cuba would be ordered to proceed."

Nick heard a gasp from some students.

Walters looked up at his class and then back to the memo. "Also, U.S. reconnaissance flights over Cuba indicated the Soviet missile sites were nearing operational readiness. With no apparent end to the crisis in sight, U.S. forces have been placed on DEFCON 2—meaning war involving the Strategic Air Command is imminent."

This time a collective gasp went up from all the students. Sarah and Nick glanced at each other, the fear evident in their eyes.

Tim raised his hand.

"Yes, Tim," Walters said.

"My cousin is stationed at SAC at Offutt Air Base in Omaha. He called last night and said they are on twenty-four hour standby."

Walters nodded. "The entire world is on twenty-four hour standby today. DEFCON 2 is the last stage before DEFCON 1, which is all-out war."

A hush fell over the classroom when Walters said the word. The silence was broken by the ringing of the bell. The students sat still, looking at one another. It rang a second time.

"Everyone, under your desks!" Walters ordered.

Nick dove under his desk, looking over at Sarah. She was sitting under her desk with her hands over her face. He looked around the room and saw students huddled under their desks with hands over their heads. Fear gripped Nick like never before as his mind went to missiles crossing the Atlantic Ocean, heading for Washington, D.C., New York City—and Iowa.

Within ten seconds the bell rang twice again and everyone slowly climbed out of their hiding places, sitting at their desks with ashen faces, staring at Mr. Walters.

Walters sat on the edge of his desk and peered out over the classroom. "Now's a good time to have a moment of silence and pray for God's mercy in the days to come."

Nick lowered his head, closed his eyes and said a silent prayer. He heard someone sniffling and peeked out at Debbie, the short blonde girl sitting next to him. He saw the tears racing down her cheeks. He glanced over at Sarah, who was staring at him, a look of total fear in her eyes.

Mr. Walters made an attempt to talk about the Mongols invading Europe, but his heart wasn't in it. "We have ten minutes left before the bell rings. Go ahead and talk to your neighbor, but quietly. When the bell rings, leave quietly and in an orderly manner." Walters looked at Nick. "Nick, can you and Sarah join me out in the hallway, please?"

Nick met Sarah and they walked together into the deserted hallway. Walters closed the door and faced them. "I talked to Sheriff Logan last night on the phone, about what you and I discussed yesterday, Nick."

Nick looked at Sarah. "I told Coach about last Friday night at Shady Oaks."

"Sheriff Logan is going to call his counterparts in the surrounding counties about the green pickup with the Walker County plate," Walters said. "He also is going to have the Walker County sheriff investigate any missing license plates."

"So he's taking this seriously?" Nick said.

"He's skeptical, but he's taking it seriously, yes," Walters said.

Sarah stared at Nick and Mr. Walters. "Does that mean the man might come back . . . to Acorn?"

Walters put his hand on her arm. "If the man you two saw on Friday night was him, he's growing bolder. He took a chance walking into that diner, but he had to know you two were in there. That means he's been following one or both of you, according to Sheriff Logan."

Nick grabbed Sarah's hand and hugged her.

"The Sheriff is going to put someone outside of your house around the clock, Sarah, until we catch this guy or he goes away."

"What about Nicky?" she said, sniffling. "Isn't he in danger, too?"

"Possibly, but the sheriff doesn't have the manpower to assign someone to watch Nick's house. You have to be vigilant, Nick, and never—and I mean never—go anywhere alone, especially at night. That means no walking home from practice. I'll drive you home if you can't get a ride."

Nick nodded. "Thanks, Coach. I may have to take you up on that. I'll talk to my parents tonight."

Walters grew serious. "Nick, I have to ask you something. Do you have a gun at home? A hunting rifle, anything?"

Nick shook his head. "No, my Dad doesn't like guns and won't have one in the house."

Walters pursed his lips. "Talk to your parents tonight. You need to have a weapon of some kind in your house—just in case."

Sarah was standing motionless, her hand over her mouth.

"How about you, Sarah?" Walters said.

She stared at Walters and nodded. "My Dad has a hunting rifle and a shotgun."

"Tell him to keep them handy, just in case. Guys, I don't like asking you to do this, but we're dealing with a psychopath, a killer, do you understand?"

They both nodded.

"And Nick, don't take any more chances. If you see him or his truck again, call me or Sheriff Logan immediately, but do NOT follow him or confront him," Walters said. "Understand?"

"Yeah, Coach, I understand," Nick said.

Walters relaxed his shoulders, the tension of the last hour leaving his body. "This is a real bad time, for everyone, but especially you guys," he said. "But we'll get through this, together."

Nick held Sarah as the bell rang and the hallway flooded with students.

CHAPTER 51

As Mr. Walters pulled up in front of the Paxton house with Nick, he looked up and down the street for any sign of a green or black pickup truck.

"Keep your eyes open, Nick. If you see anything make sure you call Sheriff Logan, okay? And if you can't reach him, call me."

Nick nodded. "Okay, Coach. Thanks for the ride. I'll talk to my parents tonight about picking me up from practice from now on."

"And about getting a gun," Walters said.

"Yeah, that may be a little tougher," Nick answered.

"If you want me to talk to your father, let me know. This is important, son."

"Okay, I'll let you know. Thanks again, Coach."

"Put ice on those ribs and I'll see you tomorrow."

Nick opened the car door and slid out. Mr. Walters waved as he pulled out into the street and drove away.

Nick looked up and down the street but saw nothing unusual. He walked up his sidewalk and opened the front door. As he closed it, he set the deadbolt lock. It was six o'clock and he heard the rest of the family in the kitchen. He put his books in his room, took a deep breath and joined them.

"Hi, Nicky, wash up for dinner," Eloise said.

Nick went to the bathroom and washed his hands. He threw water on his face and looked at himself in the mirror, seeing the dark circles around his eyes. He dried his hands and face and walked back into the kitchen and sat down in his usual spot. He smiled when he saw his favorite dish on the table, goulash.

"I made your favorite tonight, Nicky," Eloise said, patting his hand. "Let's say grace."

Everyone lowered their heads as Clint said thanks for the food. The two younger boys looked up when he added a request for peace in the world.

"Amen," Clint said.

"Amen," Eloise added. "I hope everyone in the country is sending up prayers tonight for peace. Hand me your plates, boys."

As Eloise loaded up Ethan and Bo's plates with goulash, Nick glanced at his father. Clint was putting butter on his bread.

"Dad, Mr. Walters wants me to ask you something," Nick said.

"Yes, what is it?"

Nick cleared his throat. "Well, he doesn't want me walking home from school alone anymore for a while."

Eloise stopped scooping goulash and looked at him. "Why? What's happened?"

"Did you see the man again?" Clint said.

Nick hadn't told them about what happened the previous Friday night, about the man in the white hat and green pickup, so he proceeded to tell them the entire story.

"Why didn't you tell us on Friday night?" Clint said, his eyes narrowing.

"Because I didn't want to worry you, especially about something that could have been nothing."

"Are you in danger, Nicky?" Eloise said, staring at her son.

"Mr. Walters thinks I could be, and Sarah, too."

Eloise and Clint glanced at each other.

"Then one of us will pick you up after practice every day until this nightmare is over," Clint said.

"Thanks, Dad. Mr. Walters said he could drive me home if you guys couldn't pick me up. He drove me home tonight."

Eloise put her hand on Nick's hand. "Why didn't you call us, Nicky? Your Dad could have picked you up."

"Mr. Walters offered to drive me home. We've been talking a lot lately and I think he wanted to check out the neighborhood."

"Well, he's a wonderful man, your coach," Eloise said. "We should invite him to dinner some evening. Is he married?"

"Uh, I don't know," Nick said. "I never thought about it."

"Well, it doesn't matter. We'll invite him over sometime next week."

"Uh, there's one more thing he asked me to talk to you about, Dad."

Bo and Ethan were shoveling goulash into their mouths as they stared at Nick and their parents. Little Ethan had a system down pat where he would get his mouth at table-top level and scoop the goulash straight into his mouth.

"Ethan, sit up straight," Eloise said. "You're a big boy now, so don't shovel your food into your mouth anymore."

Bo began laughing, goulash falling out of his mouth.

"Bo, close your mouth, son," Clint said, sternly. "What's the other thing, Nick?"

Nick squirmed in his chair and scratched his head.

"Son, what's the other thing?" Clint said again.

Nick looked at his mother and then at his father. "He wants us to get a gun."

Eloise dropped her fork on her plate and put her hand up to her mouth. Clint stared at Nick, not saying anything.

"Just as a precaution, Mr. Walters said."

Clint wiped his mouth and put his napkin on the table. "We will not have a gun in this house. Ever."

Eloise reached over and put her hand on Clint's arm. "Clint—"

"No! Not with two small boys in the house," Clint said, staring at his wife. "And you know why, Eloise."

Nick stared at his parents, noticing the look in his father's eyes. He couldn't tell if he was angry or sad, or both. He glanced at his brothers, who were sitting still, mouths open and eyes wide, staring at their father.

"But, Dad, he—"

"I don't care what your coach said, we won't have a gun in this house!" Clint stood up, threw his napkin on his plate, and stormed out of the kitchen.

Nick stared at his father as he walked out of the room.

"Mommy, what's wrong with Daddy?" Ethan's eyes were wide open.

"Bo, take your brother into your bedroom for a few minutes and play. I need to talk to Nicky, alone," Eloise said.

"Aw, Mom—"

"Now, Bo. You and Ethan can finish your dinner later. Go."

Bo shook his head and got up from the table. "C'mon, squirt."

Ethan climbed down from his chair and followed his brother, staring at his mother the whole way.

Once they were out of the kitchen, Eloise turned to Nick. "Nicky, we've never told you about your father's childhood," she said, holding his hand. "Your father had a younger brother."

"He did? I didn't know that."

"When your father was seven, just about Bo's age, he and his little brother were in the garage playing when they found a pistol that their father had hidden behind some boxes."

"Oh, no," Nick said.

"Your father didn't think it was loaded and pointed it at his brother," Eloise said, tears welling up in her eyes. "It went off."

Nick let out a gasp. "Oh, my God, Mom."

Eloise wiped her eyes. "His brother was only four years old, just a little older than Ethan is now. He died instantly." Eloise blew her nose, the tears running down her face.

Nick felt his eyes getting wet and wiped away a stray tear. "I didn't know, Mom."

"That's why I won't have a gun in this house, Nick." Clint was standing in the doorway. "Don't ever ask me again, son."

Nick stood up and hugged his father. "I'm sorry, Dad, I didn't know."

Clint put his arm around Nick and stroked his hair. "I know you didn't, Nicky. It's okay. Let's finish up with dinner so we can watch the news. Eloise, can you have the boys come back in?"

Eloise hugged Nick as they all sat down to finish dinner.

CHAPTER 52

Nick stood in the coach's office prior to football practice and told Mr. Walters about his conversation with his father the evening before, but left out the part about the shooting.

"Well, Nick, we can't force your father to get a gun. Do you have a baseball bat, something you can use as a weapon, if, well, you know . . ."

"Yeah, I have a couple of bats—Louisville Sluggers," Nick said. "Uh, Coach, there's one more thing."

Walters sat silent, waiting for Nick to continue.

"I think he drove by my house last night."

"The green pickup?"

Nick nodded. "Right after dinner. We were watching the news and I checked the street from our front window. I saw the pickup driving slowly as it passed our house. It was too dark to see the driver, but it was definitely a green Ford pickup."

"Why didn't you call me?" Walters said.

"Well, I tried, but there was no answer."

"What time did you call?"

"Around six forty-five, thereabouts, I think."

Walters nodded. "I was here talking with Coach Davis until seven thirty. Sorry. Did you call Sheriff Logan?"

"No, I didn't," Nick said, shuffling his feet. "I didn't think it was important enough. I didn't even tell my dad."

Walters stood up and walked around his desk, putting his hand on Nick's shoulder. "Son, this is not a game, this is real. If the man was on your street, the Sheriff should have known about it. The man was driving by your house for a reason, Nick."

Nick lowered his head. "I know, I screwed up, Coach. My mind went blank and I didn't know what to do."

Walters patted his shoulder. "I'll call the sheriff tonight after practice and let him know the guy's in the area. Maybe he can send a patrol car out to your neighborhood tonight to watch for him." Walters looked into Nick's eyes. "Did you tell Sarah?"

"No, I didn't want to scare her. She's already a bundle of nerves, Coach."

"Okay, probably for the best. The sheriff has someone watching her house night and day, so she should be safe. But this proves that the guy's becoming much bolder, almost taunting us to catch him."

Nick saw the worried look in Walters' eyes. "Coach, what should I do?"

Walters walked back and sat down. "Right now, get ready for practice. We'll talk afterwards and I'll try to get the sheriff down here. Are your parents picking you up tonight?"

Nick nodded. "Yeah, at six."

"Your father?"

Nick nodded again.

"Good. It's time we spoke about what's going on. Have him come into my office when he gets here. I'll try to have the sheriff here at six, too."

"Okay," Nick said. "Coach?"

"Yeah, Nick?"

"Thanks. My Mom wants to invite you over for dinner some night, and your wife, if, well, uh . . ."

"I'm not married, Nick. Still waiting for the right woman, I guess. Tell your mother I'd love to come over some time, and meet the whole family."

Nick smiled. "Great, I'll tell her."

"Okay, get ready for practice. See you on the field."

Nick's father was waiting in the school parking lot when Nick walked out with Coach Walters. They walked up to his car as he rolled the window down.

"Mr. Paxton, I'm John Walters," the coach said, extending his hand.

"Glad to finally meet you, John," Clint said.

"Would you have a few minutes to come into my office and talk?" Walters said. "About the situation Nick and Sarah are facing."

"Sure, I'll follow you in."

The two men and Nick walked back into the school and down the steps to the locker room. It was almost deserted except for one or two players getting dressed, and Coach Davis in his office.

Walters turned the light on in his office and invited Clint and Nick to sit down. "Mr. Paxton—"

"Call me Clint, please."

"Okay. Clint, I've invited Sheriff Logan to join us but he's running a little late, so maybe we can get started. How much time do you have?"

"Just a few minutes. I have to get Nick home for dinner. My wife doesn't like it when we're late."

"Okay, I'll get right to the point," Walters said. "Nick is in danger, Clint. There's a psychopath roaming around this area, which I'm sure you know about."

Clint nodded.

"For some reason, we think he's targeted Nick and Sarah Rogers. Nick saw him drive by your house last night. He should have told you."

Clint looked at Nick. "He was on our street? Why didn't you tell me, Nick?"

"I'm sorry, Dad. I should have, but—"

"He tried to call me," Walters interrupted, "but I wasn't home. This man is growing bolder by the day, almost taunting us. Maybe he wants to get caught, or maybe he's so arrogant that he thinks he's untouchable, who knows? But we have to take precautions, and that's why I asked Nick to talk to you about getting a gun."

Clint stiffened noticeably. "He asked me and I said no. We won't have a gun in our house."

"I understand your concerns, Clint, but—"

"No, you don't, John," Clint said. "That's final."

Walters stared at Clint. There was silence for several seconds. "Okay, no gun. How will you protect your son and your family, Clint?"

"You let me worry about that, Coach Walters," Clint said, his face turning red. "You stick to teaching and coaching, and let me worry about my family."

Walters sat back in his chair, rubbing his chin. "Okay, Mr. Paxton. I'll talk to Sheriff Logan about having a patrol car in your neighborhood until this man is caught. I'm just trying to look out for your son."

Clint's shoulders softened, the red leaving his face. "I appreciate that, Coach Walters. I really do. Nick thinks the world of you, as a coach and a teacher. I'm sorry for being so adamant, but I just can't have a gun in my home."

Walters stood up and reached his hand out to Clint. "Thanks, Clint. You have a smart boy here, and one helluva football player. Have a good evening."

Clint shook his hand. "Thanks, John. Son, you ready to go home?"

Nick nodded to his coach as they walked out of the office.

"Sorry to put you through that, Dad," Nick said as they climbed into the car.

Clint patted him on the knee. "He's a good man, Nicky. You're lucky to have him as your coach."

"Yeah, I know. Thanks, Dad."

CHAPTER 53

The team bus pulled out of the Acorn High parking lot for Woodland at four thirty. Woodland was three counties away and it took over an hour to drive there under ideal circumstances, but Friday afternoon was anything but ideal. It had snowed heavily overnight and because of the frigid temperatures, the roads had ice on them. The bus was delayed half an hour while the driver put chains on the tires, to navigate safely over the black ice. There were two buses for this road game: One for the players and coaches and one for the equipment, cheerleaders and school officials. The player's bus always took the lead. It was just starting to get dark when they pulled out onto Highway Six.

"You're driving me crazy, Nick," Tim said, sitting next to Nick and watching him constantly look back for the second bus. "They'll be fine, don't worry so much. The Sheriff has two patrol cars behind them and a whole line of cars following. It would take one of those missiles in Cuba to get to her."

Nick turned back around, tapping his cleats on the metal floor. "I know, Tim, but I have a bad feeling about tonight. The weather, the icy roads, and that psycho out there somewhere, watching and waiting."

"What's he going to do, kidnap her in front of the entire school, parents and the sheriff's department? Relax and think about the game, pal. You've got a lot on your shoulders tonight."

Nick looked at his best friend. "Yeah, I know. That field is going to be frozen solid, like hitting concrete. I'm worried about my ribs holding up."

Tim let out a sigh. "Yeah, it's going be a rough night, all right."

Nick looked up and saw Coach Walters walking down the aisle towards them.

"Tim, can I change seats with you for a few minutes? I need to talk to Nick about something," Walters said.

"Sure, Coach. I'll go sit in back until you're done," Tim stood up and walked to the back of the bus.

Walters sat down next to Nick. "How you doing, Nick? I could hear your cleats tapping all the way up in front of the bus. You okay?"

Nick stopped tapping, feeling the heat rise on his neck. "I just have a real bad feeling about tonight, Coach. I can't explain it, but . . ."

"That's understandable, with everything that's happened lately, and now this freezing weather. It's not going to be a pleasant night out on that field. You worried about your ribs?"

"Yeah, a little. I mean, the field is going to be like an ice rink and if I fall the wrong way, I don't know."

"Did you get them taped up real tight before we left?" Walters felt Nick's left side.

"Yeah, so tight I could hardly breathe. They feel okay now, though."

"Good. I'll keep an eye on you and if you need to come out, let me know. I don't want to injure them any worse than they are. You'll let me know, okay?"

"Okay, Coach."

"We're counting on you tonight, Nick," Walters said. "You should have some nice big lanes to run through on the outside, so make sure you plant your feet on cuts because it's going to be difficult with the icy field."

Nick nodded. "Coach, do you think Sarah is safe in the second bus?"

Walters put his hand on Nick's knee pad. "Nothing's going to happen to her tonight, Nick, she has too many people around her. You just think about the game, okay?"

"Yeah, okay Coach. Thanks."

Walters slapped him on the knee and stood up. "And let me know how your ribs are holding up." He walked back up the aisle.

Tim sat down next to Nick. "What was that about?"

"Aw, nothing. Coach just wanted to ask about my ribs, that's all."

Tim laughed. "That's 'cause you're the big dog tonight, buddy. Most of the plays we've been practicing are yours. You're going to be a tired, worn out big dog after the game."

Nick smiled weakly. *Yeah, I know, and that's only half of what I'm worried about.*

CHAPTER 54

Jimmy parked the green pickup on the other side of Palmer woods, out of sight of prying eyes, and checked his watch. Eight o'clock. He figured the football game in Woodland would be half over by now, so he had plenty of time. He grabbed his backpack and opened the door. The snow was falling a little heavier now, the cold air biting his face. He pulled his parka hood over his head and trudged into the woods.

It was a struggle getting through the woods due to the heavy snowfall, but once he reached the other side he knelt down and peered at the gray house with the white trim. It was dark, inside and out. He looked around for a sheriff's cruiser, but saw none. It must have been dispatched with the girl to Woodland, as he had figured, a smile creasing his face.

He waited for ten minutes to make sure it was safe, then emerged from the woods and crossed the dark street and skirted the house until he was in the back yard. He looked around for any lights coming on, listened for barking dogs, but it was dark and silent. He slowly walked to the back porch, climbed the three steps and took his snow boots off, placing them next to the door. He looked in all directions one more time, and then tried the doorknob. It was locked, as he expected. He took out a kit from his backpack and pulled out a long, thin pick. It took him ten seconds to open the simple lock.

Jimmy entered the dark house, enjoying its warmth after being so long in the cold, and took his flashlight out of his backpack. Shining it on the floor, he walked carefully to the stairs leading to the upstairs bedrooms. He took one step at a time, keeping his eye out for any cats or dogs, but there was only silence. He came to the top of the stairs and saw three doors. He knew that her bedroom was facing the street, so walked slowly to the first door. When he opened it he smelled a man's cologne, and closed the door, knowing it was the parent's bedroom. He walked to the second door, sniffing it for any signs of her. He opened it slowly and stood in the doorway, breathing in the aroma of the blonde cheerleader. Her smell was in the walls, in the room, the smell of a young female. His left eye began twitching as he pointed his flashlight around the room, being careful not to shine it at the window. He saw the full bed, with a floral bedspread and throw pillows. A girl's room.

His heart was beating fast as he slowly walked to the dresser, shining his flashlight on the items on top. He saw a picture of the football player and her, in her cheerleader's outfit. He stared at the picture, the long blonde hair tied up in a ponytail, the long muscular legs. He put the picture in his backpack and then opened the top drawer of the dresser and saw the panties. He picked up a pair and put them to his face, rubbing it around, taking in the smell, the aroma, the texture. He put them in his backpack and opened up the second drawer, but saw only tee shirts and socks. He closed it and opened the third drawer, smiling when he saw the black sweater with the large 'A' on the front, her cheerleading sweater. He picked it up and put it close to his face and breathed in the faint smell of perfume and sweat. He put the sweater in his backpack and pulled out something else, placing it in the third drawer where the other sweater had been. He smiled as he thought about her finding it.

Then he closed the drawer, walked out of the room and down the stairs to the back door. He slipped into his boots, closed the door and retraced his footprints in the snow, knowing that by morning the falling snow would make them invisible. He walked down the driveway and checked the street before walking quickly back into the dark woods.

Once at the bottom of the woods, Jimmy, breathing hard, peered through the snow to his left. He had one more thing to do before the night was over. He trudged into the thick of the woods, the snow crunching underneath his boots. He pulled out the folded up duffel bag from his backpack as he walked. This would be unpleasant, but necessary. When he reached the spot, he began removing snow, tree limbs and brush until he saw the brown tarp. A bare foot stuck out from underneath.

CHAPTER 55

As the team climbed back into the bus for the long ride home, Nick and Tim sat next to each other as before. Players walked by and slapped Nick's shoulder pads.

"Great game, Nick!"

"What a stud!"

"The hundred yard man!" Allen Neal yelled from across the aisle.

Nick smiled, but no one saw him holding his ribs, except Tim.

"They hurting pretty bad?" Tim said.

Nick nodded. "Yeah, that ground was so darn hard. That last play in the first half, when the big linebacker from Woodland hit me, I thought that was it. I could hardly breathe, just like when I first hurt them against Taylor Falls."

"Did you tell Coach Walters?"

Nick shook his head. "No, I taped them up a little tighter at halftime, but didn't want to tell Coach. At halftime it was only seven to nothing, so it was still a tight game."

"Well, you played a helluva game, bad ribs or not. I hit the ground hard a couple of times on tackles and it was like falling on the sidewalk. I'm gonna have bruises on my bruises."

Nick smiled, but it faded quickly. "Did you see Sarah get on the second bus?"

Tim shook his head. "No, the cheerleaders were still outside cheering when we got on the bus. Are they still out there?"

Nick wiped the moisture-covered window and looked out. He saw lots of people standing around, but didn't see the cheerleaders. "I don't see them. I hope they got on their bus."

"I'm sure they did, just to get out of the cold if nothing else. Want me to go check on them?"

Nick saw the bus driver closing the door. "No, looks like we're about to leave. I'm sure she's okay."

Coach Walters walked down the aisle, checking on everyone, making sure all the players were on the bus. He came to Tim and Nick.

"I saw you holding your ribs, Nick. You okay?"

"Yeah, they're sore but okay," Nick said. "That was one hard field, Coach."

"I want to take a look at them when we get back to Acorn. Come see me in my office, okay?"

"Okay, Coach."

"Oh, and nice game tonight, Nick, and Tim," Walters said.

"The hundred yard man!" Allen Neal said from two rows up. "What a stud!"

Walters laughed and looked at Nick. "You came through tonight, Nick. Nice job, son."

Walters returned to the front of the bus and told the driver to go. The bus pulled out of the Woodland parking lot onto a residential street, headed for State Highway Six and Acorn. Nick looked behind him and saw the second bus following them. He caught a glimpse of one or two cheerleaders through the foggy window, but couldn't tell if one of them was Sarah. He turned back around and closed his eyes. *Just get us home to Acorn.* He opened his eyes and looked out the window again. He saw something that made him freeze. He wiped the foggy window with his hand and stared out into the darkness. He knew he'd seen it, passing on the right, but it was gone.

"What's wrong, Nick? You look like you saw a ghost," Tim said.

Nick was shaking as he looked at Tim. "I just saw a green pickup."

"Oh, hell," Tim said. "Better tell Coach."

Nick slowly made his way to the front of the bus and bent down to talk to Coach Walters in the first row. After several seconds, he walked back to his seat.

"What did he say?" Tim asked.

"He has a walkie-talkie and is going to talk to the Sheriff's deputies. We'll probably stop up ahead somewhere."

The yellow Acorn Public Schools bus pulled into the next gas station, with the second bus pulling in next to it. Two Oak County Sheriff's patrol cars parked in front of the buses, their flashing blue lights piercing through the night air.

The doors to the first bus opened and John Walters emerged, walking quickly to the patrol cars, meeting the Sheriff's deputies half way.

Nick opened his window and watched, and listened.

"One of my players saw a green pickup about a mile back. Did you notice it?" Walters said, looking at the first deputy.

"No, we weren't looking for a green pickup," the deputy said.

"Why the hell not?" Walters said loudly. "Sheriff Logan said he had all you guys on the lookout for a green Ford pickup."

The deputy seemed flustered. "In Acorn and the surrounding area, yes, but not seventy miles away. There are plenty of green pickups in rural Iowa, Coach."

Walters relaxed his shoulders, glancing back at Nick, who had his head out of the bus window. "Yeah, you're right. Guess I'm a little paranoid right now. Well, keep your eyes open for one the rest of the way home, okay Deputy?"

"Sure, we will, Coach. You okay? You seem agitated," the deputy said.

"Yeah, yeah, I'm okay. See you in Acorn."

"Coach, it's late, cold, and these roads are dangerous, so we need to get these kids home as quickly as we can," the deputy said. "We can't afford to stop again."

Walters nodded and headed back to the bus. He climbed in and told the driver to continue to Acorn. He stopped to talk to Coach Davis, who was not happy, and then walked down to Nick and Tim.

"They didn't see it, and weren't too happy about stopping to talk about it," Walters said. "They made a good point—lots of green pickups in rural Iowa. I think we're getting somewhat paranoid about this guy."

Nick felt the heat on his neck again. "Sorry, Coach, I was just, you know . . ."

"I know, Nick. Keep your eyes open. Let's get you guys home."

Nick watched Walters walk to the front of the bus as it pulled out onto the road, behind one Sheriff's patrol car, it's flashing lights off. The other patrol car drove behind the second bus, with many parents following behind.

"Heck, Nicky, you caused quite a stir back there," Tim said.

Nick glanced around the bus and saw everyone looking at him. "Coach is right, I'm becoming paranoid. How many green pickups do you think are in this part of Iowa, a hundred or more?"

"Probably more," Tim said. "I hope they catch this guy soon, before you go nuts, Nicky."

"Yeah, me too, Timmy. Me, too."

CHAPTER 56

The snow was falling harder, the wind almost at blizzard force, when the two buses and the caravan of cars pulled into the Acorn High parking lot. Coach Davis and Coach Walters hurried the players off the bus and into the locker room to get undressed and showered. The parents and cheerleaders were either standing in the driving snow or sitting in their cars, waiting. There would be no cheers for the team tonight when they emerged from the locker room.

Nick slowly took his uniform off, asking Tim for help with his shoulder pads and jersey, his sore ribs causing a lot of pain. Tim helped him rip the tape from his ribs, which left large red welts in a circle around his body. Trudging to the showers, he stood under the hot water for several minutes, enjoying the heat on his frigid body. It helped the inflammation in his ribs, and he was able to move a little easier once he dried off and began dressing. He saw Mr. Walters walking up to him as he was pulling on his sweater.

"Nick, your ribs feeling any better?" Walters said.

"Yeah, Coach. The hot water really helped. I think they'll be okay."

"Okay, let's hurry it up so your parents can get you guys home. This snowstorm is getting worse."

Nick combed his hair, threw on his heavy jacket and walked out of the locker room and up the concrete steps to the parking lot. There were no cheering fans waiting, only a few people blowing into their hands, stomping their feet, waiting for the players to emerge. He spotted his parents and waved to them, putting up one finger. He had to talk to Sarah before going home. He looked around and finally saw her standing next to her father outside of their car. He quickly walked to her.

"Hi," Nick said, blowing into his hands, his breath cloud filling the air. "It's so cold."

Sarah hugged him and kissed him lightly on the lips. "You were so good tonight, Nicky."

Nick winced from the pain in his ribs when she hugged him. "Thanks, it was a really tough night."

"Are your ribs okay, son?" Sarah's father asked, clapping his hands together to stay warm.

"Yes, thank you Mr. Rogers."

"Well, we better get home and get warmed up," Mr. Rogers said to Sarah.

"Okay, Dad," Sarah said, turning to Nick. "Can I see you tomorrow, Nicky?"

Nick smiled. It was the first time they would hang out on a weekend since becoming a couple. "Sure, after I shovel the sidewalks downtown in the morning."

"Can I come down and help you?"

Nick laughed. "I'd love the help, but I think there's going to be a foot of snow by morning. I'll be okay. Do you want me to come over to your house afterwards?"

She kissed him. "Yes, I'd love that. Sleep tight, Mr. Hero."

She opened the car door and got in. Nick watched them drive off and then walked to his parent's car, thick exhaust coming out of the tailpipe. He opened the door and slid in next to Ethan, who was asleep on Bo's lap. He ruffled his youngest brother's hair and then punched Bo in the shoulder softly.

"Hey, little man," Nick said to Bo.

Bo yawned wide and said, "Hi, nice game, let's go."

Clint put the Buick in gear and headed out of the nearly deserted parking lot.

"Great game, Nicky," Eloise said from the front seat. "That field looked so frozen, so hard. How do you feel?"

Nick put his hands on his ribs. "Sore, really sore, Mom. Might have to soak in some hot water when we get home."

"Okay, I'll draw you a bath when we get home. I don't remember it snowing this hard in October before, do you Clint?"

"A time or two, but a long time ago. I played a couple of times in these conditions and, like Nick said, it was tough. The ground was like solid ice."

"What position did you play, Dad," Nick said, not remembering hearing his father talk about his younger days.

"Same as you, son, only we called it tailback then. I guess you got your speed from me. I was pretty fast back then, like you."

Nick smiled at this. "You ever score three touchdowns in one game?"

Clint smiled wide. "Yes, a couple of times, but I don't remember them being quite as dramatic as yours."

They turned the corner onto their street, the Buick's tires spinning slightly on the icy street. Clint drove slowly up the hill, not wanting to spin out. He finally reached their house and pulled into the driveway, there was at least a foot of snow covering it. He slowly drove to the garage and put the car in park. He got out and began cleaning snow away from the garage door. He lifted up the door, pulling it out and up until it was fully open, and then got back in the car. Just as he was about to put it in gear, he heard a scream from Eloise.

"Oh, my God—what is that?" she yelled.

Bo and Ethan yawned and opened their eyes. "What's wrong, Mommy?" Bo said.

"Nothing, go back to sleep," Eloise said, her voice shaking.

Nick leaned forward and peered into the dark garage, illuminated by the Buick's headlights. He saw something lying on the cement floor of the garage. He rubbed his eyes and looked again. He recoiled when he realized what it was.

Clint sat in the driver's seat, frozen, his mouth open.

"Dad, it's—"

"A body," Clint said.

"Stay in the car." Clint slowly got out and trudged through the snow to the garage opening. He took several steps into the garage and suddenly backed up. He ran out of the garage and vomited into the snow.

Nick watched in horror, unable to take his eyes off of the naked body lying in the garage.

"Eloise, get the boys and go into the house and call the Sheriff," Clint yelled. "And don't go in the garage, you either, Nick."

"Nick, help me with Ethan and Bo," Eloise said, climbing out of the front seat.

Nick woke his brothers up as his mother opened the rear passenger door. She picked Ethan up as Bo yawned and slid out of the seat to follow her, oblivious to what was happening.

The wind was howling now, the snow coming down sideways, cutting into Nick's face as he got out of the car. He stepped close to the garage but Clint stopped him.

"No, I don't want you to see it," Clint said.

"Who, what—"

"It's a girl, naked . . . and mutilated," Clint said, turning to throw up again.

Nick stared at the body and then stiffened. "He was here."

Clint stood up, wiping his mouth with his sleeve. "Who?"

"Him, the man in the green pickup."

Clint and Nick looked out through the blinding snow into the darkness.

"Or maybe he's still here," Clint said, picking up a shovel from the garage. "Shut the garage door, Nick, and let's wait until the sheriff gets here."

Nick slowly closed the garage door, pulling it down, all the while staring at the body ten feet away. He closed it and turned into the bushes next to the garage, feeling queasy. He made an attempt at vomiting but nothing came out.

CHAPTER 57

Two Oak County Sheriff cruisers pulled into the Paxton driveway, lights flashing. They kept the lights on as they got out and approached Clint and Nick, their weapons drawn, pointing down. Two deputies stood next to the patrol cars, holding rifles and turning in semi-circles as they looked around the area.

"Clint," Sheriff Logan said as he approached the garage. "What's going on here?"

The wind-driven blizzard had subsided somewhat, but the snow was still falling.

"We got home about twenty minutes ago and I opened the garage door . . ." Clint looked ashen as he tried to get the words out.

"And, what happened?" Logan said, staring at Clint.

"This," Clint said, as he lifted the heavy garage door.

Sheriff Logan peered into the dark garage and saw the body lying face up. He slowly approached it, looking around the garage, his firearm out front, ready to shoot anything that moved. He got within several feet of the naked body and held his nose. He backed away as slowly as he'd approached, re-tracing his steps.

Once outside, he bent over and held his hands to his knees, breathing hard. "That's the Walnut Hills girl," he finally said.

"How do you know?" Clint said, staring at him.

"The blue-and-white pompoms in either hand." The Sheriff took his handkerchief out of his back pocket and put it up to his nose. "And it looks like there's something in her mouth."

"Oh, my God," Clint said, wiping his snow-covered face.

Nick stood motionless, the snow covering his hair, face and jacket. He stared at the body in the garage, his mind going a hundred miles per hour. He suddenly bolted to the back porch and ran inside. He ran to the phone and picked up the receiver and dialed zero. After several seconds the operator answered.

"How may I help you?"

"Mabel, it's Nick Paxton. Connect me to the Rogers', please. It's an emergency."

"Okay, Nicky, hold on," she said.

A few more seconds went by as Nick paced up and down, snow falling from his jacket onto the kitchen floor.

"Hello?" a man said.

"Mr. Rogers, it's Nick Paxton." Nick was breathing hard, trying to keep under control. "Is Sarah with you?"

"Of course she's with me, Nick, Why—"

Nick heard a scream in the background. "Mr. Rogers? Mr. Rogers?"

Nick heard the phone drop, but he could hear shouts and screams in the background. He pulled at his hair, his heart racing. "Hello? Hello?" he screamed into the phone.

"Oh, my God," he heard a man yell in the distance, barely audible.

Nick was sweating from the anxiety and his racing heart. He was about to hang up when Mr. Rogers came back on the line.

"Uh, Nick, I have to hang up," Rogers said.

"No! Mr. Rogers, what happened?"

Rogers cleared his throat, which was raspy. "Sarah found a . . . a sweater in her dresser."

Nick waited. *A sweater?*

"It was smeared with blood," Rogers said. "It's a Walnut Hills cheerleader's sweater."

Nick almost dropped the phone. He couldn't speak, his mouth was dry, and his heart racing. "Mr. Rogers, the Sheriff is here at my house right now. The Walnut Hills girl—the girl is in our garage."

"What? How?"

"Mr. Rogers, the man was in your house tonight, and he was here. He's doing this, he's playing with us. I'm telling the Sheriff right now to send someone to your house."

"He's . . . he's already here, Nick. They followed us home from the game and are in the house now. I have to go, Nick."

Nick heard a click and the phone went dead. He glanced up at his mother, who was standing in the doorway, her hand covering her mouth. Nick ran out the back door and down to the garage. The deputy stopped him before he could go any further.

"Slow down, son. Wait right here," the deputy said.

Nick looked inside the garage and saw Sheriff Logan take something out of the girl's mouth. It was brown and looked like a piece of paper. Nick watched as Logan unfolded the paper.

"What is it, Sheriff?" Clint yelled.

Logan slowly walked out of the garage and stood in front of the head-lights of the Buick, reading what was on the paper. When he was finished, he looked up at Nick.

"Sheriff, what is it?" Nick asked, breathing hard.

"It's a newspaper article about," the Sheriff hesitated, "your coach."

"Davis?" Nick said.

"Walters. Someone wrote 'Next' on it."

CHAPTER 58

Jimmy drove by the school parking lot and saw the two coaches' cars still there. He made a U-turn and parked across the street, hidden by the large oak tree, the moonless night and the falling snow. He had completed most of his work for the night, but had one more thing to do. He waited patiently until he saw two men emerge from the underground locker room. He ducked down as the two cars drove out of the parking lot onto the street, waiting until they turned the corner before starting up the pickup and pulling out into the street.

Jimmy had watched Walters get into a blue Pontiac, so he followed it from a safe distance. At the Highway Six junction, the older coach turned left and Walters turned right. Jimmy turned right at the junction and followed the blue Pontiac's tail lights. He kept a safe distance behind, the snow and sleet helping to hide him from Walters.

The Pontiac turned left onto a county road a mile outside of Acorn, so Jimmy made the left hand turn and continued to follow Walters for another three miles until the Pontiac turned onto a country gravel road that was covered with half a foot of snow. The Pontiac drove slowly for another mile before turning left into a driveway. Jimmy stopped on the road and peered through the darkness and snow at the dark farm house at the end of the lane until the tail lights of the Pontiac went out.

Jimmy smiled to himself as he made a U-turn and returned to the highway. Now he knew where Walters lived, but first he had to drive back to his father's farm and take care of business there. He would get little or no sleep tonight, but he was used to that. Jimmy knew that tomorrow would be the day of reckoning and his newest and last treasure would finally be his.

CHAPTER 59

At nine o'clock in the morning, Sheriff Logan's office was packed with people. Nick sat against the wall, listening to the chatter, waiting for his turn. The reporters turned off their lights and folded up their cameras, satisfied that they got the news for that night. After they left, only Nick and his father, Sarah and her father, and John Walters were left in the room. Nick looked at Coach Walters, saw the drawn face and wanted to reach out to him, but knew he couldn't.

Sheriff Logan closed the door to his office and sat behind his desk, looking at each person in his office. "Who wants to go first?"

Mr. Rogers stood up and approached the Sheriff's desk. "I want to know what you're going to do about this, Logan. He was in our house, in my daughter's bedroom, for Christ's sake!"

Sheriff Logan held up his hands. "Okay, Larry, I know you're upset—"

"Upset? Upset? He was in my daughter's bedroom, doing God knows what!"

Logan stood up. "Larry, sit down so we can discuss this calmly. Please, sit down."

Larry Rogers' face was red, his eyes open wide, but he sat down and folded his arms across his chest. Sarah put her hand on her father's arm, her lips trembling.

Logan walked to the front of his desk and sat on the edge. "This man is not only a psycho, he's smart. He waited for everyone to be out of town before he made his move. He knows what we're going to do before we do."

Nick glanced at his father, who was sitting stone-faced next to him, a glassy look in his eyes. Then he looked at Coach Walters, who was also silent, staring at the sheriff.

"He knew we would pull the deputies away from your house when you went to the game in Woodland," Logan said. "He planned it all, right down to the Walnut Hills sweater, to placing her body in the Paxton's garage, and he even had an old clipping of the coach that he used to send his message. He's smart, he's dangerous, and he's a complete psychopath."

"How did he get into our house?" Rogers said. "And without leaving footprints or fingerprints on the snowiest night in ten years. Who is this man?"

Logan shrugged his shoulders. "We don't have a clue who he is, Larry. He's a chameleon, changing the color of his truck, the way he dresses. He's very smart."

"I know he's smart, goddamn it!" Rogers yelled. "But what about my daughter?"

Coach Walters cleared his throat. "I think I know who he is."

Everyone in the room stared at the coach.

"What?" Logan said.

"I think I know who he is, I said," the coach repeated.

Logan walked towards Walters, standing a foot away from him. "How do you know who he is? Do you know him?"

Walters stared into the sheriff's eyes. "I used to."

Nick's eyes and mouth were wide open. He glanced at Walters, then at the sheriff.

"I knew him when I was a kid, in Adams County. It was twenty-some years ago," Walters said.

"And when did you figure this out," Logan said, wide-eyed.

"When you showed me the news clipping. He's the only person that would save that clipping. And—"

Logan's frustration was evident. "And what?"

"He has, or had, a black Ford pickup the last time I saw him."

"Which was how long ago?" Logan said.

"It was nineteen fifty-eight, so it would be about the right year for the pickup I saw that night."

Logan grabbed the news clipping, which was wrapped in plastic, from his desk. He looked at it closely, reading every word. He slowly looked up at Walters.

"This is about you in the Army, at Normandy. Why would he save that?"

Nick stared at his coach. Normandy? Coach was there on D-Day?

Walters coughed, rubbed his hair and glanced at Nick. "I knew him when I was in grade school. He was my teacher."

Logan blinked several times. "Who was your teacher? Who the goddamned hell is this guy?"

"His name is, or was, Clarkson. Damien Clarkson."

Logan pressed a button on his phone. "Laura, get Sims in here, now."

"Why do you think it's him, this Damien Clarkson?" Logan said.

Walters' shoulders sagged as he looked at Nick. "We had a . . . a relationship."

Logan's mouth was open, his eyes blinking. "What?"

Walters sat down in the chair, holding his head in his hands. "He molested a friend of mine when we were twelve years old, at a class function at his house. I was confused, and didn't know what to do . . ."

Nick felt the tears welling in his eyes. He fought against them, but they tumbled out one by one.

"He was a homosexual, is that what you're telling me?" Logan said.

Walters threw up his hands. "I don't know, I was twelve. He jerked my friend off in his bed one night." He looked at Sarah, the sadness in his eyes overwhelming.

Logan began pacing around the office. "How old was he back then? When was this, anyway?"

"Nineteen thirty-seven."

Logan had a confused look on his face. "That would make him, what, in his fifties now?"

"Probably, maybe sixty," Walters said.

"And he suddenly switched to girls, in his fifties?"

Walters stood up and slammed his palm against the wall. "I don't know, goddamn it! Ask him, if you ever catch the son of a bitch!"

"Okay, okay, let's step back here," Logan said. "I'm sorry, Coach Walters, I'm just trying to understand. Again, why would he keep that clipping after so many years?"

Walters stared at the sheriff.. "Because he's my father!"

CHAPTER 60

After advising Larry Rogers and Sarah that a deputy would remain outside their home twenty-four hours a day until the man was caught, Sheriff Logan turned to Clint and Nick Paxton.

"I don't have the manpower to assign another deputy to guard you twenty-four seven," Logan said. "I've asked for help from neighboring counties but so far I haven't gotten a favorable response. The thing in Cuba has everyone on edge and every law enforcement department in the state, hell, in the country is on high alert. Anything is possible right now, including the fact that we all might not be here tomorrow."

"We can take care of ourselves," Clint said. "Just put our house on your regular patrol route if you can."

"This man is capable of anything, Clint," Logan said. "Do you have a weapon in your home, a hunting rifle—"

"No, and don't ask us to take one. We won't have guns in our house," Clint said, edging forward in his chair.

"But as a precaution—"

Clint stood up. "No! Let's go Nick."

Nick stood up, ready to follow his father.

"I need Nick to stay here for some more questioning," Logan said. "He and Sarah, and Coach Walters, are the only people that have seen this man face to face. We need to do a composite sketch on him to send out to surrounding areas."

Clint turned to Nick. "Are you okay with that, son?"

Nick nodded. "Yeah, I'm okay Dad. Go on home and I'll catch a ride with Coach Walters."

Clint turned to look at Walters, who sat in the chair, visibly shaken. "Are you okay with that, Coach?"

Walters looked at Clint, then at Nick. "Sure, no problem."

"Thanks for coming in, Clint. The forensics team will be working in your garage for a day or two, taking prints, blood samples, that sort of stuff. They should be out of your way by tomorrow. We moved the body to the morgue last night."

Clint nodded his head, patted Nick on the shoulder and walked out.

"Mr. Rogers, you're welcome to stay while I question Sarah, but you don't have to. We can get her home afterwards in a patrol car," Logan said.

"I'll be okay, Daddy," Sarah said. "Go home to Mom and I'll be there soon."

"Okay, sweetheart, but no later than noon," Rogers said, looking at the Sheriff. "We're driving up to Sioux City this afternoon to be with our son for the weekend, and to get out of that house."

"Understood, Larry. We'll have someone at your home all weekend whether you're there or not, not to worry."

Rogers nodded, kissed Sarah on the cheek, and walked out of the office.

Sarah walked over, sat down by Nick, and held his hand. They both looked at Coach Walters, sadness in their eyes.

"Okay, thanks for staying, folks. I have some more questions for you, Coach, and our sketch artist will be working with you, Sarah, to come up with a composite sketch. You're the only one who has seen his full face. Do you think you can do that?"

Sarah nodded. "It's a face I'll never forget, Sheriff."

"Good. Deputy Sims here will take you into another room where our sketch artist is waiting. We'll be right here if you need us."

Sarah squeezed Nick's hand as she stood up and followed Deputy Sims out the door.

Logan walked around and sat at his desk, looking at Walters and Nick. "Nick, I'm going to be asking Coach Walters some very personal questions, so if you want to wait outside . . ."

"No, I want him here," Walters said, looking up. "I want him to know what happened and not have questions in his mind—if that's okay with Nick."

"I . . . I can stay. I want to stay," Nick said, staring at Walters.

"Okay, then, let's get started," Logan said, opening his notebook. "Coach, we can do this two ways. I can ask you questions and you respond, or you can tell me what happened when you were young and when you split from your, uh, father."

Walters sat up straight, staring directly at the sheriff. "Let me tell you the story and then if you have questions, we can go from there."

Logan nodded. "Go ahead, Coach."

Walters glanced at Nick, smiled, and cleared his throat. "We had a farm in Adams County, about three miles outside of Lynn. My father raised corn, oats and some cattle, but he had a live-in foreman that did all the work. My father was a teacher at Lynn Public School, a sixth grade teacher. Everything seemed somewhat normal to me up until I was in sixth grade, and in my father's class at school. I never saw him do anything to anyone else prior to that night, but I remember my mother making snide remarks about him at the dinner table.

One day in class he invited five or six boys over to the house for a get-to-gether, a game night or something. I was one of the boys, obviously, and my best friend was also there. My father had done it before in previous years, but I was never allowed to join until I was in his class. It was a badge of honor for any boy to be invited, made you kind of special, you know? And as his son, I felt very special to have my best friend and some other boys at the house."

"What year was this?" Logan interrupted.

"I was twelve, so it had to be in '37."

"When in nineteen thirty-seven—fall, winter . . . ?"

"Right after school had started, so in the fall, probably October," Walters said.

"Okay, go ahead," Logan started writing in his notebook.

"Well, we played some games, innocent stuff, for a couple of hours and then my father said that the winner of the next game could sleep in his bed with him."

"It was a sleepover?" Logan asked. "Was that legal back then?"

Nick stared at Walters, waiting for the response.

"Yes, all the boys had to get permission to sleep over. They slept in sleeping bags in the living room, you know, like camping out."

"Had he played this particular game before?" Logan said.

"I don't know, I'd never been to one of these before. He never let me come out of my room when he had these . . . things. But I heard stuff, mostly from my mother."

Logan wrote furiously. "Go ahead."

Walters glanced at Nick, half smiling. "We played the game, a trivia-type game, and I won."

Logan looked up from his writing. "So you had to sleep with your father, in his bed?"

"Yes, but he didn't like it, so he wanted to play the game again, saying it wasn't fair that I won over the others."

"Why wasn't it fair?"

"I don't know, I guess he didn't want to sleep with his own son. Who knows?" Walters said. "Anyway, we played again and my best friend, Ronnie, won."

Logan was leaning forward now. "Had you ever slept with your father before this, in the same bed?"

"No, never, and he never touched me or molested me."

Logan nodded. "So then what happened?"

"It was late so everyone pulled out their sleeping bags and spread them out on the floor of the living room, all except Ronnie. We got into our sleeping bags as Ronnie followed my father to his bedroom." Walters glanced at Nick and quickly turned away.

"Was the door closed to the bedroom?" Logan said.

"Yes. I laid there for a long time with my eyes open, wondering what was happening in my father's bedroom."

Logan and Nick continued to stare at Walters.

"Did the other boys think it was unusual, this, uh, situation?" Logan said.

"We never talked about it, except for Ronnie. He told me what happened the next day."

Logan leaned closer. "And what happened?"

Walters brushed his hair back. "Ronnie told me that they got undressed and got into bed and that my father said goodnight and seemed to go to sleep."

Logan was silent, staring at Walters.

"Then Ronnie said my father turned over, facing him, and started touching him."

"Touching him where?" Logan said.

"On his genitals. He whispered that it was a tradition and that they had to follow the rules of the game."

"Did he resist?"

Walters wiped sweat from his forehead. "I don't know for sure. My father was a big man and Ronnie was only twelve. My father was a popular teacher and highly respected. We didn't know anything about sex at that age."

Logan looked at Nick and then at Walters. "And what happened?"

"He began rubbing and stroking Ronnie until he ejaculated."

Nick held his hand to his mouth, looking down at the floor.

"That was Ronnie's first ejaculation, he said, and his whole body shuddered. He didn't know what it was and was embarrassed. He said my father got some tissues and cleaned it up, and then rolled over and went to sleep."

Logan sat back in his chair, shaking his head in disbelief. "And he'd been a teacher how long before this happened?"

Nick saw Walters calculating in his head.

"He began teaching when I was two or three, so about nine years, I guess."

"Did you tell anyone? Where was your mother at the time?" Logan said.

"My mother had left us about two months before this happened, took my younger brother and moved away, to Wyoming or somewhere out west," Walters said. "I didn't know why then, but I figured it out later. And no, Ronnie didn't tell anyone but me and I never told anyone until now. I buried it deep in my brain and tried to forget about it."

"Did it ever happen again?" Logan asked.

"He continued to have these all-boys get-togethers for years afterwards while I was still in school, and from what I heard, long after I was gone."

"So there could be literally dozens, maybe hundreds, of boys that he molested over the course of his teaching career."

"Yes, I'm sure there were," Walters said, barely audible.

While Logan wrote in his notebook, Walters turned to Nick. "I'm sorry, Nick, but I didn't want you to wonder what happened. I've kept this buried for so long, I forgot about it, until now. I hope you don't think any less of me."

Nick wasn't sure what to say, so he remained silent. He smiled weakly at Walters.

"Nick, this has to remain between us, okay?" Walters said, his eyes pleading.

Nick nodded. "I won't tell anyone, Coach."

Walters smiled at Nick and put his hand on his shoulder. "Thank you, son."

"Coach Walters, how long did you live with your father before you entered the Army?" Logan said, looking up.

"I joined in '43, when I turned eighteen, so six more years."

"And what kind of contact have you had with your father since then?"

"Hardly any. After the war, I stayed in the Army for two more terms, and never went home. I was discharged in '54, after the Korean War."

"So you served in two wars, World War II and Korea?"

"Yes."

"And you were part of the invasion of Normandy on D-Day in June of '44?"

"Yes, I was in the 101ˢᵗ Airborne group. We parachuted into France on D-Day."

"Were you ever injured, shot?"

"Yes, in the leg in Europe and in the buttocks in Korea."

"So you got the Purple Heart for those injuries? That's what the news article said."

"Yes, for both."

"Any other medals?"

"The Bronze Star and Silver Star."

Nick continued to stare at his coach, his eyes and mouth wide open. *Coach Walters was a war hero.*

Logan reread the news article and then looked at his notes. "Wait a minute, Coach. You said your father's name was Clarkson, Damien Clarkson, correct?"

Walters nodded. "Yes."

"But your last name is Walters, and it is Walters in this news clipping. How do you explain that?"

Walters glanced at Nick before answering. "I changed my name when I went into the Army. I used my mother's maiden name of Walters."

"You legally changed it?"

"Yes, right before I enlisted."

Logan was writing everything down. He finally glanced up. "Why did you change your name, Coach?"

"I was embarrassed to be his son. I knew that someday the truth would come out and I didn't want to be associated with him."

"Okay, fair enough, and what did you do when you were discharged, Coach? You must have been," Logan looked at his notes, "twenty-seven or twenty-eight at the time?"

"Twenty-eight, I think. I went to college on the GI Bill, at Iowa State University in Ames."

"And you studied teaching?"

"I majored in history," Walters said, smiling at Nick, "and got my teaching credential in '58."

"And when did you come to Acorn to teach?"

"It was my first job, in the fall of '58."

"Did you ever see your father after you were discharged?"

Walters fidgeted in his chair. "Once, right after I got the job at Acorn, in the summer of '58. I drove out to his farm in Adams County to see him. I'd heard that he'd been fired from the Lynn Public School district, and I wanted to see how he was doing."

"Why was he fired?"

Walters glanced at Nick. "Someone finally said something about the molestations."

Logan stared at Walters for a long time. "Was it you?"

Walters pinched his nose. "Yes, I sent them a letter when I was at Iowa State and gave testimony at the hearing."

Logan wrote furiously. "Just a moment, Coach."

Walters turned to Nick. "Well, now you pretty much know everything about me, Nick."

Nick smiled. "You were at Normandy, in two wars, two Purple Hearts. Wow, Coach, I don't know what to say. Can I tell Tim? He thinks you walk on water, wait till I tell him about this."

Walters smile faded. "Unfortunately, I have a feeling everything is going to come out in the news very soon."

"Everything?" Nick said.

Walters nodded. "The news people don't miss anything."

Logan looked up. "Did anyone else testify at this hearing?"

"Yes, a few other men who were younger than me, and then a flood of boys came forward later."

"How about your friend, Ronnie?"

Walters rubbed his eyes. "Ronnie died in the war, at Guadalcanal, in '42."

Logan nodded. "I'm sorry. Is that one of the reasons you turned your father in?"

"Partly to avenge Ronnie, but mostly to get it off my chest. It was burning a hole in me. And becoming a teacher myself made me realize that he had to pay for what he did."

"Did your father spend any time in jail?"

"Two-and-a-half years, I believe," Walters said. "He got out the year before I graduated from Iowa State."

Logan took more notes and looked up. "So what happened when you visited your father on his farm in '58?"

Walters' shoulders slumped slightly. "He was a shell of what he once was. He'd let the farm go to pot, except for one corn field. He was getting disability income from the state and a small settlement from the school district. He'd grown old and depressed, even mentally impaired. He was only fifty-six then, but he looked sixty-six."

"How did he act towards you? Did he know that you were the one that turned him in?"

"He knew, and he was bitter. I was there only about an hour. He showed me his cornfield, his 'treasure' as he called it. He said it was the only thing worth living for."

"A cornfield? Why a cornfield?"

Walters shrugged his shoulders. "I don't know. He was mentally impaired, not all there, I guess. He showed me where he'd built a fallout shelter in the middle of the cornfield." Walters raised his head, his eyes wide.

"Coach, you okay?" Logan said.

Walters was staring off into space. "The cornfield," he said. "He had a fallout shelter in the middle of the field. He said nobody knew about it, only him, and now me."

Logan suddenly stood up. "A hidden shelter, in the middle of a cornfield. A great place to take his victims."

Walters put his head in his hands. Nick stared at his coach with mixed feelings of respect and sorrow.

There was a knock on the door as Deputy Sims brought Sarah into Sheriff Logan's office, with the sketch artist following behind. She sat next to Nick, who grabbed her hand and kissed her.

Logan looked at Sims. "What did you come up with?"

Deputy Sims laid a large white piece of paper on Logan's desk. Logan stared at it for a long time, glancing up once or twice to look at Walters. He slowly picked up the sketch and turned it around so everyone could see it.

"Sarah, is this the man you saw the day of the Fall Festival?" Logan said.

Sarah nodded. "I'll never forget his face."

Logan turned and showed it to Walters. "Coach, this doesn't look like a sixty-year-old man, although there is a resemblance . . . to you."

Sarah stood up. "Sixty? The man I saw wasn't sixty, he was, well, more Coach Walters' age."

Walters stood and looked at the sketch more closely. The man in the sketch didn't have the old eyes, the wrinkles that he had seen on his father's face four years earlier. He turned to Sarah. "Are you sure you saw him in the light? This couldn't be my father. Maybe twenty years ago, but not now."

"Mr. Walters, I stared at him for I don't know how long that day. His face will never leave my mind—never."

Walters shook his head. "This doesn't make any sense," he said to Logan. "This isn't my father, it looks more like . . ."

Logan leaned forward. "More like who, Coach? You?"

Walters blinked several times, shook his head and said, "It can't be."

Logan stood up. "Coach Walters, it can't be who?"

Walters turned to look at Logan. "My brother."

A gasp came from Sarah. Everyone in the room was wide-eyed, mouths open.

Logan glared at Walters. "What goddamned brother? You never said anything about a brother, Coach Walters."

"Yes he did, Sheriff," Nick said. "He said his mother took his brother and moved out west."

Logan checked his notes and nodded. "Good catch, Nick. I missed that."

Walters sat down, his mind a thousand miles away.

"Coach, goddamn it, who is this man in this sketch?" Logan said, loudly and forcefully.

Walters looked up at him. "I think it may be my little brother, Jimmy."

Logan stared at Walters. "Go on."

"He went with our mother when she left our father. I never saw him again," Walters said. "I was only twelve when she left and he was two years younger."

"So you haven't seen your brother since he was ten years old?"

Walters nodded. "They moved out west somewhere, Montana or Idaho, I can't remember."

"Why do you think it could be your brother if you haven't seen him in so long?"

"My father told me, during my one visit to him, that my mother wrote letters to him off and on, telling her about their new life and about Jimmy . . ."

"Yes, what about Jimmy?"

"About how he was always in trouble and how mean he was to her, and other things."

"What other things?"

Walters shifted in his chair. "She didn't say, just that he was gone a lot and wouldn't come home for days."

Logan was silent for a full minute, staring at Walters. "So Sarah saw this man," he said, holding up the sketch, "but he hasn't been seen since he was ten years old. Who is the man in the green pickup that everyone's been screaming about? Is he your father, or your brother—or maybe you, Coach?"

Walters glared at Logan. "You know it wasn't me, Sheriff, and I resent you even saying such a thing."

Logan backed off. "Sorry, Coach, I know it wasn't you, but who the hell is it?"

Walters put his head in his hands, tugging at his dark hair. "My father liked boys, that's obvious," he said. "And he's old, older than his years. I don't think he could have done these things." He looked up and fixed his eyes on Logan. "So it has to be my little brother, Jimmy."

"Sims, get everything you have on Jimmy or James—" Logan stopped and looked at Walters. "Coach, did he use your father's last name or your mother's?"

"I don't know, Sheriff. I'd check them both."

"Pull up any records of a James Walters or a James Clarkson. Hell, pull up the records of the whole damn family and see what comes up. Pronto!"

"His middle name is Adam. James Adam Walters, or Clarkson," Walters said.

"On it, Sheriff," Sims said, closing the door.

"Coach, we need to pay a visit to your father's farm, immediately. Sarah, you and Nick need to come with us to help identify the man you saw, if he's around. I'm so damned confused right now, I don't even know who we're looking for.

"Laura, call Clint Paxton and Larry Rogers and let them know their children are with us and not to worry. Call me on the radio if you have any problems. And tell Evans and Smith to meet us outside with two cruisers. We're going to Adams County. Let's go folks," Logan said.

Sheriff Logan, Coach Walters, Nick, and Sarah walked out of the Sheriff's office, through the building, and out to the two waiting cruisers.

"Coach, you ride with me. Nick and Sarah, you ride in the second cruiser," Logan said. "Smith, follow us closely, and no lights or sirens. Understood?"

Deputy Smith nodded and hustled Nick and Sarah into the second cruiser, putting them in the rear seat. Logan and Walters went with Deputy Evans and got into the first cruiser, Logan in front and Walters in back. They sped out of the parking lot onto Main Street. It was Saturday morning, and all the farmers from the surrounding area were in town shopping. They moved slowly through town, past snow drifts piled up along the street, and sped up when they reached Highway Six.

CHAPTER 61

It took them over an hour to drive the forty miles to Adams County, the previous night's snowstorm making a mess of the roads. Walters directed the Sheriff to an isolated dirt road about three miles outside of Lynn, still covered with snow. The sheriff's cruisers drove slowly down the road, piled high on either side with snowdrifts. They emerged into a clearing where a two-story farmhouse and dilapidated barn stood, surrounded by cornfields. The house was gray from years of neglect, the white paint almost gone, except for patches here and there. The barn, once bright red, was old and brown, with boards missing on all sides.

The cruisers plowed through the snow, pulling up to the house. There were no vehicles around and no signs of life.

Walters and Sheriff Logan got out of the first cruiser, their breath visible in the cold morning air. They waited until the second cruiser pulled up alongside. Nick and Sarah got out and joined them.

"Did it look this bad when you were here four years ago, Coach?" Logan said.

"No, it was still in decent shape, but the paint on the house was starting to chip away and the barn showed signs of neglect, but not this bad."

Nick and Sarah huddled together to ward off the cold wind blowing across the barren fields. They looked around and saw a cornfield in the distance, the stalks brown and dying.

"Does anyone live here anymore?" Nick said. "It looks abandoned."

Sheriff Logan blew on his hands and walked up the two steps and knocked on the door. The two deputies were behind him, rifles pointed at the door.

"It wasn't this bad when I was here last," Walters said. "I wonder if my father is even alive by the looks of everything."

After a full thirty seconds, Logan tried the door. It opened, so he walked into the mud room, the deputies following close behind. Walters, Nick and Sarah remained outside, watching. After several minutes, Logan came out of the house shaking his head.

"There's no one here and it looks like it hasn't been lived in for a while," he said. "Except for a sleeping bag in the upstairs bedroom, and a few empty cans in the kitchen."

"Vagrants, you think?" Walters said.

Logan shrugged his shoulders. "Let's check the barn."

The four people walked through the deep snow to the barn. The big sliding door was closed, but had no lock. One of the deputies shoved it open, the smell of paint hitting their nostrils immediately.

"You smell that, Coach?" Logan said. "That's fresh paint from inside."

They walked in slowly, looking up and down and around, but saw nothing. They saw the paint cans scattered around the open area. Logan picked one up and looked at it.

"Green automotive paint," he said.

They continued to search the barn, looking for telltale signs. Nick looked behind some boxes and jumped back.

"Sheriff, look at this," Nick said.

They all stood and looked behind the mildewed boxes. Two cases of chloroform sat under a blanket, partially hidden. Logan and Walters looked at each other and nodded.

"No doubt this is where it all happened," Logan said. "But the question remains, who's behind this?"

Walters walked outside and stared at the cornfield just a hundred feet away. "The answers are out there, Sheriff."

"Sheriff, over here!" Deputy Evans was pointing to an area behind the barn.

Logan and Walters walked through the deep snow to where Evans was standing.

"What is it, Evans?" Logan said.

"Look over there," Evans said, pointing.

Logan took a couple of steps forward and saw a brown Chevrolet parked behind the barn, covered in snow. He bent down and brushed the snow away from the front license plate.

"Montana plates," he said, looking at Walters. "Isn't that where your brother lived, Coach?"

"Yeah, probably. Somewhere out west."

They began walking towards the cornfield, the deputies with their rifles pointed down. They reached the edge of the field and stopped.

"Coach, this is where you take over," Logan said.

Walters walked up and down the edge of the cornfield, looking for a path, but found nothing. The snow had hidden any signs of an entry point.

"Sheriff, over here," Nick yelled from twenty feet away.

They all walked to where Nick was standing. "What is it, son?" Logan said.

"Footprints," Nick said, pointing to the snow in front of him.

"You're right, son, and they're fresh. Deputies, have your weapons ready," Logan said. "This is where we start."

Deputy Evans took the lead and began walking through the dying, brown cornstalks, following the fresh footprints. They continued walking for several minutes, single file, the breath clouds rising above the stalks. Sarah and Nick held hands, huddled against each other as they walked. Deputy Evans suddenly stopped and raised his right hand, made into a fist. Everyone stopped walking.

"What is it, Evans?" Logan said.

"A clearing just ahead, an open area." Evans pointed.

They all walked to the edge of the clearing and stopped. They saw a pile of dead cornstalks lying in the middle of the clearing.

"Is this the clearing you talked about, Coach?" Logan said.

"Looks like it, but it was summer when I was here. It looked a lot different then."

"There should be snow on top of those cornstalks, but there isn't any," Logan said.

"He's here," Walters said, "or has been here recently."

Logan turned to Nick and Sarah. "You two stay here with Deputy Smith. Don't move unless I tell you to, understood? Smith, you stay with them, and keep your eyes open."

Nick and Sarah nodded, still huddling against each other.

Logan, Walters and Evans walked into the clearing and approached the pile of dead stalks. Evans pointed his rifle at the field, making circular motions, looking for any movement. After a minute, Logan turned to Walters.

"Let's see what's under that pile of stalks, Coach."

Walters nodded and they began taking the dead stalks off one at a time. They both stopped when they saw the padlocked door.

"This is it," Walters said. "The fallout shelter my father told me about."

Logan bent down and looked at the padlock. "Evans, give me a pick."

Deputy Evans reached into his shoulder bag and took out a long, skinny piece of metal and handed it to Logan, who began working it into the large padlock. After a few seconds he heard a click and the padlock opened. He laid the pick on the ground next to the opening.

"The moment of truth," he said, looking at Walters.

The two men lifted the heavy door and peered into the darkness beneath it. The smell that wafted up was overpowering and they let the door fall back with a bang.

Walters held his nose. "Sheriff, there's something dead down there."

Logan held his handkerchief to his nose. "No shit."

Walters looked at the sheriff. "Should we continue or get some backup?"

"Let's go in," he said. "Evans, you first."

Logan and Walters opened the heavy door again, throwing it to the ground, exposing the open cavern below.

Evans, rifle and flashlight pointed in front of him, began to slowly walk down the concrete steps.

"God, it's rancid down here," he said, his voice echoing off the solid concrete walls.

Logan and Walters glanced at each other, the fear and trepidation palpable on their faces. They couldn't see Evans in the darkness but listened for any sound.

"Evans, what do you see?" Logan yelled.

"A door, with another padlock. I need the picks."

Logan turned to Deputy Smith. "Keep an eye on everything, Smith." He picked up the lock picks and began the walk down the steps, holding his flashlight in front of him. Walters watched from above, holding his nose from the stench.

Nick and Sarah watched the proceedings from the edge of the cornfield, huddled against each other, shaking from the cold.

"What's . . . what's going on?" Sarah said, shaking uncontrollably.

"I . . . I don't know," Nick said, blowing on his hands.

"Coach, come down here," they heard Logan yell.

Nick and Sarah saw Coach Walters descend into the cellar. A minute later they heard a man's scream and feet scrambling up the cement stairs. They watched in horror as Walters emerged, diving onto the frozen ground.

"Coach, are you okay?" Nick yelled.

Walters lifted his head, breathing heavily. He rose to his knees, looked behind the two teenagers and froze.

"Smith, behind you!" Walters yelled.

A man in a red cap stuck an ice pick into the deputy's ear, ending his life instantly. He grabbed the rifle and pointed it at Walters, still kneeling on the ground in front of the fallout shelter.

"Hello, Johnny," he said. "Goodbye, Johnny."

Nick lunged at the man and hit him just as he fired at Walters. The bullet hit Walters in the shoulder and spun him around. He lost his footing and fell face first down the cement steps.

The man in the red cap pointed the rifle at Nick, at the same time grabbing Sarah's arm and pulling her to him. "Get up, kid."

Nick slowly rose to his feet.

"Move to the shelter . . . now," the man said, pointing his rifle at Nick.

Nick stood motionless, staring at Sarah. "Sarah . . ."

"Move, let's go," Jimmy said. "One false move and you're a dead boyfriend. Give me an excuse."

Nick walked towards the fallout shelter, glancing behind him at Sarah, who was shaking in fear.

"Close the door," the man said. "And fast."

Nick bent over and slowly picked up the heavy door, his ribs burning as he lifted it and closed it over the shelter.

"Now lock it," the man said.

Nick stared at the man. "No, I won't. They'll die."

The man in the red cap fired a shot that barely missed Nick, passing his head by inches.

"Then you can join them. It's your choice."

Nick glanced at Sarah and bent down and locked the padlock, sealing his coach, the sheriff and the deputy into the shelter. He stood up and stared at the barrel of the rifle, pointing directly at his head.

"Goodbye, kid," the man said.

The man fired the rifle just as Nick ducked to his right, the bullet grazing his neck, sending a shock wave through him. Nick rolled in the snow, the second shot just missing him. He got up and dashed into the cornfield. He felt the third bullet pass by him, inches away from his right ear. He ran into the field, until the brown corn stalks hid him from the man. Then he heard Sarah's scream.

"Sarah!" he yelled. "Sarah!"

Nick ran back, retracing his steps until he reached the clearing, but the man and Sarah were gone.

Blood seeping from his neck, Nick followed the footprints through the cornfield towards the farmhouse, listening for any sounds, but heard nothing. Finally reaching the edge of the field he stopped and peered out into the clearing. He saw the green truck next to the barn, with Sarah already in the passenger seat, her hands behind her. The man in the red cap was just getting into the driver's seat when Nick began running towards them. He stopped running when he saw the rifle pointed at him. He lunged to his right just as the shot rang out, the bullet ripping through his parka. Nick felt a searing pain in his right arm as he looked up and heard the man turn the ignition on. The truck began fishtailing through the snow until it got traction and sped down the snow-covered road. Sarah sat in the passenger seat looking back at him, absolute terror on her face.

Nick scrambled up and ran as fast as he could through the snow but the pickup was already out of sight.

"Sarah!" he yelled again. *Sarah.*

CHAPTER 62

Nick put his hands on his knees, breathing hard. He stood up and put his hand to his neck, feeling the blood. He then looked down at his parka where the bullet had ripped through, grazing his arm. He took the parka off and felt the blood from the new wound. It stung like crazy but Nick put his parka back on and fell to his knees, not knowing what to do.

The man had Sarah.

He stared at the road, fighting back the tears that were fogging his eyesight.

Suddenly he remembered Coach Walters, locked in the fallout shelter with the sheriff and his deputy. He ran towards the Sheriff's cruiser and opened the driver's door, reaching for the radio. The receiver was lying on the seat, ripped from the radio. *Damn.* He raced to the second cruiser and found the same thing. He checked each cruiser for a weapon but came up empty.

Nick leaned against the cruiser, putting a handkerchief to his neck, his mind going a mile a minute. *Deputy Smith! He had a gun in his holster!* He ran back to the cornfield, looking for the footprints that marked the entrance point. He found it and raced through the snow and brown cornstalks, following the footprints until he came to the clearing. Deputy Smith was lying face down in the snow, which was now soaked with the blood coming out of the deputy's right ear. Nick turned him over and almost threw up when he saw the open eyes staring at him. He closed the deputy's eyes and unhooked the pistol from the holster. He ran to the fallout shelter and pounded on the door.

"Can you hear me? It's Nick," he yelled, his head close to the door.

He heard sounds from below, but couldn't make anything out. He pounded on the door again, waiting for a response. Someone pounded back.

"I'm going to try to shoot the lock off, so stand back from the door," he shouted as loud as he could.

He stood up and aimed the gun at the lock and tried to pull the trigger, but nothing happened. He looked at the gun and remembered hearing some guns had a safety. He found it, flicked it up, and pointed it at the lock again. When he pulled the trigger the unexpected recoil sent him back several feet. He missed the lock, shattering some wood on the door. He pointed again, this time using two hands, kneeling in the snow close to the lock. He fired and heard the bullet hit metal. When he opened his eyes, he saw the shattered padlock. He grabbed it, unhooked it from the door, and slowly tried lifting the door, using all of his strength. Blood continued to seep out of his neck as he pulled with all of his might, but he couldn't budge it. Suddenly, the door flew open, sending Nick backwards onto his back. He scrambled up to see Sheriff Logan standing at the top of the stairs, breathing heavily.

"Where's Coach Walters," Nick said.

"He's hurt bad. Evans is getting him now." Sheriff Logan stepped out of the rancid-smelling hole and took several deep breaths. "He was shot in the shoulder, lots of blood, but luckily the bullet went straight through without hitting bone." Logan looked at the wound on Nick's neck. "Did he get you, too, kid?"

"Yeah, he nicked me, but I'm okay."

Logan tilted Nick's head to the side and looked at the wound. He wiped the blood from his neck with his handkerchief. "Looks like a superficial wound, son. You'll be okay, just keep pressure on it."

They heard a shuffling sound and looked behind them where they saw Deputy Evans with his arm around Coach Walters, lifting him up the steps one at a time. Logan helped them up the last few steps until they were out of the shelter. Nick saw a blood-soaked rag wrapped around Walters' left arm and shoulder. He was conscious, but in obvious pain.

"Coach, are you okay?" Nick said.

Walters nodded. "Yeah, Nick, I'll live. I heard several shots. Did he . . . ?"

Nick turned and showed him his neck. "He nicked me, but I'm okay."

Walters nodded again. "And Sarah?"

Nick stared at his coach. "He's got her."

Walters fell to his knees, the strength drained out of him. "Oh, no."

"Did you see where he took her, Nick?" Logan said.

"I followed them back through the cornfield but got there too late. He shot at me again before taking off in the green pickup with Sarah." Nick showed them the hole in the parka.

Logan put his finger through the hole. "You're a pretty lucky young man, son."

"Yeah, but he's got Sarah."

"Did he drug her, or—"

"I don't think so. She was sitting up in the passenger seat with her arms behind her, and . . . and she was staring back at me," Nick said, fighting back against the tears. "We've got to go find her, Sheriff."

"We will son. Was he in the green pickup?"

Nick wiped his eyes. "Yes."

"Well, let's get Coach Walters to the farmhouse and we'll radio it in from the cruiser."

Nick shook his head. "He ripped the radio out of both cruisers, Sheriff."

Logan slapped his hands together. "Damn!" He stood staring at the cornfield, his back to Nick. "We'll use the phone in the farmhouse. Let's go. Lead the way, Nick."

Logan and Evans got on both sides of Walters and half-dragged him, following Nick, who walked quickly through the cornfield, every few steps glancing back at his coach. Several minutes later they came out into the open area next to the barn. They continued walking until they got to the cruisers. Evans laid Walters down in the backseat of one cruiser and covered him with a blanket.

Nick leaned into the cruiser. "Are you okay, Coach?"

Walters, fighting to stay awake, said, "Okay."

"Evans, check both radios and see if we have anything. Nick, come into the farmhouse with me and let's find a telephone," Logan was already heading for the farmhouse.

Nick followed him up the steps and into the house. It was dusty and cold, as though no one had lived there for some time. Nick saw opened tin cans on the kitchen counter and dirty dishes in the sink.

Logan found the phone on the kitchen wall and picked up the receiver and put it to his ear.

"Sheriff," Nick said, holding up the dangling wire, "he cut it."

Logan looked at the wire, separated from the phone box. "I'll be god-damned. That sonofabitch!"

"Nick, go upstairs and see if there's another phone anywhere. I'm going to check on the cruisers," Logan said, rushing out of the house.

Nick walked into the main living area and saw the staircase. He glanced around the room at the pictures on the wall. He stopped to look at one of a man, a woman and two young boys. He recognized Coach Walters right away, the bigger of the two boys. He leaned in and looked at the younger boy. He noticed the dark hair and dark eyes. It was the man in the red cap, no question about it. He grabbed the picture off of the wall and walked to the staircase. It was an L-shaped staircase, with a landing area in the middle. He saw more pictures on the walls as he climbed to the second floor. He stopped at the top when he saw a picture of a man in uniform. It was Coach Walters in his Army uniform, with the 101st Airborne patch on his sleeve. He took it down, and began searching the hallway for a telephone.

He checked each room, but found no phone. The last room was at the end of the hallway, the door partially open. He pushed on the door and peered into the room, dark as night because of the shades being pulled down. He saw a light switch and turned it on. When he looked to his left at the bed he stumbled backwards. A young girl, naked, was lying face up, her eyes open, but lifeless. Looking around the room, Nick saw strands of rope strewn around the room. He froze when he saw the bottle on the dresser. He slowly walked towards it and read the label. Chloroform. He backed away, glancing again at the body on the bed. He covered it with a blanket and then ran down the hallway and down the staircase, almost stumbling at the bottom. He raced out of the kitchen and flew down the outside steps.

"What the hell?" Logan said, standing next to one of the cruisers. "You see a ghost, son?"

Nick was out of breath. He pointed to the second floor. "A dead girl on the . . . the bed, blood everywhere. Ropes." Nick took a deep breath, "And chloroform."

"Slow down, son," Logan said. "Was there anyone else inside?"

Nick shook his head.

"Evans, go check it out upstairs," Logan said. "Did you see a phone upstairs, Nick?"

Nick shook his head again.

"What's that in your hand?"

Nick stood up straight and showed him the pictures. "The family when the boys were small. Coach is the taller one, and the one that took Sarah is the other boy."

Logan stared at the picture. "Sure looks like Coach Walters." He looked more closely at the picture. "And the shorter boy sure as hell has the eyes that the sketch artist drew after talking with Sarah. What's the other picture?"

Nick held it out to the sheriff. "Coach when he was in the Army."

Logan nodded his head. "Yeah, this was the picture in the news article, the one that was . . . was in the mouth of that poor girl."

"He called Coach Walters 'Johnny' right before he shot him, Sheriff. He said 'Hello Johnny, goodbye Johnny,' and then shot him."

Logan looked back at the cruiser that Walters was lying in. "Sure as hell looks like his little brother is the guy we're looking for. Now we have two questions we need answers to: Number one, who's the girl upstairs, and number two, where the hell did he take Sarah?"

Nick sat down on the steps and put his head in his hands. "Sarah."

Deputy Evans walked outside and stood next to Sheriff Logan. "I think it's the girl from Walker County," he said.

Logan's eyes grew wider. "Why do you think that?"

"The birthmark on her neck, I remember it from her picture," Evans said. "She's been violated beyond belief, Sheriff."

"How so?"

"She's been ripped open, front and back. And she has something in her mouth, like the last one."

"Another note?" Logan said.

"No," Evans said, rubbing his forehead, "her panties, soaked in chloroform."

Logan shook his head and rubbed his fingers through his hair. "That appears to be his calling card, his signature, the goddamned animal."

"What do you want me to do, Sheriff?" Evans said.

"I have to get the Coach to the hospital in Acorn before he goes into shock. Stay with her until a team gets out here. When I get to the office I'll send a forensics team out, along with some back-up. In the meantime, watch over the three bodies. Nick, you hop in the back seat and try to keep Coach Walters awake. We can't let him go into shock."

Nick got into the cruiser and shook Walters, who was just about out. Walters opened his eyes slowly and tried to focus.

"Coach, you need to try to stay awake."

Walters mumbled something.

"I can't understand you, Coach."

"Sit me up," Walters said.

Nick lifted him up into a sitting position and held his head. "We're ready, Sheriff."

Logan started up the cruiser and pulled out onto the driveway, headed for Acorn. He had his siren blasting and blue lights flashing.

"What did you mean by three bodies?" Nick said from the backseat.

Logan looked at him. "The girl upstairs, Deputy Smith and the Coach's father."

"Coach Walters' father? Where is he?"

"I forgot, you didn't know," Logan said.

"Know what, Sheriff?"

Logan ran his fingers through his thinning hair again. He glanced back at Walters, who was fading in and out of consciousness in the back seat. "We found his father in the fallout shelter, with a rag stuck down his throat. He had a note pinned on his shirt that said 'Die in hell, pervert.'"

Nick sucked in a breath, glancing at Walters. "Was he dead?"

"Oh yeah, very." Logan said, glancing at Walters again, "Appears he's been dead for a day or two. He smelled pretty ripe when we got down there."

Nick took several deep breaths. "How could Coach's brother do that to his own father?"

Logan shrugged as he pulled out onto the highway, headed for Acorn. "How could he do any of the crap he's done? He's crazy, son. Oh, and there's one more thing."

"What's that," Nick said.

"The rag shoved down his father's throat was soaked in chloroform. He poisoned his own father with the crap he uses on the girls."

"Stop the car," Nick said. "Stop the car, now."

Logan pulled over onto the side of the highway and watched Nick get out, bend over, and put his hands on his knees.

Once Nick was back in the car, he turned to Logan. "We have to find him before . . . before he . . ."

"I know, son. We'll find him, but I hope it's in time."

Nick closed his eyes. He was afraid his worst nightmare was about to come true.

CHAPTER 63

They pulled into the parking lot of the small emergency care facility on the outskirts of Acorn. Sheriff Logan, his blue lights still flashing, put the car in neutral and ran into the facility. In a few seconds two men with a gurney came running out. They slid Walters onto the gurney and disappeared back into the emergency care center.

"Nick, I need you to stay with Coach Walters while I get down to my office and get things coordinated. Can you do that, son?" Logan said.

"Sure, I'll stay with him. I'll call my parents from inside."

"Good boy. They'll want some answers, since it's a gunshot wound, so just give them the truth, no screwing around. I'm guessing they'll have to transfer him to Council Bluffs as soon as possible. He's lost a lot of blood."

Nick nodded. "I'll have my Dad follow Coach wherever they take him. Sheriff, what about Sarah? What are we going to do to find her?"

Logan stopped and ran his hand through his hair. "I need to find out what Sims has uncovered about the family, see if there might be a relative or friend in the area where the guy could have taken her. He's lost his hide-out, so he has to go somewhere. Just stay with Coach and I'll get back to you, son."

"Okay, Sheriff."

Nick watched Logan peel out of the parking lot, his siren wailing and lights flashing. He turned and walked into the emergency care center and up to the front desk.

"A man was just brought in," Nick said to the receptionist. "Where can I find him?"

The elderly lady pointed down the hall. "Second door on the right. Is that Coach Walters, the Acorn football coach?"

Nick nodded. "Yes, Ma'am."

"He looks in bad shape. What happened?"

"Gunshot to the shoulder, lost a lot of blood," Nick said. "I gotta go. Thanks."

"We have paperwork to fill out, son," she said, calling after him.

Nick waved to her as he hurried down the hallway to the second door on the right. He entered and was immediately told to get out. He saw the wound on the Coach's left shoulder where the bullet had ripped the flesh. Walters was awake and saw him.

"Let him stay, please. He's with me," Walters said.

"He can come in later, sir. Right now we need this room sanitized, so he has to go outside," the doctor said.

A nurse walked Nick out and told him to wait in the lobby. Nick walked back to the gray-haired receptionist, who was holding a pen and some papers.

"You need to register your father in," she said, looking at his neck. "And someone needs to look at your neck. You have a nasty gash there. What happened to you and your father?"

"He's not my father, he's my coach," Nick answered. "I don't have any personal information except his name."

"Okay, son, we can get that from him after he gets out of surgery, but you need to sign this form as the person that brought him in. Regulations."

Nick signed several forms and handed them back. "Can I use your phone to call my parents?"

"There's a phone right over there," she said, looking at the forms. "You're Nick Paxton?"

"Yeah."

"Why, my grandson talks about you all the time. You're a big football hero around here, he says."

Nick smiled weakly and walked to the phone. He sat down and dialed zero.

"How may I direct your call?"

"Mom, is that you?" Nick said.

"Nicky? Hi. Yes, I'm filling in for Mabel today. She got sick and . . . where are you?"

Nick rubbed his forehead, wondering how much to tell his mother. "I'm at the emergency care center outside of Acorn, Mom."

"Why? Did you get hurt? What happened?"

"Mom, Coach Walters got shot in the shoulder. They're fixing him up now."

"Nicky! Are you okay? What happened, baby?"

Nick didn't want to go over everything on the phone. "Mom, I can't talk right now. I need to talk to Dad. Can you patch me through?"

"He took Ethan and Bo with him to his office in Council Bluffs. They were going to get some lunch. Nicky, I'm worried about you. The Sheriff's office called and said you were going somewhere with the Sheriff, something about the kidnapper."

Nick rubbed his forehead and ran his fingers through his hair. He felt the tears welling up. "Mom, I just can't talk right now. I have to go see how Coach is doing. I'll call you later."

He hung up the phone and rubbed his red eyes. When he looked up a man in a white coat was standing in front of him.

"Nick Paxton?" the man said.

"Yes, I'm Nick."

"Mr. Walters wants to talk to you. We're going to have to transfer him to Council Bluffs to the hospital over there. We're going to give him some pain medication in a few minutes, so you'd better talk to him now. Follow me, son."

Nick followed the man to Walters' room and walked in. Walters was propped up in his hospital bed, brand new bandages on his left shoulder. He was awake and alert.

"Nick, come here," Walters said.

Nick walked to the side of the bed. "How are you, Coach?"

"They say I have to have my shoulder operated on, something about torn ligaments, muscle, whatever. Nick, we need to talk." Walters called the nurse over. "Can you leave us alone for a few minutes?"

"Okay, but only for a few minutes. No getting out of bed, Mr. Walters," the nurse said, walking out of the room and closing the door.

"Nick, what happened after I blacked out?"

Nick told him about the girl in the upstairs bedroom, but didn't say anything about what they found in her mouth. "The Sheriff thinks it's the girl from Walker County."

Walters shook his head. "I can't believe my brother did all these things. He killed my father, Nick. He's sick, demented."

Nick stood next to the bed, silent.

"Any word on Sarah or where they went?" Walters asked.

"No, but the Sheriff is at his office now, hoping to get some information on where he might have taken Sarah. Do you have any ideas, Coach?"

"He doesn't know anyone in this area that I know of, except me and our father, and we haven't seen each other in many years," Walters said. "Nick, he knows that I'm a bachelor and live alone, and I'm sure he knows where I live. Hell, he seems to know everything about everyone."

"Yeah, so?" Nick said.

"He needs a place to hole up, to take . . . Sarah," Walters put his arm on Nick's arm. "I live on a small farm just outside Acorn, not too far from Tim's farm. As a matter of fact, it's on the same road, just a mile further. I pass Tim's house every day on my way to work."

Nick was staring at him. "You think he might take her to your place?"

"Listen, son. He thinks I'm either dead or hurt real bad, which means I won't be going home for at least a day or so, or ever. We have the element of surprise if he's there. It's the only logical place that I can think of, unless he has another place somewhere. It's worth a shot."

Nick was beside himself with excitement. "I'll call the Sheriff and let him know."

"Call Tim, he knows where I live and the layout of my farm. You have to sneak up on Jimmy, catch him by surprise."

"Okay. Are you going to be okay, Coach?"

"Yeah, they're going to give me something for the pain soon. Good luck, son. And Nick?"

"Yeah, Coach?"

"Be careful. He's a madman and will do anything."

Nick shook his hand and rushed out of the room and ran to the telephone in the lobby. The nurse was at the desk as he ran by.

"Son, we have to look at your neck," the nurse yelled.

"Later, I have to make a call," Nick yelled over his shoulder.

He dialed zero and waited.

"How may I—"

"Mom, it's me. I have to talk to the Sheriff, now. Please connect me."

"Nicky, what's wrong? Are you in danger, baby?"

"Mom, this is life or death, I need to talk to Sheriff Logan. I'll tell you everything later."

"Okay, Nicky. Hold on."

Nick waited a few seconds until a voice came over the phone.

"Oak County Sheriff's Department," a female voice said.

"I need to talk to Sheriff Logan now, it's an emergency," Nick said.

"Well, he's in a meeting right now—"

"Tell him it's Nick Paxton and I know where Sarah is," Nick said, loudly.

"Hold on."

Nick began rubbing his eyes, then his hair, trying to keep his arms moving, the adrenalin surging through him.

"Nick, this is Sheriff Logan. What's going on?"

"Sheriff, he's taking her to Coach Walters' farm," Nick said, the emotion almost strangling his words.

"Slow down, son. How do you know this?"

"I talked to Coach a few minutes ago and he said it's the only place that his brother knows."

"I thought they hadn't seen each other in many years, how would he—"

"His brother thinks that Coach is dead, or at least hurt real bad, and knows he won't be home for a while. Coach lives on a farm outside of Acorn. We have to get out there, now!"

"What about his wife, kids—"

"Coach is a bachelor, no kids."

"And his brother probably knows all of this," Logan said. "Are you still at the emergency care center, Nick?"

"Yes, My Dad's in Council Bluffs and my Mom is working. I don't have a ride."

"Okay, sit tight. I'll be there in ten minutes. Do you know where the coach's farm is?"

"He lives close to my best friend, Tim Preston, about two or three miles north of Acorn, and he's been on Coach's farm, knows the layout."

"Call him and have him meet us in front of his farm in twenty minutes."

"Okay, see you in ten," Nick said, hanging up.

He dialed zero again.

"How may—"

"Mom, Nick again. I need to talk to Tim Preston, now."

"Nicky, I'm going crazy here worrying about you, honey."

"I know Mom, but I have no time, I need to talk to Tim right away."

"Okay, hold on."

After several seconds, a woman's voice came on the line. "Hello?"

"Hello, Mrs. Preston? This is Nick Paxton, is Tim home?"

"Oh, hi Nicky. He's outside helping his father. Can he call you back?"

"Mrs. Preston, this is an emergency, I really need to talk to Tim right now. Please."

"Oh, well, okay, I'll go get him. Are you okay, Nicky?"

"Yes, but I need to talk to Tim now."

"Okay, hold on."

Nick waited, pacing back and forth. The nurse stared at him, her arms crossed in front of her. Nick held his hand up. "Give me five minutes," he said.

Finally, Tim came on the line. "Nicky, what's going on?"

"Tim, I can't explain everything right now, but the guy has Sarah."

"Who's got her? You mean—"

"The kidnapper, the guy in the red cap."

"Oh, shit," Tim said.

"Tim, have you been to Coach Walters' farm? He said you'd know the layout."

"Yeah, my dad and me were there a couple of times to help him with stuff. Why?"

"We think that's where he's taking her."

"To the Coach's farm? Why the hell—"

"Tim, I'll explain later. Can you meet me and the Sheriff in front of your place in fifteen minutes?"

"Yeah, sure, but—"

"I'll explain when we get there. See you in fifteen."

Nick hung up just as he heard a siren outside. He stood up and yelled to the nurse, "Gotta go, sorry."

He bolted out the front door to the waiting Sheriff's cruiser, opened the front passenger door, and climbed in.

"We all set with Tim Preston?" Logan said.

"Yeah, he'll be out front," Nick said.

"Good. I have another cruiser that's going to meet us at his place in ten minutes. You ready for this, son?"

Nick nodded. "Let's go, Sheriff."

As the Sheriff began pulling away, they heard a shout behind them. Logan stopped and Nick opened the door just as Coach Walters ran out the door of the emergency care center, his hospital robe flowing behind him, holding his pants and shoes in his right hand, his left arm in a sling. A nurse was running after him with a needle in her hand.

"Open the door, Nick," Walters yelled.

Nick opened the door to the backseat and Walters dove inside. Nick closed the door, shrugged at the exasperated nurse, and got into the car. Sheriff Logan peeled out of the parking lot, staring at Walters in the rearview mirror.

Nick turned and stared at Walters. "What the hell, Coach?"

Walters was breathing hard, holding his left arm. "I'm not going to miss this, not because of a shot-up shoulder."

Sheriff Logan began laughing. "You are something else, Coach. It'll be a long time before I get the image of your bare ass out of my head. Hope you know what you're doing."

"I have to face my brother," Walters said, "and we have to save Sarah."

Nick grinned at his coach. "Did they give you the pain meds, Coach?"

Walters laughed. "That crotchety old nurse had my bare butt in the air, ready to plunge the needle in, but I bolted out of bed. I think she wet her pants."

"Coach," Logan said, still laughing and looking in the rearview mirror, "you might want to cover up a little. Your, uh, thing is showing."

CHAPTER 64

Jimmy pulled the green pickup onto the long, snow-covered driveway that he had seen the night before, driving slowly so as to not draw attention, even though the farm was a half mile or so from the nearest neighbor. He glanced at the girl, who was still out from the chloroform. He didn't want to have to use it, but she had become so distraught and violent when she saw her boyfriend, she'd become a nuisance. He'd had to pull over before they got on the highway to put a chloroform-soaked rag to her nostrils. She passed out immediately. He wanted to touch her then, but decided to wait until he got to his brother's farm.

It was late afternoon and the sun was beginning to fall in the western sky, the sunlight glistening off the snow in the fields. Jimmy's eye began twitching as he thought of what he would be doing that very night. He looked at the girl and was disappointed that she wasn't in her cheerleading outfit. She had on jeans and a heavy sweater, hiding all the good parts. But he had her Acorn High cheerleader sweater in his backpack, and that would get him in the mood when the time came. He licked his lips as he touched her face, so young and beautiful. He stroked her long blonde hair as he approached the farmhouse.

Jimmy pulled the pickup around to the back of the garage, out of sight. He got out and looked in the garage to make sure there were no cars. He knew his brother was either dead or close to it, and wouldn't be home tonight, probably for a lot of nights, if ever. If the gunshot didn't kill him, the fall down the concrete stairs probably did. Regardless, he wouldn't be home tonight.

He quickly walked to the passenger door, opened it, dragged the girl out, and carried her to the back porch. The door was not locked, as he anticipated, so he went inside, butt first. He smelled the girl's clean skin, the same faint scent of perfume he'd smelled on the sweater just the night before. He licked her cheek as he carried her to the living room and placed her on the sofa. He took her jacket off, thought about taking everything off, but decided to wait, if he could. He ran his hand over her hair, stroking it, smoothing it out. This would be the best night of his life.

He went back outside and grabbed his backpack from the pickup bed, along with some rope and the deputy's rifle. He reentered the house, locked the door, and put the backpack in the living room and the rifle next to the sofa. He searched the house for any more guns and found a .22 caliber rifle and a 12 gauge shotgun, but no shells or bullets. He'd have to look for those later.

He tied the girl's legs and wrists with the rope, and thought about maybe having some fun while she was still out. His eye began twitching again, more rapidly. He sat next to the cheerleader, rubbing her leg under her jeans with his right hand. *No, not yet. Not until she's awake and I can listen to her, feel her move.*

Jimmy looked around the living room and saw the trophies, the medals, the pictures of his brother saving somebody's ass in the war. He had a twinge of regret not being able to talk to Johnny after so many years, but what would they say to each other? He didn't even know his older brother, being only ten when their mother took him and moved to bum-fuck Montana. Maybe he would've liked his brother, who knows? But their father hated Johnny for turning him in, for destroying his life. Before he'd killed the old man, Jimmy had let him rant about how Johnny had betrayed him, and how he would get his revenge one day. *Sorry, old man, not in this lifetime, you sorry-ass pervert.* His mother had told him the stories of how the old man used to invite young boys over to the house and have 'game night' or some shit. How he would pick one each time and take him into his bedroom, molest him, get his rocks off. What a twisted, perverted piece of shit he was.

Jimmy smiled as he thought about what he had accomplished over the last two days. He had killed the old man in the fallout shelter two nights before by stuffing a chloroform rag down his throat until he gagged and passed out. Then he'd poured an entire bottle of chloroform down his throat, filling his lungs with the poison. The old man had stared at him with those lifeless, perverted eyes. *Screw you, old man.* Then he'd taken the last girl, the one from Walker County, out of the shelter and through the cornfield to the farmhouse, laid her on the old man's bed, naked, and done the same thing to her. She was half dead by then anyway, but it was poetic justice that she was the first female to ever lie in the old man's bed, other than his mother, and even that wasn't a sure thing.

Then he thought about last night, when everyone was at the football game. He laughed out loud when he thought of the young cheerleader from Walnut Hills, lying buck-ass naked on the floor of the football player's garage. *Bet that got them going.* He laughed until tears came to his eyes.

He stood up and walked to the fireplace, seeing a picture of the family when they were still together. Mother was fairly pretty when she was young, with kind of a Betty Grable look to her. Too bad she got old and frumpy. His eye began twitching when he thought about the night he left Montana just two months ago. Mother was getting wise to his games, to the smell of chloroform on his clothes. *She saw the news about the missing girls in Helena and Butte, always stared at me strangely.* It was only a matter of time before she turned him in, so she had to die, just like the old man, just like Johnny, and just like every girl he'd ever been with. Jimmy's face turned red as he thought about how his mother had used him like a toy when he was young, fondling him, touching his private parts, kissing him on the mouth. He'd finally had enough when he got out of high school, but she'd screwed his mind up so bad he knew he would never have a normal relationship with a woman.

Jimmy turned and stared at the young blonde lying on the sofa, so innocent-looking, but no different than all the rest. She would learn to hate him, just like the others. Women weren't capable of love, especially loving him. He felt his face getting hot, his eyes twitching violently as he thought about how they all betrayed him in the end. He smashed his fist into the picture, breaking the glass, the blood flowing from his knuckles. He looked at the cheerleader lying on the sofa. *Now see what you made me do, you bitch.* He walked slowly to the sofa, staring at her breathing, her chest moving up and down, the bulges showing through her sweater. He wanted to take her then, but the blood from his hand was flowing too fast. Take care of the wound and then he would take care of the cheerleader. He walked to the bathroom and closed the door.

CHAPTER 65

The Sheriff's cruiser continued down Highway 6, turning left at the snow-covered gravel road that would take them to the Preston farm.

"Coach, I'm sorry about your father," Nick said. "Sheriff Logan told me about what you found in the fallout shelter."

Walters was pulling on his slacks, still chuckling about flashing the sheriff. "Thanks, Nick, but he's been dead to me for a long time. I can't forgive him for what he did, not just to Ronnie, but to how many other boys over the years? He was a perverted son of a bitch and he got what he deserved. From his own son, no less."

"Still, to see your father like that must have been painful."

"Shocking, yes, painful, no." Walters was putting on his shirt but was having a difficult time because of his shoulder and the sling. "Nick, can you help me with this shirt? I can't move my left arm too well."

While Nick helped the coach get his shirt on, Logan was in deep thought behind the wheel. "Coach, what happened to your brother? I mean, how do you think he ended up the way he is? Was there anything in your childhood that would indicate he'd grow up to be such a monster?"

Walters was out of breath just getting his shirt on. "Thanks, Nick." He took a deep breath. "I don't know, Sheriff, I'm as confused as you are. He was only ten the last time I saw him and I was only twelve, so I don't remember much at all. I know our mother doted on him a lot, much more than she did me. I guess because he was small and scrawny, unlike me."

Logan looked in the rearview mirror at Walters. "We got some information back on our search of your family." Logan hesitated, clearing his throat. "Your brother, Jimmy, murdered your mother two months ago, in some suburb of Helena, Montana." Logan continued looking at Walters, waiting for a reaction.

Walters shook his head. "What a screwed up family. I don't know how I escaped all the madness. How did she die?"

Logan scratched the side of his face. He hesitated before continuing. "They weren't sure of the actual cause of death, but she died when her house caught on fire. They suspect Jimmy set it before he left. It appears he's been at this stuff for some time. We found out that the Helena police are linking your brother to multiple kidnappings and murders in Montana over the past five or six years. All young girls, mostly runaways and street kids."

Nick watched Walters shake his head as he closed his eyes. "You okay, Coach?"

Walters opened his eyes and looked at Nick. "I'm going to kill him myself. He's an abomination, an animal. If he's harmed one hair on Sarah's head . . ."

Logan watched Walters carefully. "Coach, I can't let you do that. You know that, don't you? I'm sworn to uphold the law, so we have to do it my way. If you can't agree to that then you can get out at the Preston farm."

Walters stared at the sheriff, not saying a word.

"John, are you hearing me?"

"Yeah, I hear you, Sheriff. I'll let you handle it, but if it doesn't go well, he's mine."

Logan nodded. "Fair enough. I just hope he's there at your place . . . and that we get there in time." He looked at Nick, who was deep in thought.

"Nick, you doing okay?" the Sheriff asked. "We're going to bring her home, son."

Nick turned to the Sheriff. "If you or Coach Walters doesn't kill him, I will."

"We'll get him, Nick." He looked in the rearview mirror again. "Coach, is there a back way to your farmhouse, one that he can't see from inside?"

"Yeah, but we have to park at a neighbor's farm and walk in. No road to the house except in front."

"How far do we have to walk from the neighbor's place?"

"Half a mile, but it's pretty tough terrain. Some woods, a cornfield and a creek that may not be frozen over yet. I think we could get there faster by going overland from the Preston farm. It's farther, but flat, through a cornfield. Maybe Tim or his dad can drive us close with one of their tractors or whatever they have."

"Doesn't he have a vantage point on that side of the house? Wouldn't he see us coming?" Logan said.

"Not unless he's outside. There's only one window on that side of the house, an upstairs bathroom window. Plus, I have two big oak trees that would cover us most of the way."

Logan scratched his head. "Let's talk to Tim and his dad and see what they think. We have two cruisers, one from Walnut County and one from my department joining us at the Preston farm. We'll have to move fast. You sure you can make it with your bum shoulder, Coach?"

"Don't worry about me, Sheriff. I had worse than this in the war."

Logan looked at him in the mirror. "Europe or Korea?"

"Both, but Korea was more like what we're facing today. The coldest damn country I've ever seen, snow and ice everywhere."

"What was it like in Europe, Coach, on D-Day?" Nick asked, staring at Walters.

"Well, I didn't go through the hell that the infantry went through on Omaha Beach, Nick. I was in the Airborne and they flew us in and we parachuted into France."

"If I remember my history, that was no picnic either, was it?" Logan said.

Walters stared out the window. "No, it was FUBAR, for sure."

"FUBAR, what's that?" Nick said.

Walters looked at him. "You have to excuse my language, Nick. It means fucked up beyond all recognition."

"Sort of what we have today, right Coach?" Logan said.

Walters nodded. "Yeah, this is definitely FUBAR, Sheriff."

CHAPTER 66

They arrived at the Preston farm as the sun was beginning to set. Logan pulled the cruiser onto the snow-covered lane that led to the farmhouse, then stopped abruptly.

"Is that Tim Preston?" he said, seeing a boy on the side of the road.

Nick rolled his window down. "Hey, Tim, climb in."

Tim opened the door to the backseat and slid in next to Walters. "Hi, Coach." He saw the sling. "What happened?"

Walters smiled. "Hi, Tim. Oh, just a torn up shoulder."

The Sheriff drove down the lane to the two-story white farmhouse and pulled up next to a tall man in overalls. "Is that your Dad, Tim?"

"Yes."

Everyone got out of the cruiser. Three dogs stood nearby, barking.

Sheriff Logan shook Mr. Preston's hand. "I'm Sheriff Logan of—"

"Yeah, I know who you are, Sheriff. I voted for you twice. You're earnin' your pay today, huh?"

Logan chuckled. "Yes, I guess I am, Mr. Preston."

"Call me Earl."

"Okay, Earl. This is Coach—"

"Walters, yeah I'm real familiar with him, too. How you doin', neighbor?" Earl looked at the sling. "You had some trouble, did ya?"

Walters shook Earl's hand. "Hi, Earl. It's been one helluva day, and it's not getting any better."

"How can I help you fellas?"

"We need to get to the Coach's farm without being seen," Logan said, "and we thought you could help us."

Earl rubbed his black stubble-covered chin. "I could drive you across the cornfield in my pickup over yonder, but we'd have to stop about a quarter-mile away or he'd hear us."

Logan looked at Walters. "That would work, Earl."

They all turned as they heard two police cruisers coming down the lane.

"Here comes our backup," Logan said. "Earl, can you get your pickup fired up and ready to go?"

Earl nodded and began walking toward his barn.

Logan turned to Nick and Tim. "You boys can go as far as the truck goes, but no further, got it?"

"But Sheriff—"

"No buts, Nick. I can't put you two in any danger."

"But Sarah—"

"I'll make sure she's okay, Nick," Walters said. "I promise."

"Okay, you two football heroes understand?" Logan said.

"Yes, sir," Tim and Nick answered simultaneously.

"Okay. I'm going to talk to the deputies in the cruisers for a minute. Be right back."

Earl drove up to them in an old Mercury pickup, rusted and weathered by time and the elements.

The two boys climbed into the bed of the pickup, with Coach Walters in the front with Earl. Logan walked over as the two cruisers backed up and went back down the lane.

Logan leaned on the passenger door open window. "The cruisers are going to drive down and wait on the road for my instructions," Logan said, holding a walkie-talkie. "Once they get my word they'll head down your lane to the house. If it's a false alarm, meaning if your brother's not at your place, then they'll head back home."

"What about weapons?" Walters asked.

"I got this shotgun from my deputy, so you take it. I've got my service revolver. That should be all we need." Logan handed Walters the shotgun and a box of shells. "You got any guns in your house that your brother could use against us, Coach?"

"Yeah, but the ammo is hidden away. He won't be able to use them."

Logan nodded. "Good. Earl, you and the boys stay with the pickup, out of sight. If he's at the coach's house, we'll get a ride back with my deputy. Under no circumstances do I want you or the boys anywhere near that farmhouse. Okay?"

"It's your call, Sheriff." Earl started up the pickup as Logan hopped into the bed, sitting down next to Nick and Tim.

The pickup drove past the barn and down a slope to the edge of a cornfield. Tim jumped out and opened the metal gate, climbing back into the truck when it passed. They headed into the cornfield, mowing down brown, decaying cornstalks, leaving a path behind them.

Logan looked behind him at the setting sun. "We have about twenty minutes before it gets dark. We'll wait until then to sneak up to the house. Coach knows the layout so we'll follow him."

The old, rusted pickup bounced through the cornfield and finally stopped. Sheriff Logan stood up in the bed of the truck and peered over the top of the cornstalks, seeing the white farmhouse about a quarter of a mile ahead.

"Okay, we walk from here. Stop at the edge of the cornfield until its dark, and then, Coach, you'll lead us up to the house."

Walters nodded as he got out of the pickup.

"Coach, you have any dogs around that'll give us away?" Logan asked.

"No dogs, Sheriff. It's clear all the way from the cornfield to the house, but we'll have to climb over a barbed wire fence."

"Can you handle that, Coach?" Nick asked.

"Yeah, son, I handled a lot worse in the Army."

"But your shoulder—"

"Shoulder's fine, Nick. I'll be okay."

"Coach, one more question." Logan was looking through the dim light at him. "What if he isn't there, at your place?"

Walters shook his head. "Then I don't have a clue where he might be or might be headed. You might want to send someone to the farmhouse to see if the green pickup is there, to be sure."

"I'll go, Sheriff," Nick said.

Logan looked at Nick and at Walters. "That's a good idea, Coach. Nick, can you and Tim get there, look around, and get back here in fifteen minutes? Just check to see if the truck is anywhere on the property, that's all we need."

"Sheriff, you know how fast Nick is. We can make it," Tim said, standing next to Nick.

Walters shook his head. "I don't know. What if he's there and he sees them. It's too dangerous."

"Tim knows where to look, he knows your property, Coach," Nick pleaded. "Please let us go."

Logan looked at Walters, who nodded his head. "Better ask Tim's Dad."

Earl stood, not far away, listening to the conversation. "You get in and get out, Timmy. No screwin' around."

Tim clapped Nick on the shoulder. "Let's go, Nicky."

The two boys sprinted through the cornfield to the edge, stopped and surveyed the remaining landscape.

"The fence will be easy to get over," Tim said, "but we have a lot of open lawn to run through before we get to the garage. You ready, Nicky?"

"Let's go."

They ran to the barbed wire fence, jumped it with no problem, and laid flat on the grass, peering at the farmhouse.

"Follow me, Nick."

They ran around the perimeter of the lawn to the garage, which was behind the farmhouse. They slowly walked around to the back of the garage and stopped.

"There's the pickup," Nick said, breathless.

"All right! Let's get back and tell the Sheriff," Tim said.

"You go, I'm going to check the windows to see if Sarah's in there."

"Nick, no, it's too dangerous."

"Go back and tell them, Timmy. I'm staying."

Tim shook his head and began running back to the fence. Nick watched as Tim hopped the fence and disappeared into the cornfield. The sun was almost gone, just a glimmer of twilight left. Nick bent low and slowly moved to the farmhouse, stopping underneath a window that had light coming from it. He slowly stood up and peered in through a small slit between the curtains, enabling him to see part of what looked like the living room. He saw the sofa to the right and strained to see more. Suddenly, he saw movement to his left and ducked down. His heart pounded as he gradually rose up to look in the window again. He saw the dark-haired man standing over the sofa, rubbing his genitals. Nick's heart skipped a beat as he realized that Sarah was lying on the sofa. He rose up to take another look and froze when he saw the man unbuckling his belt.

CHAPTER 67

Nick knelt below the window, trying to control his breathing. He knew he had to make a decision, and fast. Should he wait for the others to get here, knowing by then it might be too late for Sarah, or should he run into the house like a wild man, go straight for the man and hopefully catch him by surprise? He had to stop him before the man violated her. He looked around for anything to use as a weapon, but saw nothing useful. He stood up and took another look inside and saw the man leaning over the sofa, his shirt off.

Nick bolted around the house and slowly walked up the back steps to the door. He stopped, took a deep breath, and tried the doorknob. It was locked. *Damn!*

He ran around to the other side of the house to the front porch, quietly taking the four steps up to the big brown door. He opened the screen door, hoping that it didn't squeak, and tried the doorknob. It was locked, also. Panicking, he rubbed his eyes, trying to figure out how to get inside.

Nick's head suddenly jerked up. He'd seen a cellar door on the side of the house, the kind you enter from the outside and walk down some stairs, just like the fallout shelter they had been to earlier in the day. He ran to the side of the house and almost stumbled on it. After scraping the snow off, he tried to lift the heavy door and got it a foot off of the ground when it started to creak. He looked up at the window, the slit revealing the sliver of light from the living room. He plastered himself next to the side of the house, but no one looked out. His heart raced as he opened the cellar door slowly, glancing up at the window with every creak. He finally got it open far enough for him to slide under, but it was pitch dark inside and he didn't have a flashlight.

Now what? He descended the cold, concrete stairs to the bottom, reaching the opening into the cellar. It was cold, musty smelling, and pitch black. He tried to adjust his eyes to the darkness, but it was useless. He felt the walls for a light switch, but found nothing. He ventured straight ahead, totally blind, reaching forward with his hands in the darkness. He kicked something on the floor, but it didn't make any noise. It felt like a sack of something soft. He took another step forward and felt something in his hair. He swiped at it and realized it was a cord to turn on an overhead light. He pulled on it and the cellar was illuminated. He blinked his eyes, adjusting to the sudden light, and got his bearings. He saw the stairs to the main floor and walked quickly to them, looking up at a closed door at the top. He looked around the cellar for anything to use as a weapon and saw a pair of hedge clippers lying on a bench next to the steps. He grabbed them and began ascending the stairs, one at a time. Suddenly, he heard a scream.

Sarah!

Nick ran up the remaining stairs and tried the door. It was unlocked, and he opened it slowly. He was in the kitchen and began inching towards the living room when he felt something wet on his face, the smell overwhelming. Before he blacked out, he grabbed the man's arm and thrust it away from him, wiping the smell from his face. The dark-haired man was standing in front of him with the rifle pointed at his head.

"Walk over to the sofa and sit next to your little girlfriend," the man said. "And drop the clippers."

Nick dropped the hedge trimmers and walked quickly to the sofa, where Sarah was sitting with her naked legs up to her chest, covered by her cheerleader's sweater. Her jeans were in a pile on the floor. He reached over and held her face.

"Are you okay, Sarah?"

Sarah's eyes were red, the tears streaming down her face. Her eyes were wide open, like a wounded animal in the woods.

"Shut up, kid, and put your arms out in front of you." The man had two strands of rope in one hand, the rifle in the other.

Nick looked into the man's eyes and saw the eyes of a wild beast staring back at him. He suddenly started feeling woozy, his eyes beginning to fog up.

The chloroform. Dammit!

He blinked several times to stave off the inevitable.

Jimmy put the rifle on the floor, grabbed Nick's hands and looped the rope around them.

Before he could tie the knot, Nick leaned back and kicked him in the groin as hard as he could, sending him to his knees, shouting in pain. Nick took both hands and whacked him on the side of his head, sending Jimmy flying to the floor. Nick picked up the rifle and pointed it at Jimmy, who looked up at him from the floor. The image of the man became blurry as the chloroform began to take hold.

"You know how to use one of those, kid?" Jimmy said. "You ever kill a man?"

Nick weaved back and forth as he blinked his eyes, trying to keep Jimmy in focus.

Seeing this, Jimmy leaped up and grabbed the rifle from Nick's hands, hitting him in the side of the head with the butt.

Nick fell to the floor as the blackness overcame him.

CHAPTER 68

Jimmy tied Nick's hands behind him and then tied his feet together. He drug Nick away from the sofa and laid him down near the entrance to the kitchen. He looked at Sarah, who was whimpering in the corner of the sofa, her legs pulled up to her chest. Jimmy looked at her bare legs and felt the familiar stirring in his groin. He sat on the sofa and began rubbing her legs.

"My precious treasure, soon we'll be alone—"

"That's enough, Jimmy. Get away from her."

Jimmy turned and saw his brother standing near the front doorway, a shotgun pointed at him. He slowly stood up and faced Walters.

"Johnny. I didn't think I'd ever see you again."

"Yeah, I know. Move away from the girl." Walters motioned with his shotgun for Jimmy to move towards the kitchen.

Jimmy glanced down at the rifle lying on the sofa.

"Don't even think about it, asshole."

Jimmy smiled and took a step towards Walters. "It's been a long time, Johnny." He pointed towards Walters' shoulder. "Your shoulder doesn't look so good, brother. I see lots of blood seeping through."

"Don't call me your brother, you perverted piece of—"

Walters stopped as pain shot through his body. He kept his eyes and shotgun on Jimmy.

"You okay, Johnny? Is the pain getting worse?" Jimmy had an evil smile on his face.

Walters dropped the shotgun to the floor as he reached for his shoulder, letting out a loud groan.

Jimmy lunged for the rifle and grabbed it before his brother could pick up the shotgun. He pointed it at Walters and pulled the trigger, hitting him in his left thigh.

Walters fell backwards as blood began spurting out of his thigh. He dropped to his knees as he kept his eyes on Jimmy.

Jimmy slowly walked towards his brother, keeping the rifle pointed at him. He bent down and picked up the shotgun.

"Now what, Johnny? I bet that hurts, doesn't it?" Jimmy poked his brother's bleeding shoulder with the barrel of the shotgun. "You aren't so tough now, war hero."

Walters grimaced and let out a low moan. He looked up at his brother. "What happened to you, Jimmy?"

Jimmy lifted his head and laughed. "What happened to me? Our old man and our old lady, that's what happened to me. They were both perverted pedophiles and they got what they deserved." Jimmy knelt down so his face was even with Walters' face. "Question is, Johnny, why didn't you end up like me?"

Walters, grimacing from the pain and breathing hard, stared at his brother. "I got away, Jimmy. Why didn't you leave mother? Why'd you stick around?"

Jimmy stopped smiling. "I used her, just like I use every little bitch, just like I'll use that little cheerleader over there. I like it, Johnny. I'm in control. When I'm with them, I'm God."

Walters continued to stare at his brother. "I think your days of playing God are over, Jimmy."

Jimmy grinned. "Really? Who's holding the gun, Johnny? I'm God right now and I proclaim that you're about to meet your Maker." Jimmy raised the shotgun and pointed it at Walters' head.

"Drop the guns, asshole, both of them, and turn around."

Jimmy's smile faded as he turned and saw Sheriff Logan and his deputy, a rifle and a pistol pointed at him.

"I said drop the guns, Jimmy. Now!" Logan took a step closer, both hands on his handgun.

Jimmy slowly stood up, holding the rifle in one hand and the shotgun in the other. He grinned at the Sheriff. "You can't kill me, I'm God."

"Move out of the way, John, so I can send this perverted piece of shit back to where he came from."

Walters slid to his left, out of the line of fire. "Remember what you told me, Sheriff," Walters said. "You're a lawman, not a killer."

Logan glanced at Walters and in that split second Jimmy raised the rifle and fired, hitting the Sheriff in the left arm. The deputy fired his rifle and hit Jimmy in the chest, sending him flying backwards.

Walters grabbed the rifle away from Jimmy, who sat on the floor against the door, blood oozing out of his chest. Jimmy looked down at the hole in his chest and began laughing, then coughed up blood. "You can't kill God." He raised the shotgun with his right arm, pointing it at the deputy.

One more shot rang out, hitting Jimmy in the temple. He dropped the shotgun to the floor and fell sideways, landing at Walters' feet, staring up at his brother holding the smoking rifle.

Then the darkness came.

CHAPTER 69

Nick heard voices and tried to open his eyes.

"Nicky, are you awake?"

Nick heard the familiar voice and very slowly opened his bloodshot eyes. He blinked several times, trying to focus on the person standing in front of him.

"Nicky, wake up, honey."

Nick suddenly saw his mother standing over him, his father next to her. "Mom?"

Eloise put her hand to her mouth. "Yes, honey, it's Mom."

Nick blinked again, looking around the hospital room and saw someone lying on the bed next to him. "Who's that?"

"It's your coach, son." His father was patting his leg. "They brought you in together last night."

"Coach? Is he okay?" He suddenly tried to sit up, his head pounding. "Sarah, where's Sarah?" Nick stared at his mother, who was crying. "Mom, where's Sarah?"

Eloise turned and put her face in Clint's shoulder.

Nick looked at his father. "Dad, is she, is she . . ." Nick felt sick to his stomach, the dread of hearing the answer overpowering him, the pounding in his head adding to the nausea.

"She's going to be all right, Nick." His father was smiling. "She's at home recovering."

Nick wiped his face and looked over at Walters. "Is Coach, is he okay?"

Walters opened his eyes and looked at Nick. "I'm okay, Nick, but probably won't be at practice tomorrow." Walters slowly pushed himself into a sitting position, wincing and holding his shoulder.

Nick stared at his coach, an intravenous line attached to his arm, his left leg elevated on a pillow. "Coach, what happened to your leg?"

"Ah, it's just a flesh wound. My shoulder's what's killing me."

"Coach, what happened? I remember holding a gun at Jimmy and then everything went dark."

"You passed out from the chloroform and then Jimmy hit you in the head with the butt of the rifle. I didn't see it, that's what Sarah told me."

Nick felt his head, feeling the gauze. "I don't remember."

"You've been out since it all happened. You missed the good stuff." Walters blinked and lay back in bed.

"Sarah. Coach, did Jimmy, did he—"

"No, you caught him before he could do anything to her. You might want to ask her yourself."

"Hi Nicky," Sarah said from the doorway.

Nick turned and saw her. She had her long blonde hair pulled up in a ponytail. In spite of the pain in his head, he grinned. "Hi, Sarah."

She walked to his bedside and bent down, kissing him on the lips. "You saved me, Nicky. Thank you."

Nick felt his face flushing. "I saved you? I passed out, how could I—"

"You got there before . . . the man . . . could do anything to me, Nicky. You saved me," Sarah said, tears welling in her eyes. "And after you passed out, Coach Walters came in and took over."

Nick turned his head to look at Walters. "What happened, Coach?"

"Well, I guess it became an old-fashioned shoot-out. Sheriff Logan and his deputy came in just as I dropped my shotgun. They sort of took over from there."

Nick shook his head. "Why'd you drop the shotgun?"

Walters pointed to his shoulder. "The pain became unbearable holding that heavy gun up, and I just dropped it. That's when Jimmy shot me in the leg."

Nick's eyes were wide open. "And what happened to your brother?"

Walters turned and stared at Nick. "He wasn't my brother anymore, Nick. He turned into an animal, a godless, murdering animal."

"The deputy shot him first, and then Mr. Walters shot him, Nicky," Sarah said. "Just when the man was about to shoot the sheriff."

Nick lay back in bed, his head pounding from the news and the excitement. "Holy crap."

Nick suddenly sat up in bed, holding his head. "Dad, what day is it?"

Clint leaned forward. "Sunday, why?"

Nick's eyes grew wide again. "Cuba—what's happening in Cuba?"

Everyone in the room began laughing, except Nick.

"What?" Nick said.

"They blinked," Walters said. "The Russians finally blinked."

A smile grew on Nick's face. "So we're okay? President Kennedy got us out of that mess?"

"I guess you could say we went to the brink, in more ways than one," Walters said. "It's a new day, Nick, a glorious new day."

ABOUT THE AUTHOR

Ron Parham is an accomplished and award-winning author of the Paxton Brothers Sagas, including thrillers *Festival of Fear, Molly's Moon,* and *Copperhead Cove*. His novels are about ordinary people caught up in extraordinary circumstances. *Festival of Fear* takes place in southwest Iowa, where he grew up and spent his childhood. All three novels are part of the Paxton Brothers Saga. He now lives and writes in the Temecula Valley, a world-famous wine-growing region just east of Los Angeles and north of San Diego. He is currently working on his first novel of the Gas Lamp Saga, starring Jake Delgado, the private investigator from his first two novels.

VISIT RON AT:

WWW.RONPARHAM.COM

Facebook Ron.Parham50

RWParham44@aol.com

DON'T MISS BOOKS 2 AND 3 IN THE PAXTON BROTHERS SAGA!

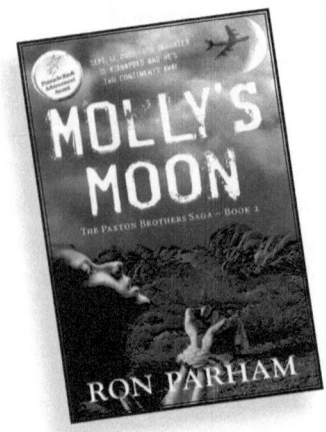

THE PAXTON BROTHERS SAGA BOOK 2

On a routine trip to Europe, widowed businessman Ethan Paxton learns of the terrorist attacks on the U.S. while landing in Amsterdam on September 11, 2001. Stuck in the Netherlands while fear grips at America's throat and the world is in chaos, he finds out his daughter, Molly, has been abducted by terrorists in Mexico while she was on a school mission trip.

Desperate, Ethan remembers an old Air Force buddy, Jake Delgado—an ex-cop who's now a broken down, alcoholic P.I. Ethan hires him to look for Molly, with Ethan's son alongside.

In a white-knuckle race against time, the men turn over the dark underside of Baja, California, searching for the girl. Their journeys converge at the Tijuana border crossing on September 13, with the diabolical kidnapper and his prostitute companion in the crosshairs.

Will the three have what it takes to outwit and outfight the terrorist to save the girls?

LEARN MORE AT:

WWW.PEN-L.COM/MOLLYSMOON.HTML

Dear Readers,
If you enjoyed this book enough to review it for Goodreads, B&N, or Amazon.com, I'd appreciate it!

Thanks, Ron

Find more great reads at
Pen-L.com

www.ingramcontent.com/pod-product-compliance
Lightning Source LLC
Chambersburg PA
CBHW020609260626
47157CB00003B/934